I0791815

DECEPTION'S EDGE
A BLADE BROUSSARD THRILLER

NANNETTE POTTER

First Edition: May 2025

ISBN 979-8-9873547-5-9 (hardcover)
ISBN 979-8-9873547-4-2 (paperback)
ISBN 979-8-9873547-6-6 (digital)

Cover design by Cherie Foxley at www.cheriefox.com.

"Judge not, and you will not be judged; condemn not, and you will not be condemned; forgive, and you will be forgiven."

—LUKE 6:37 (ESV)

CHAPTER
ONE

April 4 – 11:05 p.m. CDT
New Orleans, Louisiana

Blade steadied herself against a high table. A half-filled margarita glass tipped over, covering the table in sticky strawberry liquid, but she remained focused on the dartboard eight feet away.

"Twenty bucks says you can't even hit the board," Mick taunted over the rock music wailing from the jukebox.

The roughneck had approached Blade as she drank alone at Gators—the dive bar where she had first met Alec Quinn, four months earlier. From that moment until now, her life had been like riding on an explosive roller coaster. She'd survived multiple attempts on her life, joined forces with a secret Christian brotherhood, and met her biological mother—only to have her die with the name of Alec Quinn on her last breath. She'd spent thousands of dollars on private investigators in the last three months, chasing promising clues to New York, Liverpool, Barcelona, and even Thailand, but every one led to a dead end. The man had effectively disappeared.

Rubbing her shoulder, she smiled at Mick. "Let's make it fifty."

"It's your money." He crossed his arms.

She was used to men like Mick underestimating her. Even if she was drunk, hitting a bull's-eye would be child's play. Shifting the dart to her left hand, Blade tried to stand straight, but her world kept going in and out of focus. That last shot of tequila had burned all the way to her stomach, which threatened to erupt any second. The smell of fried food and spilt beer didn't help.

April Fool's Day wasn't a holiday, but it had been tradition— her parents pulling some ridiculous prank on her birthday until her mother passed. Now, three days had come and gone in silence. No word from her father, or Chase, or any of the Soldati. *Some family.*

"Come on, Blade," Mick goaded, leaning back against the table with an air of smug confidence. "Show us what you got."

"Let it fly, girlie," someone else shouted from the crowd of regulars, huddled around their tables, eager for the showdown.

The dart felt foreign in her grasp, a far cry from the balanced knives she was accustomed to throwing. But with a final burst of energy, Blade drew her arm back, then snapped it forward, releasing the dart with a flick of her wrist.

It clattered to the floor.

Crap, a flippin' bounce-out.

A collective groan rose from the onlookers. Blade's cheeks burned as Mick's laughter cut through the din.

"Looks like I won!" he said, taking a small victory dance around the table. "I bested the renowned Blade Broussard." He raised his arms above his head. "Knife-thrower my ass."

The pent-up rage she'd been harboring since coming back to New Orleans swept away the nausea and exploded on the rough- neck. She pushed him backwards and kept pushing until his back smacked against the dartboard. "You think you bested me? You're a nobody from nowhere," she spat.

Someone grabbed her shirt collar and dragged her back to the table. Blade swung wildly at the offender until she realized it was Gloria, the bartender and her former coworker. *What is wrong with me?*

Mick straightened, red-faced at the insult.

"Shows over," Gloria said to the crowd of onlookers who had gathered around for a little entertainment. Meager protests and grumblings followed as people made their way back to their own tables and conversations.

Mick regained his composure and took a long, hard look at Blade before walking away with a shake of his head.

Gloria wheeled on Blade. "Girl, you're a hot mess tonight. What's gotten into you? I'm not about to let you start a brawl. Not again."

"I-I didn't mean to—"

"I'm just trying to earn a living, and bartending at Gators isn't exactly my dream job." Gloria took hold of Blade's arm and pulled her close. "The last time you were here, I almost got canned. You and that Brit, taking off and leaving me to explain to the cops why there were several people with injuries. No wonder you're here alone. Get it together and consider yourself 86'd."

Blade couldn't argue. Her life was crap, and she had only herself to blame. The inheritance from her mother should have helped; Vivienne had left her millions in investments and an estate in Tuscany. But Blade couldn't rest easy until Alec was found. Her need for justice had turned into an obsession.

After paying her tab and slipping a fifty-dollar bill into Mick's breast pocket, she stepped outside into the fresh air and stood by her motorcycle, parked at the curb. It was still relatively warm outside, although a cool breeze lifted the tendrils of hair that had escaped from her ponytail.

Gloria's words hit home. Instead of celebrating her birthday with Chase and the Soldati, the people who had offered her a home and a purpose, here she stood in New Orleans again, like a broken record repeating itself. Had she subconsciously hoped that Alec would be here?

What she wanted most was to sink into her bed and sleep without the nightmares that had come back in full force since the explosion in Gstaad. Thankfully, her apartment was only five miles away. She knew calling a cab was the smart move. Her adoptive mother would be alive today if the drunk driver who'd slammed into her had made that decision.

Blade ran a finger along the shiny red finish of her Ducati Streetfighter, weighing the risk. If she left the bike behind, it might not be here in the morning. Throwing a long leg over the leather seat with practiced ease, she fastened the strap of the helmet beneath her chin, turned the key, and pressed the start button.

"Easy does it," she whispered to the bike, as she pulled out into the near empty street, her mind already on autopilot. Rather than take the freeway, she'd take the slower side streets through the Garden District, with its oak-shaded lanes and opulent mansions. There was something otherworldly about the place that captivated her. And it felt like home.

She cruised slowly, allowing the night air to clear her head. Then, a flicker of light caught her eye in the rearview mirror—headlights, distant but closing in. She pulled to the right, expecting the SUV to go around her, but the lights became brighter, closer.

Damn, they were going to rear-end her!

With a flick of her wrist, she throttled the engine. The powerful bike surged forward, creating a twenty-foot gap between her and the SUV.

The residential district blurred past her, wrought-iron

balconies and streetlights becoming indistinct streaks of color, but the space between her and the SUV didn't grow. Someone wasn't just following; they were bearing down on her. With her heart thumping hard, Blade considered her options and decided to turn left onto Washington Avenue, but at this speed, it would take all her coordination to not flip the bike.

As she began to slow and lean into the turn, the SUV's bumper clipped her rear tire, sending her and the bike flying out of control. The Ducati barely avoided a large oak tree and slammed into the porch of a small single-story home. At the last second, Blade threw herself free but landed hard—driving all the air from her lungs. Dogs began to bark as motion sensor security lights illuminated the yard.

Blade blinked once, twice, her gaze finally settling on the rear wheel of the motorcycle, still spinning. With effort, she turned her head to see a dark SUV stop briefly before speeding away just as the front door of the home opened. Blade lay still, listening to the sound of sirens in the distance.

"Hey, girl, can you hear me?" asked an elderly man, his dark legs poking out from beneath a flannel robe hastily tied at the waist.

"It wasn't," she began, swallowing hard. "Not . . . an accident."

"What did you say?" He bent over to hear her better.

She fought against the dizziness that threatened to pull her under, but the world spun wildly, and then, mercifully, everything went still.

April 5 – 10:03 p.m. KST
50 miles west of Hamhung, North Korea

The infant wailed against its mother's breast.

Wind whistled through the mountain passage and the sun had long since disappeared over the horizon. The biting cold made it difficult to keep moving forward. Pausing to rest, the ragtag group of North Koreans huddled together for warmth against a granite formation. The past sixty miles had been arduous for the family of two men, three women, and one infant.

"Stay strong, Pastor," Chase Maserati said, his voice barely above a whisper but laden with conviction. "We're going to make it."

Pastor Kwon nodded, his eyes reflecting a depth of pain and hope so intertwined it was impossible to discern one from the other. "Day of the Sun . . ." he mused aloud, his words floating like ghosts in the chilling air. "They wanted to make an example of me during our national holiday."

Chase tilted his head to the heavens, baffled by man's inhumanity to man. The Day of the Sun commemorated the birth of

Kim Il Sung, the so-called Eternal President of North Korea. Sung himself was not eternal, dying in 1994, but his family sought to ensure his power would be; they maintained a stranglehold over the country by executing those who dared disagree with the regime. Pastor Kwon had done nothing except spread the good news of love and peace, and his reward was to be martyred as a spectacle.

The Soldati di Cristo had learned of Pastor Kwon's dire predicament through their clandestine channels in China and South Korea. For centuries, the brotherhood had rescued persecuted Christians in a way no other organization could. Although the rise in surveillance and artificial intelligence worldwide threatened the secrecy that shrouded their movements, North Korea's lid on technology actually helped with their rescue operation.

Chase, the Soldati's chief operative, bristled at their current situation. The rescue operation from Camp 14 had been intended for one man, not this party of half-starved people who were slowly losing hope of escaping their nightmare. But when Pastor Kwon refused to leave without his family, Chase's get-in and get-out operation had turned into a colossal FUBAR.

There was no easy way out of a North Korean labor camp. Disconnecting the electrical current running through the fence had been child's play compared to locating Pastor Kwon, gathering his family, and making their way soundlessly through the prison grounds.

Escape routes out of Camp 14 were limited: travel down the Taedong River, walk nearly four hundred miles to China, or traverse the mountains to Hamhung. The river would have been the optimal means of escape, but it went right through the capital city of Pyongyang. The route through North Korea to China would have taken well over a month, which wasn't an option. This left only an arduous journey through the mountains, then boarding a boat that awaited them in Hamhung, on the banks of the Sea of Japan. The city was still in North Korean territory, but Commander Thomas Kazir's orders had been clear: make it to Hamhung. There was no other choice.

"What now?" asked Hakim, as his eyes skimmed over the huddled group. Six years ago, he'd been in similar circumstances as a prisoner of al-Qaeda. After refusing to renounce his Christian faith, the thirteen-year-old was about to be executed when the Soldati di Cristo had swarmed his small village and rescued the youth.

Even in the limited moonlight, Chase could see the haunted look in the young man's eyes. "Sorry you joined our band of brothers?"

"And miss all the fun? Never."

After five days of constant walking, the group still had over one hundred miles to cover. Chase was well aware of the numerous guards and potentially even military personnel hot on their trail. Pastor Kwon was regarded as an enemy of the regime for sharing the gospel and bringing hope to the people of North Korea. After days of torture in the camp, the forty-something man now looked closer to seventy, but he had refused to give up any information about current operations to smuggle North Koreans into China.

"I need you to scout ahead," Chase said to Hakim, his voice firm despite the fatigue that plagued them all. "We need supplies —anything you can find. Be swift, but careful."

Both men knew that without additional food or water, the people in their care wouldn't be able to walk another fifty miles.

Nodding, Hakim headed down the rocky trail and soon disappeared in the darkness, leaving Chase to distribute the last bottle of water among the civilians.

Pastor Kwon's lips parted in a weak smile. "Your faith, brother Chase, it gives me hope."

Chase returned the smile, unsure of what to say. Was false hope better than none?

In the last thirty minutes, the temperature felt like it had dropped twenty degrees. It was eerily silent. Even the bundled infant was fast asleep. Chase had allowed himself a few moments of rest, leaning back against an outcropping, head bowed and eyes closed, though he did not relax his guard long enough to sleep.

The silence of the mountain pass was abruptly shattered as a cascade of rocks clattered down the slope. Chase's head snapped up, his soldier's instincts instantly alert. His gaze darted to Pastor Kwon and his brother, who both froze, their eyes reflecting the sudden rush of fear. Chase held his index finger to his lips and listened, drawing his Glock 19 from its holster. He motioned to the group to stand. They needed to keep moving.

"Let's go," Chase hissed.

Pastor Kwon gathered his family, herding them forward, but before they could move ten feet, a shot rang out, splintering the rock above Chase's head.

"Soneul deureo!" a man shouted.

Pastor Kwon's brother flinched at the sharp Korean words, but immediately raised his hands in the air. Chase tossed his Glock 19 onto the ground, the weapon skidding across the stony path. The women, weak and terrorized, dropped to their knees.

Eight men emerged from the darkness, forming a semicircle and keeping their weapons trained on the group. *Soldiers—not guards.* Chase felt, once again, helpless in the reality of a stronger force mustered against innocent civilians. For an instant, he was transported back in time to northern Nigeria, where an attack by the Boko Haram had left his wife dead and him unconscious. He considered diving for his Glock, but thought better of the brash move.

A North Korean soldier, wiry and cocky, approached the younger woman. He was almost a foot shorter than Chase and wore an insignia on his olive green uniform. Definitely the man in charge. He reached down and pulled on the jacket Hakim had given the young mother to help keep her child warm. The woman pulled back, and a tug-of-war ensued, delighting the soldier. The jostling woke the sleeping infant and it let out a howl of displeasure. The soldier's face instantly turned to stone. Chase had heard of atrocities against pregnant women and newborns in labor camps, but surely not even this brute would harm an innocent child.

Without thinking, Chase made a move toward the woman, but one of the other soldiers rewarded him with a swift blow to his abdomen with the butt of his rifle. "Keep away from her," Chase gasped, now on hands and knees.

Pastor Kwon tried to intervene, speaking rapidly in Korean, before a rifle blasted through the night. The noise echoed as Pastor Kwon's brother slumped to the ground, blood pouring from his chest. The oldest woman, Kwon's sister-in-law, spoke in a low growl, pointing an accusatory finger at the pastor.

If one person was arrested for any offense against the regime, then that person's entire family was sent to the labor camp, too. This family had no choice but to come on this perilous journey. If not, they most likely would have been executed on the spot when Pastor Kwon met his own fate. But Chase was beginning to think no one would survive the next hour. He hoped Hakim had made it far enough away to escape capture and would reach the boat to report their situation.

Thank God I had the good sense to hide the sat phone.

The wiry soldier stomped on Chase's back, then ground his

face into the dirt with a heavy boot. "I am Senior Colonel Pak Yong-Sun. You are American?"

Chase, stunned to hear English spoken by the soldier, lay speechless.

"Not what you expected? You American bastards underestimate our Respected Comrade and his people. We are not ignorant peasants," Yong-Sun said, snapping his fingers.

In unison, the other soldiers brought their weapons up and aimed at Pastor Kwon and his family.

"He was to be executed as an example at the Day of the Sun celebration to honor the Eternal President Kim Il Sung." Colonel Yong-Sun stood straight and tall, his boot on Chase's back. "You will make a far more valuable example. An American, dead on the Day of the Sun—now that carries a message."

Chase tried to rise. "You filthy—"

Yong-Sun kicked him savagely in the kidney. "Bring me the baby," he ordered with an unsettling calm.

The mother, already defeated, handed her baby to the waiting soldier. Pastor Kwon's gaunt face paled further and, sensing the inevitable, he tried to shield the three women with his body.

"Fire!"

Chase closed his eyes as the smell of gunpowder filled his nostrils. From his position, he could see the lifeless eyes of the pastor, a life extinguished too soon. He prayed for their souls.

And for a miracle.

CHAPTER
THREE

April 5 – 4:26 p.m. CEST
Rome, Italy

"Chase is alive," Commander Thomas Kazir said at last in his melodic Nigerian accent. "We can't level a nation, but we can do what we do best."

In the hush that blanketed the conference room, Thomas could hear the subtle rhythm of Rome beyond the walls—the thrum of distant traffic, the faint echo of voices on the street like a murmuring tide, a violinist practicing *Ode to Joy*. People going about their business, oblivious to worldwide atrocities that only worsened daily. A reminder that God, and only God, was still in control.

He'd summoned his senior staff to an emergency meeting as soon as he'd gotten word from Korea. They all understood that every operation the Soldati undertook was risky, but the news he'd just delivered gutted them all. Hakim had returned to the mountain pass in North Korea expecting to see Chase, Pastor Kwon, and his family—only to find the bodies of innocents shot and discarded like garbage. Killed merely for their Christian faith.

Chase had been taken, presumably, by the guards of Camp 14 or the Korean People's Army. Thank God they hadn't found the satellite phone.

Across the oval table, Xiu's fingers ceased their perpetual dance over her keyboard—an unusual moment of stillness from the team's typically restless cyber expert.

"Jaysus, Mary, and Joseph." Finn shot to his feet, sending his chair crashing against the wall. "You sent Chase into that hellhole with a lad who's barely cut his teeth. I should have been sent instead."

Thomas nodded, then straightened to his full height. "It was a mistake I'll regret for the rest of my life."

Xiu's shoulders sagged. "Murdered them . . . but took the baby."

Luciano Conti, ever the stoic strategist, shook his head in disbelief.

"Let's blow the whole feckin' country to bits," Finn spat out, his Irish brogue thicker than usual. His scarred hands were clenched into fists on the large oval table, knuckles whitening, as if the demolitions expert could pulverize mountains with his bare hands.

Thomas watched his team's reaction. Except for Chase, he'd chosen—no, rescued—each one. Xiu with her unwavering focus, Finn with his explosive passion, and Luc, the cornerstone, always calculating the next move. The team had been in dire situations before. But this time, the Soldati would be operating in unchartered territory, against a regime that showed no mercy. And, as a clandestine brotherhood, the Soldati could not appeal to the Americans for help; this rescue mission would have to be secret.

"According to our network within North Korea, Pastor Kwon was going to be executed as part of the festivities during the Day of the Sun on April 15." Thomas faltered on the word 'festivities' being used to describe a public execution, but cleared his throat and continued, "Since the pastor and his family were killed, we can only assume Chase will be the prized substitute for their propaganda machine. An American in North Korea. We cannot allow his capture to become public. We have less than ten days to plan a rescue mission, coordinate with our underground network, and not cause an international incident. The clock is ticking."

Luc stood abruptly, his chair scraping against the floor. "Xiu, access a map of the North Korea labor camps and prisons."

Without a word, she complied, fingers once again dancing over the keyboard. Three of the four walls, dominated by large high-definition monitors, flickered to life. Luc strode toward the front of the room, ready to dissect any data available.

Studying one of the maps, Luc pointed to a specific area near Hamhung. "Zoom in on the area around Camp 14." His voice was steady, even calm, the analytical side of his brain overriding the emotional side. "Most likely he'll be taken to the same camp where he rescued Pastor Kwon. Both as a message to the other detainees and because of its proximity to Pyongyang."

Thomas considered what lay ahead for Chase—imprisonment and torture. But the North Koreans would keep him alive—barely —to make a spectacle of him until the Day of the Sun. He touched the scar encircling his neck. He knew that some scars ran deeper than skin or bone.

"So what's the plan, yeah?" Finn said.

Thomas straightened, feeling the mantle of command settle firmly upon his shoulders. "We wait," he said, his mind working furiously behind calm eyes. "We reconvene in ten hours. That gives our network in North Korea enough time to gather valuable intel."

"Ten hours?" Xiu's voice broke, a crack in her composed facade. "It will take over eleven hours to fly there. Another four to five hours to collect supplies. Time we simply cannot—"

"Xiu," Thomas cut her off gently but firmly. His heart

clenched at the thought of Chase holed up in a cell, but he couldn't let emotions cloud his judgment—not now. "Every choice has its consequence. We must be strategic and deliberate. Panic leads to mistakes, and mistakes lead to loss."

"Loss we can't afford," Luc added, his own voice tinged with grief.

"Exactly." Thomas walked to the front of the room and squeezed Luc's shoulder, knowing he was thinking of the recent death of Vivienne, their second-in-command and the love of Luc's life. He turned to the whiteboard, picked up a marker, and began to write. "We'll use the hours wisely—adjust plans, prepare contingencies. We've faced dark days before; we'll face this one head-on as well."

The team exchanged glances, silently acquiescing to their commander. Chase would be counting on them.

"Luc," Thomas said, the syllable laced with unspoken urgency, "we're not just up against geography and manpower. We need satellite surveillance, transportation options, escape routes, anything that—"

"Already on it," Luc interrupted, still scrutinizing the monitor. "We'll find a way in, again. And more importantly, a way out."

"North Korea's self-imposed isolation and the element of surprise will work in our favor," Xiu said.

"I'll gather a list of munitions and a wee special something that will knock their socks off." Finn rubbed his palms together in anticipation.

Thomas frowned. "We're the Soldati di Cristo—Soldiers of Christ—not mercenaries for hire. We hold ourselves to a higher standard than the rest of the world. But we all know that. Don't we?"

"Aye, Commander, but I'm still bringin' my ordnance."

"I would expect nothing less. We play this smart. We play this quiet. And we bring him home."

CHAPTER
FOUR

April 5 – 7:10 p.m. CEST
Budapest, Hungary

The orange-red skyline of Budapest slowly ebbed into the slate-blue twilight as Alec Quinn lingered, a silent silhouette against the picture window of his rented villa. From this vantage point on the hill, he could see the lights of the city but they seemed very far away. He normally stayed at the Four Seasons, with a view of the Chain Bridge and Buda Castle. At night, he'd walk along the Danube to enjoy the sight of the Parliament Building, blazing with lights. But tonight, he was trapped in this self-inflicted prison, wondering if he would ever escape the chaos brewing in his world.

Four months ago, he'd made choices he regretted. He'd been the trusted lieutenant to René Martel, the celebrated fashion mogul whose luxury empire had merely served as a glossy veneer, concealing a vast network of illegal activities that spanned continents. After orchestrating his mentor's death, then moving forward with the botched assault on the United Nations, Alec found himself off the grid, a ghost in the shadows. The fashion industry mourned Martel publicly while his criminal underworld scrambled for power, and now Interpol, the CIA, MI6, and a host of other agencies were on the hunt for him, the man who had toppled the king from his blood-soaked throne.

Yet, as the last delicate rays of sunlight surrendered to twilight, Alec allowed himself a rare moment of vulnerability—an acknowledgment of the cost of a life spent in the gray spaces of right and wrong.

"Boss." David's voice cut through the calm, pulling Alec back from his contemplation of the cityscape's jagged horizon. "There's been an incident. Blade's down."

Alec whipped around to face his lieutenant. "What the bloody hell happened?"

"Our team in New Orleans confirms Blade was targeted—it wasn't a random accident. High-speed chase, black SUV. Here are pictures of the crash site." David unfolded a tablet and tapped swiftly to bring up an image—Blade's motorcycle, a mangled carcass of metal and chrome. "It appears they clipped her rear wheel. Sent her flying—"

"Is she alive?"

"Yes. Hospitalized but stable. Concussion, some bruised ribs —they're keeping her for observation."

After deciding to let Blade live on that snowy night in Gstaad, Alec had monitored her movements for months, not out of fear—but out of calculating necessity. The black rose he'd placed on her bed in Tuscany after he breached the Soldati castle proved to be a reckless gesture. He threw down the gauntlet and she'd responded, as he predicted. She was a survivor, and as he'd always suspected, a hunter. Only one step behind him on more than one occasion. Her relentless tenacity threatened to upend his illegal empire and his freedom. They were playing the ulti-mate chess game and someone had tried to take her off the board.

"Did we identify the SUV?" Alec's mind raced, already anticipating moves and countermoves.

"Torched." David swiped to another image of a burning shell of metal engulfed in flames. "Our team arrived too late—the flames had destroyed any chance of lifting prints or gathering evidence. But we're on it."

"What a cock-up. Why didn't the team move in earlier?" Alec demanded.

"They failed to spot the SUV. When they finally saw Blade in danger, moving would have blown their cover."

"Blown their cover?" Alec's voice rose. "And why am I only hearing about this now?"

"I-I needed a clearer picture before bringing it to you."

The younger man reminded Alec of himself at that age, a competent employee who was smart and cunning. But it didn't pay to count on anyone's loyalty. René Martel had learned that lesson the hard way.

"Fire the lot." Alec strode to the bar and poured himself a whiskey. "Send in Camila to set up 24/7 surveillance. No one gets to Blade."

"Anything else?" David said.

"I want hourly updates. When it comes to Blade, don't wait for all the facts. If there's any threat to her safety, apprehend and question the person responsible. I'm keen on getting answers. Start looking into the details to track down the individual who drove that vehicle."

Perhaps this bold attack would curb her unrelenting pursuit of him. Unless she believed it was his doing. Alec exhaled deeply. He should never have baited her.

I'm a right horse's arse.

He recalled her amber eyes, the ferocity with which she drove her Ducati, her stage performance as an impalement artist. If only they'd met under different circumstances. If only he hadn't been responsible for Vivienne's death. Blade was a complex, talented woman who awoke something within him. But he had to tamp that down. *Trust no one.*

Without warning, gunfire ripped through the stillness, shards of glass splintering inward, radiating from a single, lethal point. Alec's reflexes, honed from years of living on a knife's edge, snapped him into motion just as David's body jerked, his leg blossoming red.

Both men lunged together, seeking shelter behind the heavy furniture as a stream of bullets peppered the room. The gunfire shattered window frames and furniture.

"Stay down!" Alec hissed through clenched teeth. Adrenaline surged through him as he sprinted across the room, his hand outstretched for his Sig Sauer P320. The grip settled into his palm as he crouched low, the weapon poised and ready. He fired into the darkness. But his pistol was no match for a fully automatic machine gun.

Through the smoke and floating debris, Alec caught sight of an outline—a person—and fired.

Alec saw David struggling to use his necktie as a tourniquet for his leg. In all his years with Martel, Alec had never been in an actual gunfight. Bollocks! Where was his security team? Were they dead?

The sound of returning gunfire echoed to the right. Finally. A sloppy job for an elite security detail. No doubt they would be searching the grounds, although he doubted the shooter or shooters would be found.

"You all right, sir?" one of the security team shouted.

"David's been hit. Find the nearest doctor and bring him here. We can't take him to a hospital with a bullet wound."

Alec pushed to his feet, his eyes sweeping over the destruction. He'd planned to slip through the city, like the invisible man, but his enemies had hunted him down anyway. This breach struck him as something beyond Interpol or any of the other alphabet organizations. As his pulse steadied, clarity hit him—this precise strike carried purpose. The message rang clear: nowhere offered safety, not anymore.

In this game of kings and queens, he understood the quietest whispers of financial empires, where fortunes grew and crumbled through accidents and intimidation. The most ruthless players would stop at nothing to control billions. And if the attempt on Blade's life fit their strategy, then Alec would make them regret ever stepping onto the chessboard.

"Because I'll burn their kingdom to the ground before I let them take what's mine," he vowed. "Starting with those who targeted Blade."

CHAPTER
FIVE

April 5 – 1:47 p.m. CDT
New Orleans, Louisiana

Blade first became aware of the smell—disinfectant, rubbing alcohol, with a tinge of Old Spice aftershave.

Dazzling sunlight from the window pierced through her skull as she opened one eye. Guard rails, a privacy curtain, and an IV attached to her bandaged arm. She was in a hospital room. Her body felt like she'd been run over by a truck. Blade squeezed her eyes shut.

"You just can't stay out of trouble," a familiar voice said.

Blade winced in pain as she turned her head to see Joe Mancini, her friend and mentor. She'd never seen him look so haggard. A five o'clock shadow added years to his usually immaculately shaved face. At seventy-five, The Great Mancini still exuded a youthful charm, with his thick gray hair styled after the movie star Cary Grant—the celebrity he'd used for inspiration when crafting his unique persona decades ago for his magic show.

He scooted his chair closer to the bed. His hand, disfigured by arthritis, reached for the bed control, and elevated her head. "Is this okay?" he asked before taking hold of her hand in a firm grip. "You sure know how to scare an old man half to death."

"What happened?"

"Good question. What do you remember?"

Blade tried to concentrate through the fog. "Drinking at Gators," she finally said. "Playing darts. Gloria 86'd me. How—"

"The police called me after they found your emergency contact information in your wallet. It appears you lost control of that damn motorcycle of yours and landed on someone's front porch." Joe cleared his throat, his voice rough and unsteady. "You're damn lucky to be alive."

"Yes, she is." A man wearing blue scrubs hurried into the room, his down-turned mouth marring an otherwise youthful face.

Blade struggled to sit up straighter, her body screaming in protest with every movement. She couldn't shake the feeling of déjà vu. Four months ago, a bullet had torn through her body before an explosion hurled her into an alpine snowbank. But that memory was mixed with the pain of holding her biological mother in her arms while Vivienne took her final breath. It was unsettling to draw a blank on how she ended up on her motorcycle, adding to her confusion.

"I'm Dr. DeYoung," the man said, standing at a computer station and not bothering to make eye contact. "I admitted you last night. How are you this afternoon? How's the pain, from zero to ten?"

"A six, maybe seven. But everything about the motorcycle accident is a blur."

"Not surprising." Dr. DeYoung pulled another chair to the bedside opposite Joe. "Your blood alcohol content was well over the legal limit. And you were speeding through a residential neighborhood. The good news is you didn't injure anyone else."

For once, Blade couldn't think of a comeback. A drunk driver had killed her adoptive mother when she was sixteen. It was hard to believe she would risk innocent lives by doing the very thing that had changed her own young life. But still, she was thankful no one had been hurt. "Where did I crash?"

"I'm not sure. You were brought in unconscious, no broken bones. You must have fallen on your right side. Concussion, sprained right wrist, and a bruised leg and hip. You'll be sore for a few weeks. Once the swelling goes down, we'll put on a wrist brace. Your helmet saved your life. I kept it as a souvenir for you. A reminder for the next time you decide to drink and drive."

"I'm not a drunk driver," Blade snapped, her temper flaring at the accusation.

"Your blood work tells a different story. We'll keep you here tonight—for observation." Dr. DeYoung stood up abruptly. "The police should be in shortly to ask a few questions."

Joe gripped the guard rails as support to stand. He winced with the effort, but the words boomed beyond the door to her room. "She doesn't talk to anyone without a lawyer present. You can relay that to the police."

Dr. DeYoung glared at the two, then left.

"Pompous ass," Joe said.

"He's right, Joe. I should have called a taxi."

"What's really going on, kiddo? I've never known you to be reckless—hard-headed and obstinate, but never reckless."

Blade took a shallow breath, trying to steady her thoughts. "Someone . . . hit me. On purpose." Her mind raced, connecting dots with ruthless efficiency. "This wasn't an accident, and I didn't lose control of my bike. Someone wanted me dead."

"Did you see who it was?" Joe pressed, leaning closer.

"No," she admitted, "but the only person who has a reason to kill me is Alec Quinn."

"That doesn't make any sense. You've said he's had a few opportunities to kill you. Why strike now?"

"It's possible I've uncovered something important without realizing it."

"Alec has managed to evade capture by pursuers who have unlimited resources. I doubt you've succeeded where they've failed."

Blade shrugged.

"Perhaps this was a warning." Joe put a hand on her shoulder. "You've got to put this to rest. Not for his sake, but for your sanity."

Tears welled in her eyes. "I can't move beyond Vivienne's death—the way she breathed Alec's name before she died. He holds all the answers."

"Listen to me," Joe said, his tone gruff. "I've made plenty of mistakes. I don't often give advice because I'm a lonely old man with no family and one friend. But I remember a quote I read some years back: 'The stupid neither forgive nor forget; the naïve forgive and forget; the wise forgive but do not forget.' No one is asking you to forget Vivienne's death. But you need to forgive—for you. Not for Quinn."

"It was my birthday a few days ago. Not one phone call. Not even from you," Blade whispered. "And where was I last night? At Gators, alone, drowning out thoughts about him."

She pressed the button on the bed control, lowered her head, and closed her eyes. "Maybe these past few months haven't been a waste of time and money."

"You are impossible, kiddo. I have never met a person as exasperating as you, and that's saying something."

"Can you magically make the past twenty-four hours disappear?"

"If I could do that, I'd be playing cards with the high rollers in Monte Carlo rather than wasting away in a senior living facility that smells like urine."

CHAPTER
SIX

April 6 – 9:30 a.m. CST
Shanghai, China

Fou drums reverberated through the Crimson Silk Acrobatic Troupe complex, a massive repurposed warehouse with high ceilings supported by exposed steel beams. Ming Zhang could feel each strike of the stick prodding her forward.

"Will I ever be free of this bondage?" she wondered as she watched her fellow acrobats soar through the air, their bodies twisting and turning like silk ribbons caught in a whirlwind. Some of the younger students huddled in pods, alive with whispers and hushed conversations. The troupe would join the carefully curated roster of foreign entertainers—dancers, musicians, and acrobats from twenty different countries—to perform in Pyongyang for the annual North Korean Day of the Sun festival.

The nation would televise the event across its tightly controlled airwaves, the foreigners offering a rare glimpse of the outside world for millions of North Koreans who would never cross their own borders.

Ming cringed at the hypocrisy of it all. Crimson Silk was the proverbial olive branch between the two countries, despite China and North Korea signing a defense treaty in 2021. It all came down to money, through trade agreements and aid packages. The people in China were just as repressed as North Koreans, although the progressive cities of Beijing and Shanghai gave the Western powers an excuse to ignore the human rights abuses. They never bothered to look at the underbelly of the beasts.

This time, I will send another type of message.

Standing at the edge of the rehearsal space, Ming removed a towel from her gym bag and wiped her brow. There seemed to be no end to rehearsing—twists, flips, handstands, strength training, martial arts—but this was the cost of being a celebrated acrobat in China. Grueling hours of practice were normal for everyone here. But with a new class of recruits arriving today, all the coaches would be busy acclimating the young students to their new home.

"You. Girl. Get to work!" Coach Zhou, rumored to have been coached by the renowned Russian Leonid Moskvina, shouted from the opposite side of the complex.

Ming moved onto the spring-loaded floor for a tumbling run. The scrutiny, the regimen, the surveillance, the unrelenting control. She despised it. She despised him. His brand of coaching had left its scars, invisible but deep.

For fifteen years, she had lived among the others—training, eating, sleeping—yet she trusted almost none of them. Not with *this*. Not with the truth that had reshaped her soul. There was a before and an after. Before, she had never questioned the emptiness gnawing at her. After, she had known what it was to be fulfilled. And now, she ached to share the gospel. But in China, faith had walls. Christians were only allowed to worship in official churches registered with the government. Underground gatherings carried consequences, and the weight of those consequences stretched beyond her.

So she swallowed the truth, locking it behind her lips, and did what she had learned to do best—perform.

From across the room, Qianfan motioned for her to join him. The two had been inseparable since they were eight years old. Their bond was stronger than brother and sister. It was built on the foundation of mutual trust and vulnerability. It was Qianfan who had introduced her to Christianity, and the pair had become like an island amid a sea of nonbelievers. At any hour, they could be arrested—or worse.

"Is everything all right?" she asked, her voice barely audible over the cacophony of the drums.

"Yes and no," he said, stretching his lithe body. His thin frame masked the immense strength required to be the base of the pair's acrobalance performances, supporting the perfect symmetry of lifts and balances that allowed them to create incredible paired shapes.

"That sounds cryptic." To gain time, Ming unwound her long black hair, shook it loose, and began the ritual of braiding it into submission.

Qianfan hesitated, glancing at the frenetic activity all around them. A boy on a unicycle careened into a teenage girl balancing spinning plates on her head. A loud crash echoed off the walls. He took advantage of the distraction to lean in close. "I've heard from our network."

This must be the bad news.

Ming nodded and he continued. "One of our Christian brothers has been taken prisoner by the North Korean army. A rescue mission is in the works."

"What has that to do with us?" she said, more loudly than intended.

"Keep your voice down," he said, peering around nervously. "Someone may overhear us."

Ming laughed at the absurdity of his remark. Between the

drums, the clattering of plates, the flying acrobats, and the piped-in string instruments, it would be impossible for anyone to hear their conversation.

"Rescue mission? What can we do to help? We aren't soldiers. Surely they don't think we are going to break him out of whatever hole they have shoved him in."

Qianfan furrowed his brow, clearly disappointed in her reaction. "I'm not sure, but we have our skills—and our faith."

As the drumming continued, Ming contemplated their options, her thoughts spiraling like the acrobats soaring overhead. How could they contribute to such a daring operation without compromising their own safety or jeopardizing everyone here?

Coach Zhou surveyed the area, his gaze lingering disapprovingly on their idle figures. Ming grabbed her partner's hand and led him to a partitioned space equipped with aerial silks, balance beams, pommel horses, and various acrobatic training apparatus. Crimson Silk was no ordinary acrobatic company. The government used them as a weapon to promote goodwill to other nations —especially democratic ones. What some Chinese people perceived as freedom was actually a form of servitude. Suspicion permeated the troupe's higher echelon.

Ming spun gracefully, her movements fluid and precise, as she tried to push away the fear that continually clamored forward. The Day of the Sun festival was fast approaching, and she needed to focus. Yet her thoughts kept circling back to the American, the rescue operation, and the imminent danger they faced.

"Whatever we do, we must be careful," Ming whispered as they met again in their dance, her eyes locked on his.

"Agreed." He offered her a reassuring smile as he grasped both her hands to lift her fluidly into a balanced handstand.

As Ming and Qianfan rehearsed, she reveled in their choice to depict the legend of Mu Guiying for the North Korean audience. Ming would portray the formidable woman warrior who defeated

General Yang in combat, married him on her own terms, and then brilliantly led his armies to victory—a stark contrast to North Korea's Supreme Leader. Where Mu Guiying embodied courage, strategic genius, and unwavering loyalty, the dictator represented only tyranny and fear. The audience wouldn't miss the comparison, even if they dared not speak it aloud.

Ming allowed herself a smile. She had another surprise waiting for the Korean people. The moment had come to put her faith into action.

CHAPTER
SEVEN

April 6 – 4:30 a.m. CEST
Rome, Italy

Ten hours. Time to face the team.

Still no word of an actual sighting of Chase. Commander Kazir wasn't surprised by this absence of news. Ordinary citizens from North Korea were forbidden from communicating with foreigners, but somehow, through God's grace, the Christian network was able to smuggle messages in and out of the country. Though he was sure America's Pony Express had been faster.

He strode into the conference room, expecting to be the first one there, but seated around the oval table were Finn, Luc, Xiu, and Father Sean McCann, a surprise but welcome guest.

Thomas gave the priest a bear hug before smacking him on the back. "You are a sight for sore eyes. I take it the Vatican knows of our situation?"

"Well aware. I'm here to offer whatever assistance the Holy See is able to provide—under the radar, of course."

"All right, let's begin," Thomas said, taking a seat at the head of the table. "Given that Chase is an American citizen, we unofficially reached out to the US State Department. They are reluctant to become involved, since there is no confirmation from Pyongyang that Chase is in custody. Even if they do hear officially, any publicity or diplomatic overtures would only worsen Chase's chance of survival. And we've got fresh intel from North Korea. No visual on Chase yet, but my bet is on Camp 14."

"Camp 14 would be fortuitous." Luc looked up from the notepad in front of him. "We already have extensive maps of the camp and surrounding area, though they've likely changed the guard schedules after we extricated Pastor Kwon and his family."

Thomas nodded. "We expect Chase to be transferred to Pyongyang before the Day of the Sun festival, so we should investigate opportunities along the route as well as in the city."

Unable to contain her excitement, Xiu blurted, "The Chinese Crimson Silk Acrobatic Troupe will be performing at the festival. I saw them perform years ago. Impressive. Dramatic acrobatics, unbelievable feats of strength and grace, and even bian lian—where the performers seem to change masks by magic. The heavens are truly on our side today!"

"Jaysus, lass! Acrobats helping get Chase out? By teachin' him how to walk on his hands?" Finn slammed his palm on the table. "Wouldn't it be a right sight easier to storm the camp?"

"Easy, Finn," Thomas cautioned, raising a hand. "Going in with guns blazing would sign our death warrants—and likely Chase's. One of the acrobatic performers is a Christian who may agree to assist."

Finn scoffed. "What can a bleedin' acrobat do for us?"

"More than you think," Thomas said firmly. "Ming Zhang has access to the stage, to the crowd. She will create diversions, manipulate perceptions—all the elements of their craft."

"Can she be trusted?" Luc asked.

"Ming is one of us, in faith if not in mission," Thomas said. "She wants to support our operation, but she's uncertain how to leverage her role in the festivities without compromising herself or the others in her troupe. Which is understandable."

"Then we give her certainty," Xiu said, as she hit a key to display an image of the troupe. "We find a way to integrate their performance into our operation."

"Do ya hear yourselves?" Finn rose to his feet. "We're really going to trust a Chinese circus act to determine Chase's fate? And worse, wait until the last minute to act? We're the Soldati. We rely on ourselves, working together—period."

"May I make a suggestion?" Father McCann said, continuing without waiting for a response. "Wouldn't Blade's involvement be advantageous to this mission?"

"Blade?" Xiu's voice carried a note of disbelief. "There has been no contact from her since Vivienne's funeral."

"That isn't exactly true," Father McCann said. "I spoke with her about two months ago."

Luc rocked back in his chair. "Her skills are undeniable, but I feel she'd be more of a liability than an asset."

"Is that based on analysis or personal feelings?"

"Both."

Thomas considered the priest's proposition. Blade, the professional knife-thrower and Vivienne's daughter. She'd proven to be resilient and formidable—for a civilian. But she was on her own path to find the man responsible for Vivienne's death. Nothing would persuade her otherwise. Yet the mere mention of her name stirred a sense of possibility within his heart.

The debate shifted as Father McCann leaned forward, his presence commanding despite his humble demeanor. "I believe in redemption," he began, his voice deep and resolute. "And in utilizing all of God's gifts. Blade's impalement act—it's more than trickery. It's a display of precision and fearlessness."

Realization dawned on Luc's face. "Are you suggesting . . ."

"Blade could easily blend in with the performers, become part of the spectacle, with the right makeup and costume. It's the perfect cover."

Thomas could see wisdom behind the priest's steady brown eyes. "Let's explore this option. I'm not sure how Blade could help, but any potential advantage might prove crucial for our mission."

Finn's jaw clenched visibly, the muscles working beneath his stubbled cheek. "You forget Shen's death was her fault."

"I forget nothing," Thomas fired back. "She didn't know if we were the good guys or bad. Anyone could have tripped the alarm. And I think she proved to be an asset in preventing the threat to the United Nations."

Father McCann stood, clearly intending to douse the brewing storm. "You're a team, but this isn't the moment to allow your feelings to overshadow the mission. Valuable minutes are slipping away. There is no reason why there can't be a two-pronged approach to the problem."

The group exchanged glances, the tension easing slightly as strategy overtook emotion.

"If you agree," Father McCann began, "I'll go to New Orleans and speak with Blade personally, while you continue to devise other options."

"How do you know she's there?" Luc asked.

"The Soldati isn't the only brotherhood to have tentacles in every region of the world."

"Father, that's two days of travel." Thomas measured his next words carefully. "We only have nine days till the festival."

"I'm aware of the stakes. But it would be inappropriate to deliver news of Chase's capture, not to mention asking Blade to put herself in danger—again—over a text or phone call." Father McCann gave the team a sheepish grin. "Shepherd One is available, if you give me the green light. And if Blade agrees, communication with you will remain possible en route. We'll have privacy on the papal jet."

Thomas sighed. All options had to be considered. "Make the arrangements, Father. And Godspeed."

He quickly took his leave, closing the door softly behind him.

"While you've been *talking*," Luc said, "I've made arrangements to operate out of Seoul. We'll be somewhat close to Pyongyang, although the logistics are a nightmare. There is no easy way to travel to North Korea directly from Seoul, and crossing the DMZ is out of the question. Time is not our friend."

"Is our plane fueled and primed to leave?" Thomas asked.

"Aye," Finn said. "The jet is fueled, loaded, and ready to roll, but I'm still not sold on including Blade."

Xiu stood and walked slowly toward Thomas. "We can extract Chase without Blade," she said softly. "We've faced worse odds."

"Have we?"

Finn reached over to squeeze his commander's shoulder. "We're in this together. Always have been, always will."

CHAPTER
EIGHT

April 6 – 4:14 p.m. CDT
New Orleans, Louisiana

The walls of the coffin pressed in on her from all sides. No matter how she twisted and turned, there was no room to move, no way to push the lid open. She could sense only darkness and the smell of damp earth. She opened her mouth to scream, but dirt poured into her lungs, choking her.

Blade awoke, drenched in sweat, gasping for air. For a moment, the panic remained as her gaze swept through the shadowy bedroom. Home. She was home.

She'd been thinking of her adoptive mother, Marie, as she fell asleep. Her mother had always hated enclosed spaces, yet her father had insisted on a burial rather than cremation. Even after twelve years, the thought of her mother buried underground periodically gave her nightmares. With a groan, she sat up, pressing her palm against the fiery ache in her hip—until her wrist reminded her it was injured, too.

According to the clock on her bedside table, it was a little after four in the afternoon. Joe had dropped her off a few hours ago and refused to leave until she was settled. After taking a dose of ibuprofen, she'd finally convinced him to go, craving the solitude of her apartment after the chaos of the last thirty-six hours.

In the gloom of late afternoon, she wished the doctor had prescribed something stronger. Exhaustion, pain, and—dare she admit—fear finally took its toll. Tears ran down her cheeks. Someone had tried to kill her and might try again. She'd never felt so alone in her life.

Joe had encouraged her to report the SUV and attempt on her life to the police, but Blade saw little point. Without evidence or witnesses, they'd dismiss her claims as paranoia or outright lying. No detective had even bothered to interview her about the crash; instead, an unemotional officer had simply handed her a DWI citation upon discharge, promising a court date to follow.

Gritting her teeth, Blade wiped her tears and forced herself to stand. The tan carpet felt soft beneath her feet as she steadied herself and pushed off the bed. She wouldn't cower beneath the covers like a frightened child. What she needed was a hot shower to wash away the hospital smell, then food.

A floorboard creaked somewhere down the hall. Blade went rigid, her pulse quickening as she strained to listen. Somebody was inside her apartment. Joe, returning to check on her? She held her breath, waiting for any sound of movement. The quality of the silence that followed told her everything she needed to know—whoever was out there wasn't her friend.

Damn, my phone is charging in the kitchen.

With trembling fingers, Blade reached into her nightstand drawer and removed a knife. The cold steel calmed her nerves. The bedroom carpet silenced her footsteps until she reached the bedroom door. Quickly, she peeked around the door frame into the hallway. It was empty.

Either her imagination was getting the best of her or she was having lingering effects from the concussion. Still, she'd call Joe and ask him to drive over.

Gripping the knife firmly, she moved down the hallway to the kitchen. The sun filtered through the blinds in slanted beams, striping the hardwood floor. A creak sounded from the living room, too deliberate to be the building settling. The hairs on Blade's arms stood on end. Her first instincts had been correct. And whoever it was, they weren't hiding their presence anymore.

Blade rounded the corner, poised to strike. A figure, dressed in black from head to toe, stood outlined by the window. Blade didn't hesitate. She let the knife fly. The intruder shifted, and the knife stuck solidly in the door.

"Thought you'd be tougher, Blade," the woman hissed as she whirled and seized her from behind, placing her in a choke hold.

Blade's breath hitched as the arm tightened around her neck. An image of Ellis, the woman who had attacked her in Florence, flashed before her. Ellis, too, had underestimated her.

Instinct kicked in and her countless hours of savate training took over. She snapped her hands up, grabbing the attacker's wrists. Without overthinking, she twisted violently, slamming her elbow into the attacker's ribs. The woman's grip loosened, giving Blade space to maneuver.

She unleashed a *chassé latéral* to the assailant's thigh, and the woman stumbled backward. The two stood face-to-face.

"And you look just like Catwoman in your ridiculous outfit," Blade said, adrenaline pumping as she assumed a boxing stance.

Catwoman closed the distance and threw a punch. Blade ducked and countered with a devastating roundhouse kick that sent the assailant stumbling back. She fought on, delivering a barrage of kicks and jabs with her left hand, but her injuries were slowing her down.

Wiping blood from a split lip, Catwoman grinned and retrieved the knife from the door.

Changing tactics, Blade sprinted for the kitchen. She yanked a steak knife free from its wooden block on the counter, whirling to find the woman almost upon her. "Big mistake," Blade said, leveling the blade between them.

They circled each other warily. The woman feinted left, then slashed Blade across her ribcage. Blood seeped from the deep cut. Blade parried, but pain radiated through her torso. *I can't hold her off.*

Catwoman pressed the advantage, driving Blade back against the refrigerator. Blade dodged another swipe of the knife, then kicked out with a *chassé bas*, her foot connecting with the woman's knee.

With a grunt, the woman staggered sideways. Blade slashed at her torso, but sliced only through cloth.

Catwoman launched herself forward, delivering a vicious kick to Blade's ribs. The impact knocked the breath from her lungs. She collapsed near the sink, the knife falling from her limp fingers. Dazed, she looked up to see the woman looming above her, blade raised to strike.

Blade squeezed her eyes shut, bracing for the killing blow that never came. Instead, she heard a sudden scuffle, a crash, and a startled cry that wasn't hers.

Her eyes flew open as Father McCann grappled with the assassin. He had the woman in a headlock, his face contorted with rage as he rammed her repeatedly into the refrigerator door.

"Get. Away. From. Her!" he bellowed, emphasizing each word with another slam.

The woman clawed at his arm, legs flailing, but his grip was iron. With a final heave, he hurled her across the kitchen. She crashed into the chairs, toppling the small dining table.

Catwoman's stunned reaction to facing off against a priest was nearly comical. As she struggled to her feet, her glare flickered between Father McCann and Blade, reassessing her chances. But she said nothing, bolting out the door, swift and silent.

Father McCann leaned over, hands on knees. "I haven't done anything like this since high school football."

"Remind me to stay in your good graces," Blade said. She rocked on her heels, adrenaline fading to leave her spent and numb. A gentle hand on her shoulder made her flinch.

"It seems that, once again, God's timing is perfect," Father McCann said softly as he helped her stand on shaky legs and led her to the sofa.

She sank down onto the cushions, every muscle in her body screaming in protest. "What if she returns?"

"Lord, I hope not. I don't think both of us together could defeat her. Do you need a doctor?"

Blade shook her head, then winced at the spike of pain the motion caused. "I've had enough of doctors and hospitals for the past two days."

"What is going on? Who was that?"

"I have no idea, but I suspect Alec Quinn has a hand in this. I was run off the road night before last." She rubbed her forehead as if she could erase the memory. "And then today—another attempt. Whoever's behind this wants me dead."

"We had no idea you were hurt, or I wouldn't have come." He immediately caught his blunder. "That didn't come out right. What I meant to say was I would have come, but not to enlist your help."

"I'm so tired," she said, struggling to maintain control. "I don't want to sound ungrateful, but why in the hell *are* you here?"

He perched on the edge of the coffee table so he could look her in the eye. "It's nice to see you again, too."

CHAPTER
NINE

April 6 – 4:58 p.m. CDT
New Orleans, Louisiana

Blade winced as the needle pierced her skin, but she clenched her jaw and tried not to think about the assassin who'd just tried to kill her. She had refused to go to an urgent care or hospital and would have used butterfly stitches to close the wound herself had it not been for Father McCann's intervention.

Their eyes met briefly as Father McCann paused his work. "Are you sure you don't want to change your mind?"

"Positive. Besides, I've already taken a pain pill, which should kick in soon. You're good with a needle and thread. Do they teach this in priest school?" Blade asked, keeping her attention fixed on the overhead kitchen light. She had to keep talking to keep her fears at bay—and to avoid the inevitable—the answer to why Father McCann was here in the first place.

He was quiet for a moment as he focused on the stitches. "I briefly considered going into the medical field before I accepted my calling."

"Lucky for me you came along when you did. I'd be dead, and we both know it."

"Luck had nothing to do with it. When will you accept that truth?"

So far, God had been nonexistent in her life. Two mothers dead, a career in the toilet, an estranged relationship with her father, several attempts on her life. There was never a doubt—she was on her own. Changing the subject, Blade said, "Ever have a girlfriend? Before becoming a priest, I mean."

Her question seemed to catch him off guard, and he paused mid-stitch. As he glanced up, his cheeks flushed a crimson red, and Blade realized she wore only pajama shorts and a sports bra.

"Uh, yes," he stammered, quickly returning to his task. "I had a few in high school, but nothing serious. My heart was always drawn more toward the Church."

Blade's laughter spilled out, unchecked, whether fueled by the pain meds or the remaining adrenaline. "Forgive me, Father," she gasped, "but I've never seen a priest blush before."

Flustered, he pulled on the thread with a jerk.

"Ouch!" Blade yelped. "You did that on purpose."

He shrugged. "Desperation makes a man dangerous. Wise words to remember." He carefully tied off the final stitch.

"Thank you," Blade said softly. "I owe you."

"You may be paying that debt sooner than you think. Got anything to eat?"

After rummaging through the refrigerator, Father McCann whipped up a meal of fluffy omelets, biscuits straight from the can, and a bowl of fresh fruit. Blade couldn't remember the last time she'd enjoyed food this much. Afterwards, they lingered at the table, steaming cups of coffee in hand, the silence between them comfortable.

She hated to break the spell, but she'd stalled long enough. "Why did you really come to New Orleans?"

He hesitated and removed his glasses to clean them. "It's complicated."

"You wouldn't be here if it weren't."

"Chase is in trouble, real trouble," he finally said as he carried the dirty dishes to the sink. "He was leading a family out of North Korea when he was captured. The entire party was murdered, except for Chase."

The news hit her like a punch to the stomach, and she fought to steady herself. Chase, her trusted friend and ally. She wrapped her hands around the cup of coffee, hoping its warmth would quash the sudden chill in her body. Last December, it had been chilly on the castle turret where she and Chase soaked in the beauty of Siena. Wisps of fog had lingered over the hills. She recalled his invitation to stay with him, and her stupidity in leaving. All for a failed quest to find Alec and the truth.

Blade exhaled a long held breath. "What . . . what happened to Chase?"

"Our best guess is the North Koreans will probably execute him on the Day of the Sun festival on April 15."

"*Execute* him? That's unbelievable." Blade went to the cupboard and pulled out a whiskey bottle. She poured out half a glass and took a swig, then poured a second glass and offered it to Father McCann. "What are the Soldati doing?"

"There's a tentative plan in place, but considering your injuries, I don't believe you're in any condition to help."

"Tell me what you had in mind."

As Father McCann related the plan to use the Chinese acrobatic troupe to facilitate a rescue attempt, Blade paced restlessly within the small living area as she considered the possible scenarios and outcomes of such a mission. "Nine days? That's cutting it close," Blade muttered, thumbing the scar along her jawline. How could they possibly devise a plausible plan on such short notice?

Mistaking her concentration for reluctance, he leaned in. "Chase would not hesitate to help you, no matter how impossible the task might seem. You're needed—period."

His words struck like a sharp slap across the face. "No power on earth could keep me from North Korea. Chase means more to me than . . ." She swallowed hard, past the lump that had formed in her throat.

Father McCann nodded. "We fly out of New Orleans in ninety minutes and rendezvous with Thomas and the team in Seoul. We'll sort out the details en route."

"All right." Blade turned to face him. "Before we drive to the airport, we need to make a stop."

"What do you mean?"

"If we'll be working with Chinese acrobats during a performance, then Joe Mancini's our expert. He's forgotten more about the art of illusion than most magicians will ever know in their lifetime. If we intend to pull off a rescue mission under such improbable circumstances, Joe might be our ace in the hole."

"You expect me to sell another civilian to Thomas? To Finn?"

Blade nodded. "Would you leave a sword master out of a sword fight? There's only one drawback. He'll be hard to convince."

"Convince about what?" Joe said, standing in the doorway. "If whatever question you have in mind will get me out of that old folks' home, I'm in."

Blade hurried to her mentor and held him tight. "It's about time you showed up."

Joe had a bag in one hand and a six-pack of root beer in the other. His eyes darted from her to Father McCann, noting the white collar. "I'm late to the party—again. What's this all about?"

"It's dangerous, and I can't guarantee we'll be safe," Blade said.

"You're not safe here either, judging by the state of your apartment. A change of scenery might do us both good." Joe passed out the bottles of root beer.

"Even if that scenery is in North Korea?"

Joe reached out and clinked his bottle against hers. "As someone once said, 'Twenty years from now, you will be more disappointed by the things you didn't do than by the ones you did do.' I'm not sure if I'll be around in twenty years, but I'm due a little adventure right about now."

April 7 – 4:52 p.m. ULAT
Somewhere above Mongolia

Through the cabin window, Alec studied the storm clouds that surrounded the Gulfstream as it soared over Mongolia. His own internal storm thundered anew—Budapest proved he was not invincible. Only luck or fate had saved him from a bullet. He could think of nothing else.

He'd first assumed that agents of Daystar LLC, René Martel's corporation, were behind the attacks on him and Blade. After further analysis, that seemed improbable. Alec knew from first-hand experience that cutthroat board members would stoop to murder, but they wouldn't want to dirty their hands on a wanted man or a woman who made no overtures for control of Daystar.

Alec didn't need a vivid imagination to conjure up enemies—there were plenty who'd prefer him dead and forgotten. Martel had built a criminal empire cloaked beneath the moniker *the Spaniard*—a name Alec had appropriated after his mentor's death. No one had ever confirmed the Spaniard's true identity, but Alec had always suspected Martel's original investors knew. Which was why he had eliminated them. No loose ends, or so he thought. Perhaps one of the investors had talked, and he now faced a new challenger to his position. Still, the most likely contender was Maximillian Krüger—a smug opportunist clawing for Martel's empire in court. By eliminating Alec and Blade, Krüger would silence any challenge to his inheritance and clear the field of interference.

Weighing against this explanation was the fact that Krüger depended on his mother for support, and neither of them possessed the wealth needed to track him down. Alec's intelligence far exceeded what any half-baked private investigator could uncover. Something didn't add up. But whoever had planned these attacks would pay—with their lives.

Camila's intel about Blade worried him most—her journey to Seoul, traveling with a priest. What would draw her to Seoul, and with a priest, of all people? The situation presented a proper riddle, one he needed to solve quickly.

Camila's message, both cryptic and brief, conveyed only the most essential information. She promised to rendezvous with him at another hideout in Seoul, where her team would vet the location, guaranteeing its impregnability. Alec trusted her implicitly; she was the most competent surveillance expert he knew, with a network of contacts that rivaled his own. Her Spanish beauty and intellect attracted him, but he always kept business and pleasure separate. And truth be told, she paled in comparison to Blade Broussard.

A soft knock interrupted his reverie. "We should be landing in about forty-five minutes, boss," David said, hobbling into the conference room on crutches.

Alec slammed a fist on the mahogany table, the sudden noise startling David. "Bloody hell, what's Blade doing in Seoul of all places?" he muttered under his breath, his frustration boiling over.

Fumbling for a response, David thrust a folder across the table. "The financial reports you requested."

"Sit before you fall down," Alec ordered as he opened the folder and began to peruse the report, which didn't improve his mood. Millions lost last month, putting pressure on his already strained resources. "Why are we hemorrhaging money in Thailand and Southeast Asia?"

David shifted in his chair. "Since you shut down all operations involving children, profits have plummeted."

Alec glared at the younger man, but facts remained facts. He'd crossed lines into drug running, prostitution, and other illegal activities, but child exploitation was firmly off the board. That wasn't the policy of his predecessor, who appeared to lack any conscience whatsoever. Alec's associates had balked at this decision, but it was nonnegotiable. The few who resisted the change met their ends like rabid dogs.

His own childhood, spent on the streets of Liverpool with no supervision, had left him with scars too deep and complex to contemplate. Predators such as René Martel preyed on the vulnerable. He counted himself among the lucky few who made it off the streets and into the boardroom. A stark contrast to those posh toffs from Eton who had never experienced a single day of hardship in their privileged lives. Alec remained an anomaly.

"Set up a meeting with my associates—all of them—for tomorrow. Profits must go up. If anyone hesitates, eliminate them."

David nodded and turned slowly, maneuvering his crutches before walking unsteadily out of the room, leaving Alec alone—just as he preferred it.

The plane banked, with Seoul sprawling below like a circuit board of light and shadow. Alec's thoughts switched to Blade. She was impulsive, with a penchant for rushing into situations without considering the consequences. He remembered their first meeting at Gators in New Orleans, how she'd stepped in to defend him, regardless of the risk. She had trusted him, and he'd betrayed that trust.

Alec blamed his upbringing for his lack of emotional depth. His addict mother had left him alone for days at a time, while his grandparents were oblivious to the reality of life on the streets. And yet, he was following Blade to Seoul. This feeling, this connection between them both thrilled and terrified him. There was absolutely zero chance of a relationship with Blade, not after Vivienne's death. But deep in his soul, if it still existed, he wanted to prove he was worthy.

I'm turning into a right daft wanker.

He peered at the tattoo on his forearm. The black rose—symbolizing strength and power—was utter hogwash. Intelligence-gathering, cunning, and a bit of luck were what he needed to defeat their common enemy.

Alec stalked into the main cabin and sat opposite David. "Surveillance equipment installed?"

"On both Mila Krüger's home and Maximillian's apartment. Every movement, word, and whisper recorded."

"I want updates by the hour, no matter how trivial."

"Yes, sir. I've hired the best."

"Be sure that you have."

As the runway loomed closer, a knot tightened in Alec's chest, cold and sharp. Seoul stretched out before him, a city he'd never visited nor had any desire to. It was unfamiliar and foreign—a place where enemies easily vanished among the ten million residents. A city where the Buddhist temples and palaces of the past collided with the skyscrapers and high-tech subways of the present.

Alec's bright, immense world had shrunk to remote hideouts surrounded by a security detail. He hadn't clawed and killed his way to the top, only to see his position threatened by thugs or an upstart spoiled bastard. If his ruse of running worked, his enemies would reveal themselves within the week. And he'd be ready.

Yet, in this metropolis, he sought only one. As Alec reclined in the leather seat, he recalled an earlier encounter with Blade, as she sat across from him in this very jet. The two had sipped champagne while toasting to new beginnings. He'd been so flippant and disingenuous—the joke was on him. The amber-eyed beauty had stolen a piece of his heart and common sense. Traveling to Seoul posed significant risks. But like a moth to a flame, he couldn't resist the magnetic pull. What to do about Blade remained a mystery—even to himself.

No matter the cost, to protect Blade, the streets of Seoul would run red before he was finished.

CHAPTER
ELEVEN

April 8 – 5:33 a.m. KST
Seoul, South Korea

The steady beat of the windshield wipers set Blade's nerves on edge. She peered out the passenger window, seeing nothing but a few bright lights through dense trees and foliage. Joe sat beside her, eyes closed, his breath soft and steady. Father McCann rode shotgun beside Xiu, who must have drawn the short straw for this assignment. Xiu's cold reception made it clear that Blade was not wanted or needed on this operation.

As they pulled into a curved driveway, the understated beauty of a *hanok* nestled among Mongolian oak trees and Japanese maples did not disappoint. Strategic lights illuminated the single-story structure, its clean lines and gentle curves in harmony with the nature surrounding it. The tiled roof sloped downwards, its edges curving up at the corners.

Thomas stood in the open doorway. Rain dripped steadily from the *cheoma*, forming small streams before splashing onto the wooden porch. Opening the car door, Blade moved stiffly into his waiting embrace. He held her gently, then eased back to take a better look. "Father McCann reported your injuries, but I didn't expect this."

His gaze swept over her, noting the brace on her right wrist and the small bruise forming on her cheek. "Welcome home. And happy birthday."

Tears welled up with sudden emotion. The Soldati had offered her a place within the brotherhood four months ago. But she'd been so consumed with finding Alec and seeking revenge for her mother's death that she'd foregone the opportunity. Perhaps being part of a family meant you were always welcomed home.

"Come inside, where you can properly introduce us to your friend," Thomas said.

The interior was minimalist, with polished hardwood floors, rice paper screens, and modern amenities discreetly integrated into the design. Several sofas and chairs had been shoved into a corner and replaced with eight-foot plastic tables covered with maps, spreadsheets, paper cups, candy wrappers, and assorted electronic equipment.

Luc sat hunched over a map with reading glasses perched on his nose. His face lit up when he saw Blade. He rose and strode over. "Did you catch the *bastardo*?"

Blade shook her head.

"Figures."

That one word summed up her deep sense of failure and inadequacy.

Luc turned away, but before he could take a step, Joe brushed past Blade. He stood eye-to-eye with the Italian. "I'm not sure who you are, pal, but I think you owe my friend an apology."

"Joe—"

"She hasn't told me the entire story. But I do know Blade. She's not a quitter, and she's the best person I've ever had the privilege to meet. We're here to help. So a little respect is in order."

A lump formed in her throat. Joe was always in her corner.

Luc tried to stare the older man down, but Joe wasn't intimidated. Decades of performing onstage made him impervious to hecklers, drunks, and bullies.

"What I said was uncalled for. I'm not myself," Luc said finally, by way of apology.

"It's been a tough week." Thomas extended his hand to Joe. "We've all been a bit tense. The rest of our motley crew is Finn, our demolitions expert, and of course you've met our IT genius, Xiu."

"And I'm just a pinch hitter," Father McCann said as he walked toward the kitchen. "Coffee anyone?"

"Nice to meet most of you," Joe said, running a hand through his thick hair. "I could use a shot of caffeine."

"We have less than seven days to develop a plan, coordinate with our Chinese friends, and break Chase out of Pyongyang without creating a diplomatic incident. Would you like a few hours' sleep before we start?"

"No," Blade and Joe said in unison.

Thomas's grin filled the room. "I thought not. Luc, give us a *brief* rundown of where we stand."

Luc rolled his shoulders and the energy returned to his voice. "We received confirmation that the Crimson Silk Acrobatic Troupe will provide assistance. Ming Zhang is the principal performer and our ally. She has her own network of Christian spies we can tap into. The troupe is currently rehearsing in Shanghai." Luc pointed to a map pinned to a wall. "Chase is definitely in Camp 14, identified by the red X on the map. It's heavily fortified since Chase extracted Pastor Kwon and his family from the same camp. It will be almost impossible to stage a rescue attempt at that location. There is no other choice but to wait until he is in Pyongyang. I'm currently working on obtaining any intel about where the North Koreans could hold Chase."

"Can you tell us more about Ming Zhang?" Blade asked, taking a seat in an empty chair.

"It's been right difficult to get a read on her," Finn said, looking directly at Xiu. "I don't fancy this plan of involving the Chinese. Their government can't be trusted—just ask Hong Kong and Taiwan. Ming seems to be enmeshed in Chinese diplomacy. Not what I'd call reliable."

"You idiot," Xiu said, her voice rising an octave. "You understand nothing about living under Communist rule. Spies everywhere, little to no personal freedom. You Westerners have it easy. Ming is merely trying to keep her family alive."

Finn held his arms up in mock surrender. "Didn't mean to set you off, *darlin'*. But we could be walking into a trap, or worse. Chase's life is hanging by a thread on these sketchy details that I'm not comfortable with."

Blade locked eyes with Xiu, reading the mix of animosity and fear in her expression. Xiu was in love with Chase, and if there had been any doubt before, there wasn't now. Blade was still conflicted about her own feelings toward him, but there was definitely an attraction between them. She pitied Xiu because, deep down, she knew he did not reciprocate Xiu's feelings. Blade could still feel the heat between them when Chase had held her in Siena.

"My usual kit of C-4, Semtex, detonation devices, and demolition charges is a go," Finn said. "Oh, and I've got a wee surprise if the occasion calls for it."

Thomas's brow furrowed. "Finn . . ."

"Aye, we don't use live ammo unless absolutely necessary. But rubber bullets and smoke grenades? They're not goin' to cut it in this situation, not by a long shot. We go live, or we go home in a box."

The truth of this statement silenced the room. A grandfather clock ticked away the seconds.

"Isn't that always the case?" Thomas said, reminding the team of their reality in one simple sentence. "This is no ordinary mission, and some of us may well lose our lives. We are still grieving the loss of Vivienne and Shen. I don't intend to lose Chase, too. What I was going to say, before I was interrupted, is that we will use whatever force necessary—no less, no more. Understood?"

Without waiting for a response, Thomas glanced at his watch and cleared his throat. "I've a scheduled phone call with a contact at the CIA in a few minutes. If there's another avenue to retrieve Chase, we'll take it. Until then, we must trust Ming."

Trust. It felt like throwing a knife blindfolded—hoping it would strike true but knowing it could just as easily clatter to the floor. A knot formed in her stomach. So much was riding on the unknown.

"Joe, Blade, what do you need besides something to keep you awake?" Father McCann asked as he handed out steaming cups of coffee.

"We'll begin with whatever video you have of the Crimson Silk act," Joe said, leaning against the wall, taking a sip of the hot brew.

Blade smiled at her mentor. "Maybe a smart television or large monitor? That would allow us to study YouTube videos for ideas on how to incorporate their performance into a rescue attempt. Is there any way to communicate with Ming?"

"No," Xiu said. "Ming is under constant scrutiny."

"Then figure it out," Blade countered. "We can't wait until the last minute to magically meld into their production."

Luc tore his focus from the maps littering the table and pushed his glasses to the top of his head. "Xiu, how do you feel about a field trip to China?"

CHAPTER
TWELVE

April 8 – 11:07 p.m. KST
Myohyang Mountains

The North Korean soldiers were thin and small by Navy SEAL standards, but they were disciplined and fit. Chase barely kept up the pace, stumbling after three days of little sleep, food, or water.

To Chase's surprise, no one beat or starved him. He received the same rations as everyone else—just enough to keep the group marching.

The party emerged into a clearing, where Chase spotted vehicles roughly a click away. Two soldiers, gripping his arms, steered him toward an ancient flatbed truck with wooden sides that folded down. A sharp sting of a cattle prod jolted his body, his muscles spasming as they tossed him onto the truck bed. Laughter erupted from the soldiers as they leveled their rifles at him. His hands, bound tightly behind his back with flex cuffs, throbbed in time with his racing pulse.

Chase watched the colonel hop into an olive green jeep and drive off, probably to report his good fortune in capturing an American. A pair of soldiers entered the truck cab, while the rest joined him in the back. As the truck rumbled into motion, Chase tried to forget the biting cold and take in his surroundings. The countryside was dark and desolate. Clouds obscured the stars, and the new moon cast everything into shadows and gray outlines. North Korea had access to very little electricity, which had worked in his favor when he broke Pastor Kwon out of the labor camp. But now that the roles were reversed, Chase knew the reality of such a backwards country would also hamper any attempts to rescue him.

"Hey, where are you taking me?" Chase yelled above the roar of the engine.

An older soldier jabbed him with the butt of his rifle. Not too hard, but enough to make a point. Stay quiet or else.

"Ireona." A soldier poked the sleeping Chase in the shoulder.

The truck downshifted, its speed dropping to a crawl. Chase craned his neck for a better view. Camp 14 loomed ahead, exactly as he'd feared. His only hope lay in Hakim following orders and contacting headquarters. He knew Thomas and his comrades would move heaven and earth to get him out.

His thoughts drifted to Blade, recalling their last meeting in Siena. The Soldati's sanctuary served as a refuge for the wounded and a final resting place for those who had laid down their lives to protect persecuted Christians for millennia. He should have told her how he felt about her, but—

Chase shifted uneasily when the truck came to a halt. He heard the gate open, and the truck moved once again. Sixty square miles of hell would be his home for the next week. If Pastor Kwon was correct, Chase had until April fifteenth to live. Not long to organize a rescue attempt. And now, his captors would be vigilant.

After a few minutes, Chase smelled the stench of a pig farm. It was hard to imagine a place that had food readily available yet starved its inhabitants.

The truck stopped outside a bleak, cement building that looked out of place amid the surrounding farmland. Colonel Yong-Sun emerged from the shadows, arms wide in mock cheerfulness. "Our esteemed guest has arrived. Welcome, Mr. Chase Maserati." As he translated the message into Korean, the soldiers laughed like those at a game show responding to an applause sign.

How does he know my name?

A rough hand yanked Chase from the truck bed. With his wrists tied, he was unable to break his fall. Pain shot through his shoulder as he landed on the hard-packed dirt. The soldiers whistled and catcalled as a young soldier—not more than a teen— kicked him viciously.

"Meomchwo!" Yong-Sun shouted, and the soldier stopped mid-kick. The colonel barked more orders, and the soldier who had jabbed him earlier hauled Chase up.

"Idonghae," the older man said, poking Chase with his rifle. Ignoring the throbbing ache in his limbs, Chase walked unsteadily toward the building, the chilliness biting into his bruised flesh.

Once inside, Chase found himself in a dim room lit only by a single oil lamp flickering on a grimy desk. The room stank of rotting flesh, and Chase gagged once, forcing himself to choke back bile. Chains rattled in the darkness, hinting at the building's other unfortunate occupants.

"We have pressing matters to address." Yong-Sun turned to the soldiers. "Chain him up and let us begin our initial . . . discussion. I've prepared a demonstration of our hospitality. You may find it illuminating."

Chase gritted his teeth, refusing to give the man the satisfaction of a reply.

Without a direct order, the soldiers removed Chase's flex cuffs and replaced them with irons. Cold metal bit into his wrists and ankles. As the guards pulled on the chains attached to a pulley overhead, Chase's body rose until his toes barely touched the floor.

From the blackness, two guards hauled in a man, unconscious and covered in blood and grime. Chase inhaled deeply as if someone had delivered a sucker-punch to the gut.

It was impossible.

"Please, no," Chase whispered, his heart breaking.

"We found your friend and the satellite phone on the mountain. Did you think us foolish? To believe you were alone?" The colonel crossed to the captive and pulled on a handful of hair to raise his head. "He only gave up your name. No more. But I believe you, Mr. Maserati, will be the key to my success."

A low moan escaped Hakim's lips.

Hakim had suffered more in his nineteen years than most people did in a lifetime. "You animals!" Despite the pain, Chase fought against the restraints. "I will kill you!"

The colonel clapped his hands. "You can try. I would expect nothing less from an American soldier. But before I send you to Pyongyang, you and this prisoner will be—how you say?—our entertainment."

In seconds, Chase had cast aside Christianity and fallen back on his military training. Forgiveness? Turning the other cheek? That had no place here. This country's heart was steeped in darkness, its people conditioned to despise outsiders—especially those from the West.

He lifted his chin, inhaling slow, steady breaths. He had to stay focused and ready for any crack in their defenses, any moment of weakness. The jeers and laughter swelled around him, feeding off Hakim's screams. Chase shut his eyes.

Mercy had just left the building.

CHAPTER
THIRTEEN

April 9 – 6:14 a.m. KST
Camp 14, North Korea

This is worse than hell week.

Chase didn't have the strength to fight the guards as they shoved him back into the dank cell, his muscles seizing from the waterboarding. His nasal cavity felt like it had been cauterized with a red hot poker. Although he'd been taught as a Navy SEAL to endure interrogation, years had passed since his training officers had laid him on a board, strapped him down, and put him through the session. That had only been for a minute. Today's ordeal felt like being trapped in a time loop, each second echoing the last with no end in sight. He'd nearly broken, but the Christian network in China and North Korea remained intact.

As the door closed behind the guards, he forced himself to focus. Chase took stock of his surroundings. His vision was useless in the pitch black, but his other senses compensated. The rough texture of the concrete beneath his hands. The musty smell of damp and decay. The distant drip of liquid from somewhere in the cell block.

He'd really landed in a pile of manure this time. He closed his eyes, allowing himself to relax. Inevitably, he was visited by the ghost of Cheyenne, the wife he'd lost too soon. He reached out, as if to touch her cheek after a night of lovemaking. Her soft peals of laughter echoed all around him, like a warm blanket on a snowy Tennessee day. God, she had been beautiful.

Guilt still plagued him.

His memories always replayed the same scenario. The Boko Haram barreling into the small village in Nigeria, guns blazing. The defenseless villagers running in all directions. Cheyenne trying to calm everyone. And only one Glock to defend them all. But just as he'd moved to return fire, his wife had knocked him out with a frying pan. When he awoke, the villagers were either killed or kidnapped, and the Boko Haram were gone. Cheyenne lay lifeless, her blood soaking into the thirsty earth. She had sacrificed herself to save him from certain execution. His anger at God for not allowing him to die with her had propelled him to a life of self-destruction until Vivienne and the Soldati had offered him a path to redemption.

Chase crawled to the door and leaned against the hardwood. "Hakim?" Chase croaked into the black void, hoping against hope he was still alive. "Damn it, Hakim, say something." Silence answered his call. Had the sadistic bastards taken him somewhere else to work him over? Or had they simply put a bullet in his head to break Chase's spirit?

Exhaustion and pain overcame him, his vision blurring as his eyes refused to stay open. He resisted at first, instinct urging him to stay awake, to remain alert for any weaknesses, but his training did little against the relentless pull of rest. As consciousness faded, he saw a woman standing on the edge of a turret, her reddish hair whipping in the wind.

"Blade," he whispered. "Hurry."

Hours later, the cell door clanged open with a violent screech of metal on metal. Rough hands yanked Chase to a standing position, then pushed him down the corridor to the dreaded interrogation room. Colonel Yong-Sun grinned like a carrion feeder, savoring its next meal, taking perverse delight in Chase's misery.

"How are you finding your accommodations?" Yong-Sun asked, gesturing toward the cell block. "It's not quite up to American standards, but we do our best."

"It's a bit drafty," Chase replied dryly. "Could use some curtains."

"Ready for our session?"

"Go to hell."

A pair of hulking guards pinned Chase's arms down as the colonel sauntered closer. "You are the first American I have had the pleasure of teaching. Four glorious days together—to reeducate you. Experiments make for improvement. In your case, I plan to use a different strategy each day to gather what intelligence I need."

Chase's gut clenched. He refused to show fear, squaring his jaw as they strung him up by chains, the manacles biting deep into his already raw wrists.

"Today we test your resolve," the colonel sneered. "Bring the prisoner in."

Guards dragged Hakim's bloodied, swollen form into the harsh light of the room and placed him on a wooden table near the window. He was barely recognizable as human, his face an abstract mask of bruises, lacerations, and shattered bones.

"Wake him," the colonel ordered as he removed his tan cap with the Korean People's Army emblem front and center. He slapped it rhythmically against his leg, like a drill instructor calling cadence, setting a steady, unrelenting pace.

A guard reached for a bucket of water and poured it over Hakim. A soft moan escaped his swollen lips, but he didn't move. The guard tried to rouse the semiconscious Hakim with brutal shakes and slaps.

"You bastard!" Chase bellowed. "You'll pay for this! I'll see you damned for eternity."

The colonel only laughed, seemingly entertained by Chase's fiery rant. "History tells us your Christian apostles met martyrs' deaths—burned alive, cast into a cauldron of boiling oil, crucified, beheaded. One, I'm told, was flayed to death, his skin peeled away strip by agonizing strip."

The guards moved with mechanical precision as they lashed Hakim's broken body to the table. The colonel slowly produced a scalpel from his jacket pocket, the blade gleaming as he rolled it between his fingers.

"I think we'll start with this question." The colonel sat down in a metal chair, crossing his legs, his shiny knee-high boots reflecting the light. "Why was Pastor Kwon important to you?"

"I could ask you the same question. Is your Supreme Leader so intimidated that he would imprison Pastor Kwon and his family for nothing more than expressing their Christian faith?"

A guard struck Chase with a right hook. *"Dak-chyeo!"*

The colonel snorted. "If I were you, I would not speak of our Supreme Leader again. I have no wish for you to be beaten before your execution. It would not be dignified. But if you cooperate, if you provide us with valuable information . . ."

"Will you let my friend go?"

"You are in no position to bargain. But I can promise to make your remaining days more comfortable."

Chase held Hakim's gaze, silently pleading for forgiveness for the horrors to come. His mind raced, weighing the options. Even if the Soldati managed to determine their location, staging a rescue attempt remained impossible. He knew the risks of betrayal, but survival carried its own worth. The network of Christians in North Korea and China was too vital to sacrifice. Then he turned to his tormentor, defiant and resolute.

"Do your worst, Colonel. Some things are worth more than this life."

CHAPTER
FOURTEEN

The burbling fountain that was the centerpiece of the private terrace did little to alleviate Alec's oncoming migraine, but he needed some fresh air to drive away the jet lag.

Upon landing at Gimpo International Airport, Camila's security detail had whisked Alec and David to their new home for the next few weeks.

Alec had expected to stay miles from Seoul, holed up in a ramshackle *hanok* in the middle of nowhere. Instead, they were taken to a high-rise in the posh Gangnam district, known for its luxury fashion boutiques, upscale restaurants, and towering skyscrapers.

Nothing like hiding in plain sight.

When he'd expressed skepticism about Camila's choice, she had patiently pointed out the building's multiple entrances and interconnected underground parking that allowed for Alec to move freely without detection. There were hundreds of people on the streets at all hours of the day, making it easy for him to blend in with the crowd. The penthouse was equipped with state-of-the-art security, including biometric locks, reinforced doors, and a comprehensive surveillance system. The tower's high-profile tenant list adhered to a strict privacy policy that added an additional layer of anonymity. No one would be bringing him a pasta bake to introduce themselves.

Two cups of coffee and the morning sun did nothing but intensify the pounding in his head. Alec's call to his associates had played out as expected—excuses, empty assurances, and promises to boost profits. But the Spaniard had no patience for failure. Midway through the conversation, Alec gave the order: his contact in Albania was to be eliminated. The wet, gurgling sounds over the speaker served as a brutal reminder of who was in control. Satisfied, he leaned back, certain the money would start flowing again—steady and relentless, just like that damnable water fountain.

Alec heard the French door open, and David maneuvered through, a grin splitting his face. "We got the bloody bastard."

"Get to the point," Alec said, massaging his temples.

"I've just reviewed the surveillance footage from Mila Krüger's home. She's talking with her son and their lawyer about Blade. There is definitely something off about Mila. See for yourself. I've forwarded the media file to you."

Alec straightened in his chair, his senses sharpening. Mila Krüger—Martel's ex-lover—insisted her son was Martel's only heir. When he learned the bastard had hired a legal team to gain control of Daystar LLC, Alec began to investigate mother and son. Maximillian was a tosser, but his mother was a shadowy figure, rumored to have her elegant fingers in all sorts of sordid pies. If she was sniffing around Blade, it meant trouble.

He reached for his laptop and opened the file, while David took a seat at the table. Alec started the video and the scene sprang to life. Amid the opulence of a lavish living room, Mila

Krüger sat with the effortless poise of a woman who belonged in the spotlight—a striking blonde who, even now, could grace the pages of a high-fashion magazine. He'd met plenty of women like her, who spared no expense in maintaining their flawless skin and sculpted figure. He imagined Mila and Martel were like catnip to the ravenous paparazzi. His former boss had always loved being in the spotlight with a beautiful woman on his arm.

Maximillian, dressed casually, reminded Alec of an untested college graduate with a chip on his shoulder. There were traces of Martel in the young man—the facial structure, coloring, build—but did he possess his father's ruthlessness? And the lawyer, with slicked-back hair and wearing an expensive Italian suit, looked more like a mafioso than a reputable barrister.

As their conversation unfolded, Alec's eyes narrowed at the mention of Blade.

"What a pity my cousin didn't die," Maximillian said.

Alec would have found it comical to watch Mila and the barrister positioned as bookends on an overpriced sofa while Maximillian poured himself a drink from the bar. Except this scene played out with the precision of a staged performance at the West End of London, and the dialogue centered on Blade.

"It's been four months since René died, and we don't have a court date yet," Mila said, picking at a loose thread of her Oscar de la Renta tailored tweed dress. "Meanwhile, the board of directors is naming a new CEO this week. Can't you do something?"

The lawyer sighed as if explaining the ABCs to a five-year-old. "The investigation into René Martel's death remains open. And Genevieve Broussard's account of the evening is suspect. Once the police finish their inquiry, who knows? Ms. Broussard could be facing murder charges."

"That is nonsense." Mila reached for a martini on the coffee table. "We must be ready."

"There is no 'we,' mother." Maximillian turned from the

window. "You're here as a courtesy. I could have met Elias at his office."

So, the young wanker is asserting himself.

The lawyer cleared his throat. "René Martel's financial empire is complicated. As we've discussed, he left a will with the majority of his holdings going to his twin sister. Genevieve, as Vivienne's daughter, may have a right to the fortune."

"Ridiculous," Mila said, taking another sip from her martini. "Max is René's son. The DNA results prove it."

"True," the lawyer conceded. "But Mr. Martel was unaware of a son. Had he known, Maximillian would certainly be named in the will, if not heir to the Martel fortune."

Max threw his drink against the wall, the shards of crystal scattering across the marble tiles. "You hid me like some dirty secret. Your lack of judgement has cost me billions!"

Mila ignored the tantrum, evidently used to her son's outbursts. "What now?"

"Genevieve was discharged from the hospital before my associate could make contact. Her current whereabouts remain unknown, but the firm has retained a private investigator. Once found, she will be convinced to renounce the inheritance."

"Why didn't you go personally?"

"I thought it more important to strategize with you in the event Ms. Broussard asserts her legal right to the inheritance."

"You idiot," Mila snapped as she uncrossed her legs to stand over the lawyer. "Our inheritance is riding on this knife-thrower relinquishing her claim. We hired you because you were purported to be the best in this type of litigation. Were we wrong?"

"You mean *my* inheritance." Maximillian stared down his mother. "As for you, find Genevieve or you're fired."

"You signed a retainer agreement and—"

Maximillian pounced on the lawyer, lifting Elias to his feet by the lapels of his suit jacket. "An agreement has no value if you're dead. Now get out." Max shoved the man toward the door and threw his briefcase after him.

The young man slammed the door and stalked back over to his mother. "Stay out of this."

Mila jabbed a firm finger into his chest. "You don't have the resources to wage war against Daystar's board. I may look harmless, but I've waited twenty-three years for revenge. I can ruin you with a snap of my fingers. I've raised you as a prince. It's time you pay homage to the queen."

"So much for familial love," David said.

Alec nodded, stopping the video. His gut told him Blade was the key to everything. "I want the name of the firm handling Krüger's lawsuit. Assign a surveillance team on Mila and her son."

He rose abruptly, the metal chair scraping against the stone patio. It was time Mila Krüger learned that he was not a man to be trifled with. This short video clip confirmed that Maximillian didn't have the resources to hire assassins to kill Blade and himself. It had to be Mila, but with her spending habits, it wasn't surprising her funds were dwindling and she was anxious to replenish them with her son's inheritance. There had to be someone else manipulating and financing this operation. But who?

April 9 – 5:22 p.m. CST
Shanghai, China

Ming wove through the bustling streets of Shanghai, conscious as always that she was likely being followed. The MSS agents were careful, but Ming could usually identify them in a crowd. China's Ministry of State Security kept a tight rein on the Crimson Silk performers, suspicious of their contact with outside influences. The upcoming meeting with the Soldati operative was dangerous. Ming had worked tirelessly to build a life for herself, to find a measure of freedom in a place where it was a scarce commodity. And now, with a single choice, she could lose it all.

As usual in her free time, she ducked into the Starbucks Reserve Roastery, a luxury she savored. Just a normal person enjoying the trappings of a theatrical coffee experience among people of all nationalities. It was perfect for the clandestine meetings with her network of underground Christian saints.

Normally, Ming would sit at the Experience Bar, a place where the baristas would chat as they hand-crafted a coffee. This made sharing information easy if she was being observed. But today, after collecting a latte, she sat at the coffee bar opposite the two-story copper cask adorned with hand-engraved Chinese stamps telling the story of Starbucks. Western influence was swiftly overtaking Chinese tradition.

Agreeing to meet with Xiu, a member of the legendary Soldati di Cristo, had been a calculated risk. The brotherhood wanted her assistance in orchestrating the escape of an American prisoner from North Korea. But Ming had her own plan for the Supreme Leader and his regime—a plan that did not involve this American captive. At least the Soldati had the sense to send a fellow Chinese woman. It would raise fewer eyebrows than a Westerner suddenly appearing at her side, and if she was caught, easier to explain.

Ming had just taken a sip of her hot drink when a petite woman with a sleek black bob entered the roastery. She scanned the room in a single glance and slid onto the empty stool beside Ming. In her black skirt and crisp white shirt tucked neatly into the waistband, the stranger appeared as if she belonged on the cover of *CEO Magazine*. Ming nearly told her the seat was taken —until she noticed the cross tattooed on the woman's ring finger.

"Nǐ hǎo," Xiu greeted softly, her voice barely audible above the din of the café. "Ming?"

Ming glanced at the woman's face briefly, then dipped her chin in a barely perceptible nod.

"Thank you for meeting with me," Xiu continued. "I've come to discuss how we can integrate a few of our operatives into your acrobatic production in Pyongyang."

This woman spoke as if it were the simplest request to grant. "I am only a principal performer." Ming's grip tightened on her cup. "With only six days until the Day of the Sun festivities, it is impossible to add anyone other than Chinese performers—unless our coaches deem it necessary. And they are loyalists."

Xiu shifted, her earnest gaze boring into Ming. "We have a

highly skilled professional knife-thrower. With the right costume, makeup, and choreography, she could blend seamlessly into your troupe."

Ming shook her head. How she envied the young professionals typing on their laptops, living in their isolated world while steam rose in lazy wisps from their drinks. Xiu had lived too long in the West, where people did not live under scrutiny and suspicion. Her acrobatic troupe was a smoke screen for the general secretary of the Chinese Communist Party, a disguised party favor that masked the true nature of Chinese life within its borders.

"If we are caught, it won't be only us who bear the consequences. Our families, our loved ones, would suffer too. I cannot —I refuse to—put them in danger. You need a different strategy."

If Qianfan were here, he would be ashamed of her words. Bibles were difficult to obtain in China, since the sales were limited to officially sanctioned churches. Qianfan had been lucky to receive a copy, and he read it daily, sharing his knowledge with Ming whenever they rehearsed together. He often recited the parable of the good Samaritan as an example of someone who showed compassion through actions—not words. Many Christians in China were willing to suffer for their faith, as was she. But the American did not fit into her vision.

Xiu's hand darted out, like a striking serpent, gripping Ming's forearm with surprising strength. Desperation radiated from her in palpable waves. "There is no other plan," she hissed. "Chase will die if you don't help us. Please."

Desperate. Xiu is in love with the American.

Ming felt nauseous. Although she empathized, this proposed rescue was a suicide mission. The North Korean regime, notorious for its ruthlessness and paranoia, would crush them if discovered. And yet, beneath the fear, a small voice whispered to her. Was this not the very reason she had embraced her faith? To bring light to the darkest corners of the world, to stand for hope in the face of tyranny?

Ming carefully extricated herself from Xiu's grasp. "You have forgotten much, sister. There are eyes everywhere. I am sorry, but your friend is not my responsibility."

Her attention lifted heavenward, the ceiling an intricate pattern of wooden hexagons that reminded her of dragon scales. In China, the dragon symbolized great power, good luck, and strength. Could this be a sign to assist the Soldati, to make a stand against the darkness, while still holding on to all she held dear?

Xiu stood up abruptly, hands clenched, all semblance of propriety gone.

"Sit down before you draw unwanted attention. Do you think you can force your demands upon me?" Ming asked. "One cannot have both the fish and the bear's paw."

Xiu's eyes narrowed into slits. "You are correct. We cannot have everything we desire in life, but you can't expect to catch a cub without venturing into a tigress's den."

Without risk, there was no chance of success. Ming studied the room, fearing she'd already been compromised, but nobody looked in their direction. A seed of an idea took shape—a way to turn the North Koreans' propaganda festival on its head. A way to hide the Soldati operatives in plain sight, to give the American a fighting shot, and still fulfill her divine purpose.

As Ming stood, a sense of peace enveloped her. She recalled a recent discussion about Proverbs 4:18 with Qianfan. "But the path of the righteous is like the light of dawn, which shines brighter and brighter until full day." It was not a coincidence that her path would lead to the Day of the Sun festival. Ming couldn't help but smile.

"Tell your knife-thrower I have something in mind. But we do it on my terms."

CHAPTER
SIXTEEN

April 10 – 10:13 a.m. KST
Seoul, South Korea

The Seoul skyline glittered like a thousand diamonds, the morning air fresh after the night's downpour. In his sleek penthouse suite, Alec paced restlessly, his footsteps echoing off the polished marble floor. His thoughts were consumed by the person who had come so close to killing him—and Blade. The walls seemed to close in around him, the space feeling more like a claustrophobic prison than a luxurious sanctuary.

"You're going to wear a hole in the floor if you keep that up, *amigo*," Camila remarked from her perch on the leather sofa.

Alec paused, his green eyes blazing with barely contained frustration. "I can't just sit here and do nothing. I'm like a bloody prisoner in this place."

Camila unfolded herself from the couch, her movements fluid and deliberate. "I might have a solution. Why don't we go for a run in the mountains? It will clear your head. We'll take a small security detail and you'll be able to think without distractions."

Alec hesitated, torn between the need for action and the nagging sense that something was amiss. But he was already dressed for a workout at the gym, and the prospect of escaping the confines of the penthouse, of doing something physical and proactive in the outdoors, was too tempting to resist. "After you," he said.

They took the service elevator down to the ground floor, emerging into the dimly lit car park. Camila headed straight for a nondescript white sedan. Her black leggings hugged her curves, and he found himself admiring the way she moved. She was attractive, with full lips and high cheekbones, but she paled in comparison to Blade. She slid into the driver's seat while Alec settled into the passenger side, his senses on high alert as they navigated the streets of Seoul. Four security guards followed in a black SUV.

Camila drove through the city to Bukhansan National Park. "One of my security guards told me about a trail we should try. Just you and I. We don't want to attract attention by having an entourage follow us."

Alec looked out the window, noticing how the electrical power lines marred the landscape. It had been too long since he'd been outdoors for any length of time. "I agree."

She parked at the Bukhansanseong trailhead, the air crisp and clean, a stark contrast to the urban sprawl they'd left behind.

"Ready to get your sweat on?" Camila asked, a mischievous smile brightening her face. "Looks like you could use a solid workout."

"Crikey, how much am I paying you again?"

"Not enough," she said, punching him in the arm.

They set off at a jog, the paved path making the slight increase in elevation moderately easy. Despite relishing the fresh air and the exercise endorphins already flooding his body, Alec felt an inexplicable unease about Camila's behavior, which felt out of character. She was never overly friendly and typically waited for orders instead of making suggestions. This environment provided the perfect setup for an ambush. Should he trust his intuition and find an excuse to return to the penthouse? No—with what they had in front of them, he needed to determine her trustworthiness sooner rather than later.

The paved path eventually opened to the forest floor, leading to steep inclines through forested areas. They jogged past a muted turquoise temple with curved eaves and ornate wooden carvings. Its beauty begged for exploration.

"We can break here," Camila said, slowing down.

"It's too tranquil for my taste," Alec said, picking up the pace. He'd learned the hard way, from a childhood spent in the alleyways of Liverpool, that quiet couldn't be trusted.

By the time they reached the Yonghyeolbong Peak, both runners were gasping for air. Not another soul in sight to see the magnificent view except for the birds singing high in the trees. After a few minutes, Camila pivoted to face him with an unreadable expression. "I know your secret, Alec," she said, her voice soft and deadly. "Or should I say I know the Spaniard's secret?"

"What are you talking about?" Alec said, keeping his voice neutral.

"You should have been an actor, *amigo*. I'm well aware of your little empire," she said, walking toward a boulder. "A change in management is due. After all, shouldn't a true Spaniard be running the show?"

The pieces fell into place with sickening clarity. Camila was the traitor, the one who'd attacked him in Budapest. She'd anticipated his move to call her. When had he become so predictable? But one question still nagged at him. How did Blade fit into this takeover? Unless . . .

"Why go after Blade?"

"Men only think with their dicks," Camila said as she pulled a gun from underneath a pile of leaves. "I don't give a damn about your knife-throwing girlfriend. This is about you, Alec. And with you gone, maybe I'll pay Maximillian a visit, too. Can't have the little bastard becoming curious, can I?"

Before she could pull the trigger, rocks slid down the hillside, drawing her attention for a split second. But that was all Alec needed. In a heartbeat, he closed the gap between them, his body slamming into hers with bone-jarring force. They careened onto the jagged terrain, grappling on the narrow trail, kicking up a cloud of acrid dust.

Alec's fingers grazed the gun, but Camila was lightning-quick, yanking it away. Her elbow smashed into his jaw with a sickening crunch. Pain exploded through Alec's skull. What she lacked in brute strength she made up for in technique. Camila fired a shot, but Alec rolled and recoiled upward, striking the gun from her grasp. It flew, the metal skipping off rocks as it plummeted over the cliff.

"I trusted you," Alec said, facing her.

"You know better."

Camila launched a roundhouse kick, but Alec anticipated the move and countered with a hard punch to her kidney, knocking the air from her lungs. She fell to one knee. This was his chance. He lunged at her, trapping her under his weight. Camila bucked under him, trying to create any amount of space between them to launch another attack.

"How did you find out about the Spaniard?" Alec hissed, keeping her arms pinned above her head.

She bit his arm—hard—in response. Hooking a leg around his body, she flipped him over to free herself, then bounded to a fighting stance. "You are too old for this, my friend."

"And you should have known better than to betray me."

The two circled each other, the mountaintop silent save for their ragged breaths and the whisper of an ominous wind. He struck her midsection with brutal force, sending her stumbling backward, blow after blow, until Camila teetered on the edge of the cliff. Alec froze, the final strike hanging in the balance, until her eyes met his. She would never give up. After all, she'd been trained by the best, which was why he had hired her in the first place.

"Adios, *amiga*." With a powerful kick, he sent her flying out and over the sheer drop. Alec listened for the scream that never came.

He slumped onto a low flat rock, his mind spinning with the enormity of Camila's betrayal. How had she discovered his secret identity? Who else knew? The questions swirled in his brain as he forced himself to his feet. The security guards left at the trailhead were on Camila's payroll—he couldn't return to the car without her.

Alec needed a cell phone. Retracing his steps back to the temple, he spotted a young couple taking selfies. Feigning an injured ankle, Alec moved slowly toward them. They both rushed over to help and Alec allowed himself to be led to a bench. They spoke Korean, so Alec gestured to borrow their phone. The young man handed it over.

After the second ring, David answered and Alec issued instructions in a quiet voice. "Grab everything from the safe, the guns and ammo, and a change of clothes for me. Meet me at the Jeongneung Visitor Center in three hours. I'll explain later." Without waiting for a response, he disconnected the call and returned the phone.

"Gamsahabnida," Alec said, bowing slightly in thanks.

A smart man recognized when to cut his losses. With enough

money in his various bank accounts to last several lifetimes, disappearing under a new identity was an option. He had the means to go underground, start fresh, and truly live—not merely exist. But first, he needed to root out the leak in his organization and uncover whoever was orchestrating Mila's attack on Blade.

Then he'd consider retirement.

CHAPTER
SEVENTEEN

April 10 – 3:14 p.m. KST
Seoul, South Korea

Blade faced the makeshift target, knife in hand, brow furrowed in concentration. The tranquil backyard garden, surrounded by trees and a burbling brook nearby, failed to quiet her fears. Unable to sleep last night, she'd spent the restless hours thinking about Chase. She'd watched enough action movies to imagine the worst. Thomas insisted the North Koreans would keep him alive until the Day of the Sun festival, but what if he was wrong? What if Chase was already dead?

She shook her head, trying desperately to dispel the distraction. Was the promise she'd made—to know him better—now null and void?

Adjusting her stance, she shifted her weight to her left side, the unfamiliar pull of muscles a sharp reminder that she wasn't operating at a professional level. She'd taught herself to become ambidextrous for her signature gunslinger throw, but her injuries made it impossible to throw accurately. Frustrated, she threw the knife into the grass near Joe's feet.

"The soreness will pass," Joe said, dropping a sketch pad to the ground. "You're lucky to have a body that can still repair itself." He held up his arthritic fingers. "It's hard to pull a rabbit out of a hat with these."

Chagrined, Blade strode over and picked up the knife. "I-I feel so helpless."

"We all do. But once this is over, I insist you see a specialist about that arm of yours."

Ever since Martel had shot her in Gstaad and the wound had become infected, the radiating pain along her right side affected every throw by a few inches. Not good when the target was human.

"Okay, okay. Any new ideas?"

"Not yet."

She sighed. With Xiu in Shanghai and no plan in place, Blade and Joe had spent hours reviewing footage from the Crimson Silk performances from start to finish. The performers were graceful yet strong, the music distinctive and haunting. Joe had even shed a tear during Ming's performance with her partner. Blade couldn't see how a member of the Soldati could slip into a role in the troupe and make it to North Korea undetected. But Joe was a world-class magician. If anyone could solve this problem, he would.

Blade glanced up at the soft crunch of footsteps on gravel. Finn emerged into the sunlight, his gaze focused on her throwing arm. He must have been spying on her from the window. The Irishman's body language spoke volumes. He was itching for a fight.

And I'm the woman who's ready to give it to you.

Facing the target once again, she gritted her teeth, drew back with her left arm, and let the knife fly. It struck the target, a perfect bull's-eye.

"Don't look so pleased with yourself. Not bad with the left,

I'll give you that—but what about the right?" Finn's brogue carried a hint of skepticism. "Are you ready for this operation, or should we be worried?"

She'd come halfway around the world, still injured, to help rescue Chase. And this was the thanks she got? Blade focused on the target, determined to prove herself. She drew back, this time with her right arm, and released. But instead of the familiar *thwack* of the knife sinking into the plywood, it deflected off and landed uselessly in the grass.

A satisfied grin spread across Finn's face. "Joe, tell your girl to go home before she gets hurt."

Her temper flared, hot and bright. "I'm not anyone's girl."

Joe kept his head down, engrossed in his sketches. "She needs a little practice. No need to get your shorts in a twist."

Pain be damned. She reached for another knife from her holster, each throw failing to hit the target. Each throw more desperate than the next.

In three quick strides, Finn closed the distance between them. He stepped directly into her path, his solid form an immovable barrier. Their gazes locked, a silent battle of wills raging in the scant space between them. Blade knew that he was thinking about the debacle in Mallorca—where his friend Shen had been killed while helping Blade escape from René Martel.

Joe snapped upright. "I've got it!" he exclaimed. "With some misdirection, you and Finn will fit in perfectly."

Blade turned sharply to Joe. "What do you mean? You and I are advisers."

"You're fooling yourself, kiddo. You've always known it would be you."

Blade wanted to disappear, like one of Joe's rabbits. If this operation's success was dependent on her, then Chase was as good as dead. But she sure as hell wouldn't admit this to Finn.

"I may not be able to throw a knife with my right hand, but

my left is just fine." She took a menacing step toward Finn. "And by the way, since I haven't seen you contribute to the team, except to complain and blame others, there is no way I'm working with you."

Joe finally seemed to notice the pair facing off as if they were gunslingers in the Wild West. "What's this about?" Joe demanded, standing abruptly. "Step away from her."

Joe moved toward the pair, the arthritis in his knees making his gait slow but steady. A storm gathered on his weathered face. Finn tried to sidestep the older man, but Joe stopped him cold with a gnarled fist to his chest. "We came here by invitation. We can also leave any time we like."

"That's fine by me, oul' fella," Finn said, his tone dry. "Using an acrobatic troupe to save Chase was a daft idea from the start. And a washed-up magician along with a knife-thrower who couldn't hit a brick wall? Pretty damn useless."

Blade had learned to shrug off criticism, but an insult to her friend and mentor was a step too far. Without hesitation, she slapped Finn's iron jaw, the sharp crack cutting through the silence.

"You're a real piece of work, you know that?" Joe said.

In the sudden stillness, the gentle rustling of leaves was abruptly shattered by the distant sound of glass breaking from somewhere inside the *hanok*.

Alarmed, Blade shoved past Finn, nearly knocking him off balance.

Finn and Joe's eyes met, a loaded glance passing between them.

"Wait," Finn hissed as he bent to retrieve two of the discarded knives from the ground, his expression grim.

Out in the open, exposed and vulnerable, they scrambled closer to the *hanok* with cautious steps. The weathered wood deck creaked beneath their feet.

As they neared the door, Finn offered Blade a knife. Shadows danced eerily across the delicate paper screens. Were the people who tried to kill her in New Orleans here? Had she put her friends in danger?

Finn hesitated, his hand hovering over the ornate metal door handle. A beat passed, a shared breath—and then, with a decisive motion, he slid the door open, ready to confront whoever lay in wait on the other side.

CHAPTER
EIGHTEEN

April 10 – 3:34 p.m. KST
Seoul, South Korea

Blade stayed close on Finn's heels, her ears thrumming, as they stepped into the kitchen. The crash of splintering furniture and a sharp "What the devil?" sent a jolt through her, instinct screaming at her to charge in. But Finn raised a clenched fist, halting her in place. The unspoken command grated, but she bit down her frustration. Better to wait than blunder in and wind up dead.

Blade looked over her shoulder to see Joe holding a knife in each hand. She motioned for him to stay put, but he slowly shook his head.

Finn signaled for Blade to go left as he rounded the corner. Damn him—but she followed his order, Joe close behind. Moving carefully, she caught sight of a body sprawled in the center of the room. Luc. Unconscious. Motionless. He lay exposed amid the wreckage—paper screens torn to shreds, overturned tables, and documents scattered as if a grenade had exploded.

And to her surprise, Father McCann, a vivid red bruise blooming on his cheek, grappled with a familiar figure. The same woman who had broken into Blade's apartment in New Orleans. Finn, adrenaline surging, lunged to take her down. But she slipped past him, her movements swift and controlled.

In a flash, the woman pivoted, her leg slicing through the air in a vicious arc. Her kick landed squarely against Father McCann's jaw, snapping his head back. He staggered, then collapsed, hitting the floor like a downed boxer out for the count. A cold knot of fear coiled in Blade's gut—this woman wasn't just dangerous, she was leagues beyond Blade's savate instructor. Even Ellis, Martel's hired killer, couldn't compare.

Finn pushed himself upright after slamming headfirst into the wall. "You bitch!" he roared with fury. He reminded Blade of a bull in the ring—not one blindly charging at the cape, but smart enough to go for the matador's legs.

They crashed down—hard. But, like a fish out of water, the assassin managed to slip out of his grasp. Snatching the nearest object, she wound a lamp cord tight around his throat, twisting it like a garrote. Muscles straining, veins bulging, she pulled with relentless force. Finn clawed at the cord, desperate to loosen its grip, but it held fast, wrenching his neck into a brutal, unnatural angle.

The assassin suddenly locked eyes with Blade and gave a slow, taunting smile that dared her to intervene. She was a predator, relishing Finn's frantic struggle against the garrote. And he was losing.

Finn wasn't going to die on her watch.

Blade sprang from a crouching position, knife in hand. The assassin held the cord taut until the last possible second—then released it before executing a perfect front snap kick that sent Blade's knife flying. She barely had time to recover before spinning to face her opponent. Her savate training was no match for the assassin's martial arts skills. If she wanted to survive, she'd have to play dirty.

Blade's fingers closed around a broken chair leg. In a swift motion, she swung it hard, slamming it into the assassin's shin. A yelp of pain escaped the woman as she involuntarily bent over, shock flickering across her face. Blade pressed her advantage, driving a knee into her nose. Blood spurted freely.

Joe had dragged Luc to safety and was now hauling Finn to his feet. It was three against one.

With a howl, the assassin charged Blade, pushing her into Finn and Joe, momentarily knocking her off-balance. Outnumbered, the woman bolted for the door.

"Joe!" Blade yelled.

He lobbed a knife into the air. Blade caught it with her right hand, aimed for the woman's shoulder, and let the knife fly. It spun end over end, its trajectory locked on target. But at the last instant, the assassin shifted, and the knife burrowed itself in between her shoulder blades. She staggered forward, taking hold of the door frame, and sagged to the floor.

Finn pushed through the debris, kneeling beside the woman. "Who hired you?" he demanded, his voice hoarse from the near strangulation.

Hatred burned in her brown eyes.

Finn shook her, his desperation mounting, but still she refused to yield.

Blade shoved Finn aside, fury boiling over, intent on ripping the truth from the woman herself.

"Tell me," she hissed.

The assassin's blood-smeared lips twisted into a grimace. "You. Are. Dead." The last word was barely a whisper before her muscles slackened. A rancid stench rose from the woman.

Finn crouched beside the body, his voice quiet. "She's gone."

Blade's breath hitched. She scrambled backward, fingers clawing at the floor until her spine connected with the wall. "I killed her," she whispered. "I-I only meant to slow her down."

Wrapping her arms around her legs, she curled in on herself. Another life snuffed out—by her hand. And with it, any secrets the assassin had carried.

Finn settled beside her, his voice measured. "She came to kill you. This was self-defense."

"Self-defense? There's a knife sticking out of her back!"

He exhaled, shaking his head. "This is war, darlin'. And make no mistake—we're fightin' one, whether we like it or not. Her? She was a casualty. There'll be more." He studied her, his next words softer. "You can walk away. Go home. Hell, wait it out in Rome. There's no shame in standing down."

Blade narrowed her eyes. "You're stuck with me—no pun intended."

A corner of Finn's mouth lifted. "Ah, well. Wouldn't be the same without ya."

"We have a problem," Father McCann said as he leaned over Luc, wiping blood from his brow with a kitchen towel. "Call an ambulance. He's not regaining consciousness."

"We need to clean this up before the police get here," Finn said, moving toward the dead woman.

"It's too late for that," Joe said. "Get out of here, and take Blade with you. I'll stay with Father McCann."

Before Blade could argue, Father McCann stood, his expression immalleable. "You three meet Thomas and high-tail it to Shanghai. I can handle things here. The police won't suspect a priest."

While Blade grabbed a few essentials and tossed them into a bag, her mind drifted to Alec. Intuition told her this attack wasn't his doing but the work of another—a relentless enemy with a vendetta that ran deeper than power and money. But who— and why?

"Ready?" Finn asked, walking into the bedroom.

Blade nodded

"I owe you big time," Finn said, the red ring around his throat vivid against his pale skin. "I thought I was done for."

"You would have done the same for me."

"Aye, I'll always have your back."

As Blade strode out of the *hanok* and into the waiting car, she made a silent vow to unravel who was responsible for the recent attempts on her life. But that vow came second to saving Chase. No matter the cost, no matter the danger.

CHAPTER
NINETEEN

April 10 – 3:49 p.m. KST
Seoul, South Korea

Alec, covered in dirt and sweat, felt like he'd taken on a rugby team—and lost.

His lungs burned as he fought to catch his breath. He'd pushed through a grueling stretch of trail, traversing boulders and fallen trees, his body reminding him of his neglect with every step. Months of complacency had left him a shadow of his former self. The realization hit hard. He'd grown soft and vulnerable—no wonder Camila had seized the opportunity to take him out. He knew with chilling certainty that his arrogance had nearly cost him everything.

For the past fifteen minutes, Alec had been studying the parking area, keeping himself well-hidden. No sign of Camila's security force or anyone else who appeared out of place. He was relieved to see David's pale face through the windshield of a gunmetal gray Kia Sorento as it glided to a stop at the Jeongneung Visitor Center. Once more, Alec scanned the area, his green eyes alert for any signs of danger. Certain all was clear, he swiftly closed the gap to the vehicle and slid into the passenger seat.

David's fingers tightened on the steering wheel. "Boss, are you . . . ?"

Alec clenched his jaw. "Just bloody drive."

He angled the air vent in his direction, drawing in deep lungfuls of cool air. Three relentless hours on the run, as if the devil himself were snapping at his heels. He should've vanished after the chalet in Geneva went up in flames, leaving Martel in the rubble. A clean slate had been within reach. If only he'd been willing to kill Blade while she lay unconscious. But he couldn't pull the trigger. Instead, he'd embarked on a game of cat-and-mouse with the enigmatic knife-thrower—one he'd enjoyed far more than he cared to admit. What he *should* have been doing was putting boots to arses, reminding the troops why they still feared the Spaniard.

As David merged onto the highway heading east toward Sokcho, Alec's gaze remained fixed on the passing landscape—and the rearview mirror. The protective detail following him and Camila to the park had probably started a search. But he doubted these paid mercenaries would bother to track him down. They were hired help, not loyal soldiers.

David broke the tense silence. "I've secured a house in Sokcho. Beachfront, isolated. I have what you asked for—money, passports, computers."

Alec nodded, his mind replaying the events on the mountain. Waves of uncertainty made his skin crawl. Camila had uncovered his identity as the Spaniard. Who else could possibly know? Besides David?

As a boy, he remembered his grandmother shaking her head, muttering, "What comes around, goes around." Back then, he'd thought her mental, but maybe—just maybe—there was truth in her words. David once worked on Martel's legitimate payroll as part of the Daystar LLC. Alec had personally vetted him, but there were ways to conceal one's past.

Martel had eventually trusted Alec to run his illegal enterprises. Was history repeating itself? Alec would reevaluate David's role after ensuring Blade's safety. Until then, he'd keep David on a short leash.

The drive stretched on for hours, the sky darkening as twilight fell. When they finally arrived at the modern glass and wood structure perched on the edge of the Sea of Japan, a light drizzle greeted them.

David hesitated as he opened the car door. "It's not up to your usual standards, but—"

Alec waved him off, striding toward the house. Two large grocery bags blocked the front door. Alec scooped them up while David quickly unlocked the door. Dropping the bags on a kitchen counter, he flung open the glass patio doors and stepped onto the wooden deck. The breeze tasted of salt and distance, biting at the back of his throat. "Perfect," he murmured.

Turning to David, Alec said, "Any beer in one of those bags?"

"It was the first item on my list."

Minutes later, they sat in the living room, each with a beer. David pulled a duffel bag closer to him and unzipped it. He carefully laid out a Glock 19 and two Heckler & Koch MP7 submachine guns on the coffee table. "I also brought your Remington 700, and a weaponized drone."

"You must've been a bloody Boy Scout as a lad."

David merely shrugged and knocked back a swig of beer.

Alec sighed. "Camila knew about the Spaniard, about my operations. She almost killed me."

David's eyes widened. "But how could she have known?"

Alec's hand tightened around the beer bottle. "That's your mission. Dig into every lead, every connection to Camila. Uncover who she talked to, who might have fed her information.

And let there be no mistake—I require intel on any other threats to my position. Are we clear?"

David nodded, setting down his beer.

Alec continued, his tone hardening. "I need to send a message. Make an example of someone to keep the others in line. Suggestions?"

"I-I wouldn't presume to offer you suggestions."

What a pile of shite.

"On the last conference call, Sombat claimed an additional twenty percent was required to expand his territory in Thailand to include Myanmar. Jimenez insisted on more cash to grease the right palms—an excuse to double his cut. He believes he can exploit our reliance on his distribution in Colombia and South America to bleed us dry. Then there's Amador, convinced his current compensation is inadequate since Mexico remains the leading exporter to the United States."

"Which one shall we target?" David asked.

"All three." Alec met David's stare, letting the weight of his words settle. "Our employees seem to forget who they're dealing with. The Spaniard isn't to be questioned or squeezed."

"Are you sure—"

"If there's a problem with my orders, then you're in the wrong line of work."

"I'll get it done."

The sound of the pounding surf could be heard through the open patio door. When Alec spoke again, his voice was soft, but laced with steely resolve.

"There's work to do, David. Tonight, we clear out the dead weight."

And be thankful I still need you.

In the distance, storm clouds gathered on the horizon, promising violence to come.

CHAPTER
TWENTY

April 10 – 6:27 p.m. KST
Somewhere over South Korea

The sleek private jet sliced through the midnight blue sky, its engines humming with an undercurrent of tension that mirrored the emotions of those inside the luxurious cabin. Blade sat on the edge of her leather seat, her body coiled tight, a spring ready to snap.

Beside her, Finn and Joe rehashed the events at the *hanok*, their voices rising and falling like crashing waves. Thomas listened, his expression unreadable, as the tale unfolded once more—the attack at the *hanok* by a mysterious woman, her unfortunate death by Blade's hand, Luc's motionless form crumpled on the blood-stained floor, and Father McCann fighting with their assailant. Finn's voice registered a hint of pride and humor at this last bit, which brought a smile to Thomas's usually stoic features.

Blade shifted restlessly in her seat, trying to ignore the twinge of pain from her battered ribs and sore arm. Chase hadn't been seen since he was taken to a labor camp in North Korea. Whether that was good or bad remained to be seen. Five days. To pull off an unprecedented rescue and bring back their friend. Chase, who had somehow become more than just a comrade-in-arms. The stakes were high—and more personal than ever.

A warmth spread through Blade as she recalled the penetrating blue eyes that seemed to see through her defenses, the sharp cut of his jaw dusted with stubble, and the magnetic force that drew them together. Until these past few hours, she'd dismissed her feelings as mere infatuation, a schoolgirl crush on someone with a purpose that didn't include her. But the truth had surfaced, undeniable and raw. When the moment had come in Siena, he hadn't pulled her close. He'd let her go, refusing to take advantage of her roiling emotions. *Damn his honor.* Damn him for being exactly the kind of man she could love.

The sharp chirp of Thomas's encrypted satellite phone shattered the heavy silence. He snatched it up, his response a low, terse murmur. Blade strained to hear, her heart hammering. After a moment, a flicker of relief softened his tense features.

After the call ended, Thomas slapped his thigh, his grin spreading wide with relief. "Good news. Luc is stable, and Father McCann plans to stay with him in Seoul."

Finn downed a glass of Irish whiskey. "Will you finally consider my plan? Storm the camp, blast our way in, and haul Chase out of that godforsaken pit?"

Thomas shook his head. "We've lost Shen and Vivienne, and Luc is incapacitated. I refuse to send you or anyone else on a suicide mission, even if it is to save Chase. We either work with the Crimson Silk troupe or we pack it in and go back to Rome."

"Suicide mission, my bloody arse," Finn shot back. "I'd blow the whole place to bits. North Korea is so backwards, no one would even realize it was under attack—not until Chase and I were well away."

Thomas shot out like a rocket, pinning Finn to the seat with strong hands on each shoulder. "Maybe I didn't make myself clear. No one else gets killed. I can't afford to lose you, too. Chase was well aware of the risks when he accepted the mission."

Finn swiped his arms away and stood, toe to toe, with the director. "So that's it? We work with the Chinese? With her?" Finn glared at Blade before continuing. "No offense, Blade, but you're hurt and a liability. We don't know who's after you or how they found us. They may be trailing us now."

Blade had never seen Thomas so enraged and defeated. The scar around his neck reddened as he slumped back in his seat. "We can't start an international incident by charging into North Korea on the offensive," Thomas said, massaging the bridge of his nose. "Xiu needs to be part of this discussion."

Thomas punched in numbers on the sat phone. As he brought Xiu up to speed, Blade exchanged a look with Joe. He looked so calm, his brown eyes observing every nuance of conversation and body language. He read people like most people read books. She wondered what his insights were now.

"Ming says she'll help us, but on her own terms. Her words exactly." Xiu's voice crackled through the phone. "I'm waiting for further word."

Thomas dragged a hand down his face. "We're running out of time and manpower. We stick with Joe's plan."

"Blade is injured and our operation might be compromised by whoever wants to harm her. I'm the next in line for this assignment, Thomas," Xiu said. "Besides, she isn't a Soldati."

"I have the skills and experience," Blade argued. "I can do this."

"But I'm Chinese," Xiu countered. "I also have skills and can move through the country without raising suspicion. It is too risky for an American."

Blade sensed Thomas scrutinizing her, calculating each woman's strengths and weaknesses, and assessing the operation. Blade met his stare.

"Enough!" Joe's sharp rebuke cut through the rising tension. "Finn and Xiu, you're worried for your friend, and I respect that. But don't allow fear to cloud your judgement. Blade is still the person who can deliver in this particular instance."

Thomas glanced between Blade and the sat phone, clearly torn between two formidable women, each convinced they were the right choice. "Xiu, your background is ideal, and your technical skills are unmatched. But you're untested in the field. And Blade, you've proven yourself capable, but your injuries are an impediment."

With a heavy sigh, Thomas turned to Finn. "I'm putting this in your hands. You'll be on the ground. Who do you want as your partner?"

Finn sat down and hunched forward, elbows braced on knees. The silence dragged on, thick and unending. "Blade," he said at last. "I choose Blade."

Xiu's sharp intake of breath was audible over the line, but Thomas overrode her unspoken protest. "Then it's settled."

Joe shrugged his shoulders, a ghost of a smile on his lips. "Better get the best damn makeup artist in Shanghai lined up, Xiu. We're gonna need a miracle."

But before anyone could say another word, a deafening explosion rocked the jet. The plane quaked violently, black smoke coming from the engine.

Blade rushed to the cabin window, fear paralyzing her in place. Part of the right wing was blown away. The plane pitched and Blade was thrown against the cabin wall like a rag doll. The stomach-churning sensation of plummeting registered dimly through shock and confusion.

As the ruined jet careened toward the unforgiving earth below, one despairing thought crystallized in Blade's mind with inescapable clarity.

How will we live through this?

CHAPTER
TWENTY-ONE

April 10 – 6:54 p.m. KST
Somewhere over the coast of South Korea

"Finn, grab the chutes!" Thomas bellowed above the screaming engine.

"Buckle up!" Joe yelled as he threw Blade into a seat.

The fuselage was still intact—for the next few minutes. Crippled, the plane kept descending. The pilot's strained voice crackled over the intercom. "Attempting to hold her steady— prepare to evacuate!"

Blade's stomach twisted. Evacuate? Out of a spiraling plane?

Finn reappeared, steady despite the bucking aircraft, tossing parachute packs to each of them.

Thomas's clipped instructions barely cut through her rising panic. "Secure your harnesses!" he ordered. "Prepare to jump!"

The plane's nose dipped sharply, metal screeching as the damaged wing buckled further. Blade had never touched a parachute before. She watched the others deftly slip their arms through the shoulder harness, then attach the strap between their legs and click the metal buckles into place. Blade's hands shook, fumbling with the dangling strap—grasping it was hard enough, fastening it nearly impossible.

Thomas pushed toward her and finished securing the parachute, his eyes locking onto hers. "You freeze, you die. We jump, or we go down with the plane." His tone softened. "You *can* do this."

Drawing a shaky breath, Blade gave a jerky nod. *One step at a time. Focus on reaching the door.* Joe was suddenly at her side, his weathered hands checking her harness once more with a soldier's efficiency.

"Done this before?" she croaked.

Joe gave a tight smile. "Back in my Army days—many moons ago. We'll make it through this."

The pilot's garbled voice cut in again. "Can't hold—jump! Jump!"

A wave of vertigo crashed over Blade and she swallowed convulsively against the sudden surge of bile clawing up her throat.

"On my mark!" Thomas shouted. A blast of frigid air tore through the cabin as he yanked the emergency release. The passenger door blew open, wind roaring through the space—and then he was gone.

The plane pitched violently, a fresh explosion rattling the fuselage. A gaping hole in the side of the aircraft revealed the rugged, unforgiving terrain below, blurred by speed and chaos.

Raw terror blurred her vision. Heights had always been Blade's Achilles' heel, an inexplicable phobia she'd never managed to fully conquer. And now this literal leap of faith.

This can't be happening, this can't be happening.

Finn glanced back, his features impossibly grim. With a final nod to Blade and Joe, the Irishman dove headlong into the hungry, howling wind.

"When you jump, keep your body stable—don't flail!" Joe barked.

But Blade's trembling legs refused to move. She stared at the empty sky, unblinking. Somewhere deep inside, a distant part of her registered her own mortality.

Joe cursed. "Move, girl!"

She forced her eyes up, counted to three, and jumped. Joe's words were lost in the deafening noise as she plummeted, hurtling through the air. Blade screamed, a long gut-wrenching wail that made her dizzy. Disorienting seconds passed before she remembered to pull the cord. For one horrifying second she thought her parachute wouldn't open—until it deployed with a bone-rattling snap, jerking her upward.

Blade tried to steady her breathing, knuckles white around the straps. The eerie silence was almost more terrifying than the chaos above.

Joe floated beside her, giving her a thumbs-up. "Steer with the toggles!" Joe demonstrated, tugging the toggles to adjust direction. Blade couldn't hear, but she copied him, fighting the instinct to panic.

"Get ready for the landing," Joe yelled. "Eyes forward! Keep your feet and knees together until you touch land, then roll to your side. Follow my lead."

Blade mimicked his movements until she understood the mechanics. Then she made the mistake of looking down. The ground rushed up to meet her, a patchwork of muted greens and browns, with a few buildings sprinkled in. The wind buffeted the chute, making her sway dangerously.

She braced for impact. With a sickening crunch, she hit the unforgiving earth and tumbled, the parachute pulling her back.

Somewhere nearby, Joe struck the ground with a grunt.

How the hell do you get out of this contraption? She clawed at the harness until she was free. Trembling, Blade staggered toward him. "Joe! Are you hurt?"

He lay motionless for a few seconds before rolling to his hands and knees. "Just my pride. Nothing like seeing a grown man eat dirt."

Not for the first time, Blade wished Joe was her father. She ached to draw him close, but knew he would only be embarrassed by the show of affection. They seemed to be in the middle of nowhere—endless farmland rolled out in every direction, cattle grazing in the tall grass. Not a soul in sight. "Where *are* we?"

"Don't know, but we need to find Finn and Thomas, fast," Joe said, rising to his feet.

A sharp whistle rang out.

Blade tensed. Two figures emerged from the shadows of a nearby barn. Her heart leapt—Thomas and Finn.

Finn reached them first, giving Joe a bear hug. "You're all right, auld fella."

Thomas joined them, his sharp gaze raking over Blade and Joe, assessing, approving. "Didn't doubt you for a second."

Blade let out a wild, breathless laugh. She caught sight of the men's expressions and laughed even harder. They'd just jumped out of a disintegrating plane into a pasture, with unknown threats dogging their heels. And they were alive.

"Oi, the pilot managed to bail out," Finn said, a huge grin splitting his face as he pointed to the sky.

"We're not out of the woods yet." Thomas held up a back-pack. "Grabbed the sat phone on my way out. Help's on the way. Let's stow the parachutes in the barn and find the downed pilot."

As they set off through the darkened fields, the hair on Blade's arms bristled. She squinted, searching for an unseen threat. The stress was getting to her. But she couldn't shake the feeling of being watched—hunted.

Blade recalled the only alligator hunt she'd ever joined, not long after landing in New Orleans. She'd jumped at the chance to glide through the fabled swamps, picturing ancient cypress trees draped in Spanish moss, the air thick with mystery. Reality hit harder—the stink of rotting vegetation, the oppressive humidity, and the raw violence of the hunt. Lines baited with rotting meat hung from low branches, snapping taut when a gator took the hook. She'd watched the beast thrash and strain, trapped and helpless, before the hunter aimed to take the final, merciful shot to the head.

Now she understood what that alligator must have felt just before it snapped the line and disappeared beneath the murky water.

Sometimes it's not about who sets the trap, but who walks away from it.

CHAPTER
TWENTY-TWO

April 11 – 10:47 a.m. KST
Camp 14, North Korea

Chase jolted awake, his head striking the rough wood above him. He sucked in a sharp breath, his lungs still burning from yesterday's waterboarding. The stifling confinement, the sheer helplessness, stoked his fury. He thrashed against the walls of his prison, but the box held firm. The hours spent in the box blurred—impossible to gauge.

With every attempt to move, agony ripped through his contorted limbs, muscles cramping and spasming. Memories surfaced of being herded from his cell to a room housing a four-by-four-foot wooden box. The colonel's order to kneel inside seemed like madness. When the lid slammed shut and locked, Chase forced himself to calm his mind. Yong-Sun, the bastard, was playing with him, trying to break him.

But it wasn't only the physical agony that tormented him. Ghostly images of Hakim floated in the dark. His bloodied legs, his screams, until mercifully, the young man fell unconscious.

Chase could have stopped the torture by giving Yong-Sun the names of Christians who had helped him. He wrestled with his choice—saving hundreds at the expense of one. *Please, God, forgive me and let him be alive.*

A door slammed, shattering the oppressive silence. The lid unlocked and flew back, flooding the space with blinding light. Rough hands seized him, hauling him out. Numb and unsteady, his legs buckled as the soldiers dragged him down a dank hallway toward his cell.

He recognized the young soldier who had kicked him upon his arrival at the camp. They threw him at the open door. Determined to prove himself, the soldier kicked Chase in the midsection. Chase rolled away from him across the cold, hard concrete floor, pain lancing through his shoulder and hip.

"You American pig!" the soldier yelled, spitting at him before shutting the door.

For a long moment, Chase lay where he'd fallen, his cheek pressed to the icy surface beneath him. The overpowering odor of urine and feces made him wonder how many men or women had passed through this cell—only to disappear.

His legs tingled as blood returned to numb muscles. His platoon leader's relentless reminders about assessing yourself and your team came to mind. With deliberate care, he moved, unfurling his limbs like a soldier raising the Stars and Stripes at dawn.

As he gradually extended to his full height, the room tilted and swayed as if he stood once again on a naval destroyer. Supporting himself against a wall, he allowed himself time to adjust. The throbbing pain over his entire body was a searing reminder of the continual beatings.

Chase shuffled to the door. "Hakim?" he rasped. "Hakim, can you hear me?"

Silence.

Chase rested his forehead on the wood. As a team leader, he should have known better than to bring the young and inexperienced Hakim on this op. Just the two of them, with no backup. It was foolhardy and arrogant to think only he could train the eager recruit. Chase clenched his fists, refusing to lose faith.

Then, so faint, he almost missed it. "Chase?"

Relief washed over him. An answered prayer. "I'm here, brother. Right here."

"Thought you were dead."

"I'm not that easy to kill. What's your condition?"

Seconds ticked by. "They bandaged my legs, but I'm shivering. No food or water today."

This stink hole reeked of disease and decay, a perfect breeding ground for infection. At least they weren't plagued by rats; starving residents had likely turned them into delicacies. Chase faced the grim truth—Hakim wasn't going to survive the week. Yong-Sun would sacrifice Hakim, who held no real value, to break Chase.

He'd encountered men like the colonel before—ruthless climbers desperate to impress their superiors, no matter the cost. Escape remained their only option, though they probably wouldn't get far without being shot.

"Stay with me, Hakim," he called out. "Don't give up the ship."

A low chuckle and cough echoed through the blackness.

Barely a week ago, Chase had recounted the story of Captain James Lawrence, a hero from the War of 1812. Hakim listened intently as Chase described how the mortally wounded captain urged his crew to fight to the last. Don't give up the ship—five simple words that took on a life of their own—were inscribed on battle flags, emblazoned on naval insignia, and served as a lasting symbol of courage and resolve in the face of certain defeat.

Since joining the Soldati, Hakim had absorbed every lesson like a sponge, mastering the training with relentless focus. Sharp, driven, and instinctive, he embodied the ideal recruit. To Chase, he was more than a mere soldier—he felt like a younger brother. And Chase would stop at nothing to set him free.

"Chase. Are you there?"

"I'm here," Chase said, his voice an urgent whisper. "Listen, I have a plan. It's risky, but it may be our one shot. You with me?"

"All the way. Till the end."

"Get some rest, kid. I'll do the same."

"Can we pray together? In-in case I don't wake up?"

Chase's throat tightened. "The Bible tells us about two thousand years ago, the Apostle Paul and Silas were shackled in a prison, probably not much different than this one. While they were praying to God, a violent earthquake shook the foundations of the prison, and miraculously the doors opened and the prisoners' chains came loose. Miracles still happen. We can't give up hope."

As the final "amen" faded into the darkness, Chase laid his weary body down on the unforgiving floor. He needed a few hours of rest, just enough to hold on to his sanity.

His thoughts kept circling back to Blade, unbidden and merciless. Those amber eyes that flashed fire when anger flared, the razor-edged smile, the quick wit that cut deep, and a magnetism so strong she pulled everything into her orbit. He should've told her what she meant to him. But regret clung like a cruel companion—silent, cold, and difficult to shake.

Cheyenne had dreamed of building a family, but Chase had thought it best to wait until his tour ended. Now he knew that a pregnancy would have kept her safe in the States, far from the godforsaken village in Nigeria. He would never wait for the perfect time again. Cheyenne wouldn't want him to spend his life alone, haunted by the past.

One way or another, he would escape this hellhole. There was unfinished business with a chestnut-haired spitfire—and come hell or high water, he'd hold Blade in his arms. His truth had been buried for too long.

CHAPTER
TWENTY-THREE

April 11 – 6:04 p.m. CST
Shanghai, China

The Shanghai sky burned orange, the setting sun reflecting off countless glass-and-steel monoliths. In the gathering twilight, Nanjing Road pulsed with life, as dozens of people used the crosswalk, most to reach the Starbucks Reserve, one of the largest in the world. Ming's heart raced as she scanned countless faces from her vantage point through the second-story café window in the adjacent shopping center. Finally, she spotted the foursome mingling with the crowd—Thomas, Finn, Blade, and Joe. Even from this distance, they seemed out of place.

Ming brought the cooling cup of tea to her lips. As she looked over its brim, she analyzed each person as they moved through the throng. Blade walked with athletic grace, a byproduct of constant practicing and performing as a professional knife-thrower. But it was her beauty and fiery hair that made heads turn as she strode toward the Starbucks entrance with purpose. Finn was unexpected. Ming was rarely drawn to Westerners, yet there was something arresting about his rugged features and broad shoulders—he stood out sharply against the tide of familiar profiles around them. Thomas followed close behind, his head swiveling left to right, watchful for any deviation. This left the older man, who must be Joe, the magician from America. Deep lines etched into his weathered skin spoke of a life both hard-earned and full of stories. It was a shame there wasn't more time to hear them.

She set the cup down carefully and reached for her phone. Years of training under the watchful eye of the Chinese government had honed her ability to detect their presence. Her hasty departure from the gym had not gone unnoticed. After running her fingers through her black hair, she smiled and took a selfie, then examined the picture closely. And there he was, a younger man dressed as a tourist, hoping to blend in except for the eyes that always gave the government spies away. She was being tailed, which was not unusual. *Stay calm, everything depends on this.*

When hearing of the airplane crash, Ming wanted to call off the rescue plan. Let the Soldati figure this out themselves. But Qianfan reminded her that they were doing God's work. Yes, saving the American was good, but the plan she had set in motion to save the North Korean people was also important.

The two had stayed awake most of the previous night discussing how best to proceed. They were performers—not administrators or coaches. After seeing Finn and Blade, she knew it would take a miracle to disguise the couple as part of a cleaning crew. And this was the easy part. The difficult part would be securing Korean People's Army uniforms.

"Please, God," Ming prayed silently, "let this work."

If only I lived in a truly free country. China might appear progressive to the outside world, but in reality, Ming felt like she lived life under a microscope. She had met with Xiu two days ago, but a direct meeting with the Soldati team was not possible.

Thank God there was Tian, her closest cousin and fellow believer, to deliver the vital instructions necessary for their operation.

There, crossing the busy intersection, was Tian. She watched her cousin weave through the flood of people with practiced ease. Within her memory lay the instructions for the entire operation. Faced with the reality of their audacious plan, doubt gnawed at her resolve. The idea of Blade and Finn infiltrating North Korea seemed ludicrous. How would they ever pass as Chinese, let alone as North Korean soldiers? The pair were like giants among locusts.

And what of Chase? Ming's stomach clenched at the thought of the American's plight. Camp 14 was known as a black hole from which few returned. She knew imprisonment intimately—if not the physical bonds, then certainly the mental and spiritual shackles that came with living under constant surveillance.

Ming's attention darted back to the street, scrutinizing every passerby for signs that Tian had been followed. The stakes were impossibly high—Chase's life, her own safety, the fate of countless Christians working within their network. They could not be compromised.

As she daintily bit into a biscuit, the wail of sirens interrupted the rush hour traffic. Ming's head snapped up, eyes widening in horror as three police vehicles screeched to a halt outside the Starbucks. Black-clad officers poured out with military precision.

Ming froze.

Chaos erupted below.

Pedestrians scattered like startled birds, their shouts of alarm rising above the cacophony of car horns and squealing tires. Ming's gaze darted frantically, searching for Tian or any sign of Thomas and his team.

Every instinct screamed at her to run, but she had nothing to fear—unless Tian or the others were arrested.

Blaring sirens pierced the air, interrupting the tense silence that had fallen over the group. Tian had just delivered Ming's plan—to add Blade and Finn into the cleaning crew and then, once in North Korea, to hide them in plain sight as soldiers. This sounded preposterous to Blade's ears, although Joe nodded in agreement. Perhaps his experience as a magician, routinely transforming the ordinary into the extraordinary, made the plan seem plausible. His world was one of misdirection, spectacle, and grandiose results.

Sirens drew closer, and Blade's heart rate spiked as adrenaline flooded her system. She exchanged a quick glance with Thomas, seeing her own alarm mirrored in his eyes.

Tian's face drained of color, her delicate features now distorted with terror. *"Tāmen zhǎodàole wǒmen,"* she breathed, her voice trembling. "They have found us."

Thomas rose, his movements deliberate and controlled. "Everyone up the stairs. Now. Move like you belong here."

Heart hammering against her ribs, Blade stood, careful to maintain her air of being a casual tourist as they threaded their way through the maze of tables and up the stairs. The aroma of coffee and pastries, once comforting, now seemed cloying and suffocating. Perhaps they were just being paranoid, and the police were responding to an accident in the vicinity.

As they stepped onto the second-floor tea bar, Blade heard the police swarm the first floor of the roastery. Customers hurried from their seats, stampeding toward the exit.

Blade sighed in relief when she spied an exit to a second-story mall. At least they weren't trapped.

"Split up," Thomas ordered. "Meet back at the hotel." He grabbed Tian's slender wrist, practically dragging her behind him as he headed to the second-floor exit. Finn followed close on their heels.

By the time Blade and Joe made it through, Thomas and Tian were running over a footbridge leading to another building. Finn turned left down a walkway. Blade spun around, ready to bolt, but the look on Joe's face stopped her cold.

"Go," Joe said, his voice gruff with emotion. "I'll only slow you down."

Realization hit Blade like a slap across her cheek—Joe's arthritis. He couldn't outrun the police. "I'm not leaving you," she said, putting her arm through his as if they were on an afternoon stroll. "If we're lucky, the police will only see a couple of shoppers."

Two police officers burst out, weapons drawn.

"Hands up!" one officer shouted in heavily accented English.

Blade's mind raced, looking for a way out, but she knew they were cornered. Slowly, she raised her hands, acutely aware of Joe doing the same beside her.

Just as the officers began to approach, a woman in a tan apron —likely a Starbucks employee—rushed out, speaking rapid-fire Chinese. The officers turned, momentarily distracted by this unexpected interruption.

Blade didn't hesitate. She lashed out with a vicious kick, her foot connecting solidly with the nearest officer's sternum. He crashed into the glass wall with a sickening thud, sliding to the ground in a heap.

The second officer spun around, weapon snapping up. His finger began to squeeze the trigger. Instinctively, Blade threw up her arms to shield her face as the gun fired. For a heartbeat, all was still, until she opened her eyes.

And saw a red stain blossoming on Joe's shirt.

"No!" Blade screamed, catching him as he collapsed. The weight of his body forced her to her knees.

Before the officer fired again, a blur of motion caught Blade's peripheral vision. Finn had returned, his face a mask of cold fury as he drove a fist squarely into the officer's temple. Both officers were no longer an eminent threat.

Blade barely registered Finn's presence as she cradled Joe to her chest. Tears flowed down her face. "Why?" she choked out.

Joe managed a weak smile. "Couldn't let anything happen to you, kiddo," he wheezed. "You're the daughter I always wished for."

Blade's throat tightened as she shook her head. She had convinced herself that Joe deserved one last adventure. She didn't know how to face any of it without him.

"I've known . . ." Joe's hand tightened around hers. "About the retirement home. So expensive. Thank you."

"I need to get you out of here."

Joe smiled. "No regrets about this trip. Better to die here, like this." His expression grew urgent. "Get out of here," he rasped. "Go!"

Gunfire exploded from inside. The glass doors shattered. Finn grabbed an officer's gun from the walkway and returned fire.

"Blade, we need to move!"

With a shuddering breath, Blade leaned down, pressing a gentle kiss to Joe's forehead. "I love you," she whispered, carefully laying his motionless head on the blood-stained pavement.

Finn grabbed her hand, pulling her to her feet while firing blindly into the store. Together, they ran over the footbridge that Thomas had used, leaving Joe behind. Bullets whizzed past them as Blade glanced back, her heart breaking as she left her friend on a cold slab of cement.

They raced through the mall and onto the street, dodging pedestrians and weaving through alleys. Blade made a silent vow. Joe's sacrifice would not be in vain. She would make it count. No matter the cost, she would save Chase—or die trying.

CHAPTER
TWENTY-FOUR

April 11 – 6:39 p.m. CST
Shanghai, China

The hotel room door clicked shut behind Blade and Finn.

Inside, Thomas and Xiu were hunched over a battered round table, their faces ghostly in the blue glow of a police scanner spitting rapid-fire Mandarin. In the corner, Tian sat curled on a brown upholstered chair that may have been cream or tan at some time in the previous decade. The orange drapes were drawn tight, shielding the room from prying onlookers.

Xiu's head snapped up, relief flooding her features. "Finn!" She practically leaped into his arms. "The scanner picked up a report of an unidentified man. DOA at the hospital. I thought—"

"It was Joe," Blade said.

She sank to the floor, her back against the door, staring blankly ahead. The words came out flat, almost detached. "I left him. I should've stayed."

Thomas crossed the room in two swift strides, dropping beside her. His shoulder pressed against hers, a silent show of solidarity.

"And you'd be in cuffs right now," he said, his tone grim. "Joe would still be dead."

"That's a bit bloody harsh," Finn said.

"Sentiment won't help us now. One man's dead. Two officers are wounded. An entire police force is on high alert. They'll be reviewing the Starbucks security footage soon. We need to go underground—fast."

Blade barely heard him. Words tumbled out. "He saved my life." She took hold of Thomas's hand and squeezed. "The officer was going to fire, but Joe . . . he shielded me with his body."

Finn's expression darkened. "I doubled back, thinking about Joe's knees—figured he'd not get far. I was right. Blade had one of the bastards down, but the other wasn't takin' any chances."

That was an understatement. Blade relived that moment—the glint of the barrel, Joe's eyes locking on hers, his powerful arms pulling her close. From her first appearance on stage at the Rising Sun, Joe had been there—gruff, wise, protective. His grizzled demeanor was off-putting to some, but to Blade, he was something akin to a grandfather.

Finn turned to Tian, who shrank further into her chair. "There's a leak," he growled, stalking toward her. "And it's not one of us."

"Enough," Thomas said sharply. "Xiu, talk to her. We need clarity, not accusations."

Finn clenched his fists at his sides, his fury barely contained. "It's not enough. Joe was a good man. He's dead 'cause you wouldn't listen! A wee bit of C-4 or Semtex, and I'd blow Chase out of Camp 14, but you're too damn stubborn to even consider the option. Even now, I can see you're not hearin' me."

Thomas sighed and stood. "The Soldati don't launch attacks on foreign soil, Finn. Not ever. No matter the circumstances. We all knew the risks. Joe . . ." He glanced at Blade, a flicker of guilt crossing his face. "You and Joe aren't soldiers. We should never have involved either of you."

Blade swallowed hard, grief and guilt warring inside her. Just as she tried to find her voice, Thomas's attention shifted to the women, whose conversation had turned sharp and urgent.

"Names," he demanded. "Everyone who knew about the meeting."

Tian's fingers twisted nervously in her lap. But she answered slowly and clearly in halting English. "Ming, Qianfan, and . . . my mother."

"Your mother? Is she part of the underground church? What did you tell her?"

Before Tian could respond, Xiu's hand shot up, her body going rigid. "Quiet!" she hissed as she listened intently to something on her equipment.

Color drained from Tian's face. "They've taken her," she whispered, horror dawning. "My mother . . . they arrested . . ."

"Christ," Xiu said.

"Uncle," Tian spat, the word a bitter curse. "Maybe he overheard. But I swear, I never mentioned Ming."

Thomas exhaled. "Small mercies. There's still a chance."

"We can't afford to screw this up," Finn muttered, pacing.

"We push forward," Thomas said, firm and final. "If Ming's still in play, we stick to the plan. It's our only shot at extracting Chase alive."

Tian lurched to her feet. "I should tell the police my mother is innocent."

"No," Thomas barked. "You're safer with us. We'll arrange for a local church to shelter you."

Tian threw herself at Thomas's feet. "Thank you. God is good."

Uncomfortable with her display, Thomas gently pulled her up.

"We're the ones who should thank you. We've put you and your mother in danger. That was never our intent. Do you understand?"

"Yes." Tian wiped away tears. "I want to help the American."

"You already have. Tomorrow, your journey to South Korea begins. You'll be free—and I promise, we'll get your mother out too."

Blade watched her, admiration stirring beneath the grief. Tian's courage reminded her too much of the pain she carried—of the mother she'd lost to a drunk driver, of Vivienne, stolen by a monster in their own family. Joe's death, the chaos, the rising stakes—it was all pressing down on her.

"The theatrical makeup artist Ming arranged," Xiu said, breaking into Blade's spiraling thoughts. "Is that confirmed for tomorrow?"

Thomas nodded grimly.

Blade forced herself upright, every muscle protesting. "What's our next move?"

Thomas met her gaze, a hint of approval in his dark eyes. "First, we prep you and Finn for infiltration. That means clothing, makeup, and a basic lesson in Mandarin. Xiu, return to the safe house, run through the comm protocols again, continue to monitor every avenue you can think of. We'll also need your hacking expertise to help us avoid the surveillance cameras. I'll escort Tian to the local pastor. We regroup at 0800 hours. Blade . . ." He paused, studying her. "You sure you're up for this?"

Her hand instinctively went to the hidden push dagger at her hip, a small weapon that had saved both Chase and herself a few months ago. "Try to stop me."

There would be a time to mourn for Joe, but that time was not now. His words echoed in her head. *The show must go on, kiddo.* What a cliche, but Joe was old-school, a man of conviction. She'd have time to mourn later, but as she looked around the room, she could see that everyone present was ready to sacrifice their lives in order to rescue Chase. In this moment, the dingy hotel room, with its peeling wallpaper and outdated furniture, felt like a place where hope was fragile but alive.

CHAPTER
TWENTY-FIVE

April 11 – 8:23 p.m. CST
Shanghai, China

The soft glow of paper lanterns cast dancing shadows across the Crimson Silk compound as Ming made her way through the winding paths between practice halls. The scent of jasmine hung heavy in the air, mingling with the distant strains of an erhu's mournful melody. Despite the tranquil atmosphere, Ming's heart raced, her memory replaying the clandestine meeting between Tian and the Soldati that had descended into chaos mere hours before.

Guilt overwhelmed her. She regretted getting Tian involved in this foolish mission to rescue the American. But Tian, in her young naiveté, had welcomed the opportunity to demonstrate her faith and impress her older cousin.

If anything happened to Tian . . . No, she couldn't think like that. They were already in too deep. Ming was reminded of her first coach, a brutal taskmaster who insisted her students learn to swim. There had been no gentle instruction, no patient guidance. Instead, ten trembling adolescents had been herded onto a rickety boat and unceremoniously tossed into the churning sea. Sink or swim—that was the only lesson. Ming still remembered the salt burning in her eyes, the panic clawing at her chest as she fought to keep her head above water. Only eight students made it back to land that day, leaving two empty desks as grim reminders of failure.

Ming recognized this as another sink or swim moment. But this time, it was Tian treading water in a sea of danger far deadlier than any ocean. Ming sent up a silent prayer, begging for her cousin's safe return.

It was well past the hour for the evening meal, and it was relatively quiet within the compound. She slipped into the darkened acrobatic studio, her practiced feet silent on the polished wooden floor. Qianfan was already there, a lithe shadow perched on the balance beam.

"You're late."

Ming approached, her eyes darting to every corner of the room to ensure they were truly alone. "We have a problem. There was a police raid at Starbucks. It was pandemonium."

A flicker of fear crossed Qianfan's usually calm demeanor. "Tian? The Soldati?"

"I don't know," she admitted. "It all happened so fast. I left the café immediately. And worse, I was followed, so I pretended to shop," she said, holding up a bag.

Silence fell between them as they considered their limited options. The path forward was clear, even though every instinct screamed against it.

"I need to make contact," she said, her tone grave.

Qianfan's eyebrows shot up. "You can't be serious. That's only for an emergency."

"We have no choice."

She led him to her bedroom, hoping their coaches wouldn't be lurking in the corridors as they usually did. Men were not allowed in the women's wing, but Ming and Qianfan had found ways to circumvent the rule. She closed the door and locked it. With trembling fingers, she burrowed under her bed to retrieve the hidden mobile phone from its resting place under a floorboard. Beads of sweat formed on her forehead.

I hope I'm not making a mistake.

She jabbed the speed dial and tapped the speaker function, lowering the volume. It rang once, twice, three times.

Finally, a male voice answered, terse and coldly efficient. "One of the Soldati is dead—the old man—but the rest of the foreigners and Tian escaped. The police are reviewing security footage. Tian's mother has been arrested for fraud. Reported by a relative."

Ming swayed, lightheaded. It was difficult to absorb the information. This nameless contact, their emergency lifeline, had delivered a gut-wrenching report. "Can you help?" she asked.

"Don't call again. And dispose of the phone."

Stunned, Ming threw it across the room. *Coward.*

She turned to Qianfan. "What now?"

Fraud charges were often leveled against Christians. The penalty ranged from beatings to being consigned to a labor camp. The informant must be her uncle, a worthless man always asking relatives to take him in like a stray dog. Her aunt insisted there was good in her brother, but if he guessed Ming was a Christian, all would be lost.

Qianfan ran a hand through his short hair. "The police are in the dark about you. I think we should proceed with the plan."

Ming shook her head. "You know what will happen to us if we're caught."

"We accepted that one day our faith would be tested. Are we going to cower forever? I'm ready to put my faith to action. Aren't you?"

Ming lay back on her pillow and patted the bed beside her.

Qianfan sat on the edge, reaching for her hand. She absorbed his warmth, hoping she conveyed feelings long denied. The unspoken threat loomed over them—not just their lives on the line, but their families and the entire troupe. One misstep and they'd all burn.

"Tian's mother knows nothing of my involvement," Ming said, barely above a whisper. "Even if we are arrested for our faith, they can't tie us to the Soldati."

"I keep thinking of the Apostle Paul," Qianfan said. "He was flogged, shipwrecked, and imprisoned. But he never strayed from his path. We have this chance to serve our brothers and sisters. We cannot let them down."

Ming nodded as she pulled him to her. Over the years, through countless performances and shared dangers, they had never crossed this invisible barrier. She could feel the sands of time running out—the specter of North Korea looming on the horizon. It would be her undoing, but she prayed Qianfan would survive.

Her hands slipped under his shirt, tracing the contours of his muscled torso. They knew each other's bodies intimately through practices and performances on the world stage. Together, they created magic. But this—this was different. Before fate closed its fist around her, Ming wanted to experience magic for herself.

As his lips met hers, tender yet urgent, fire swept through Ming's body like an inferno. She wrapped herself around him, skin touching skin. In this fleeting space between danger and desire, nothing felt more God-breathed, more achingly alive than this.

CHAPTER
TWENTY-SIX

April 12 – 2:32 a.m. KST
Camp 14, North Korea

Chase opened one eye to the creak of his cell door opening. He'd been waiting for hours, his ears alert to any sound in this godforsaken shack. Two North Korean soldiers entered, their boots thudding heavily against the concrete floor.

"On your feet, American scum." The butt of a rifle rammed into his back.

Chase recognized the voice. It was the sadistic little bastard who enjoyed kicking helpless victims. This punk had no idea what awaited him.

He complied slowly, stumbling forward as if too weak to stand. The soldiers exchanged a smug glance, lulled into a false sense of security by his apparent frailty. It was the opening he needed.

A brutal jab to the older soldier's jaw sent him crumpling to the ground, out cold before he hit the floor. The younger one reacted quickly, swinging his rifle around, but Chase was faster.

He ducked under the weapon's arc and caught the soldier in a chokehold, squeezing until he went limp in his grasp.

Dragging the unconscious bodies deeper into the cell, Chase removed their belts, boots, and socks. He stuffed a sock into each man's mouth and fashioned a rope using their belts to hog-tie them. The older soldier's boots barely fit him, but they were better than nothing. He snatched up the rifle and keys, then slipped out into the dimly lit corridor.

The gun was a knockoff of the AK-47, a weapon he was familiar with. At least it was loaded. He held it in the high ready position as he listened for any movement beyond the door leading to freedom. He cracked the door an inch and saw no one. Hooking the strap across his shoulder, Chase hurried to Hakim's door and eased it open.

The sight that greeted him turned his stomach. Hakim lay curled on the filthy floor, semiconscious, his once strong body reduced to a broken mess of bruises and blood. Chase knelt beside him, gently lifting his friend into a fireman's carry. Hakim groaned softly, the sound tearing at Chase's heart.

Hakim's eyelids fluttered, a moan escaping his split lips. "Chase?"

"Yeah, it's me. We're getting out of here."

Escape. They had to escape.

Once outside, Chase scanned the perimeter, orienting himself. He'd memorized every inch of Camp 14 before traveling to North Korea. The extraction point he'd penetrated before lay about two clicks north. This area within and around the camp was barren, purposely cleared of any obstructions, making it easy for the guards to shoot prisoners trying to escape. With any luck, they'd make it out of here before any alarms were triggered.

Taking a deep breath, Chase headed north, thankful for the borrowed boots. A shooting star streaked across the heavens, and he prayed it was a good omen.

Halfway to the extraction point, Chase eased Hakim to the ground. His calves and thighs burned with every step, muscles screaming from the strain. Hunger and dehydration were grinding him down.

Hakim mumbled, "If I don't make it—"

"Don't," Chase growled. "We're going home. You hear me?"

If the Soldati knew of his capture, where would the new rendezvous be? He recalled the maps Luc had showed him, the mountain pass they were on, the Taedong river that flowed through Pyongyang, the rural countryside. Which way to head once they escaped through the fence? The river. Thomas would be at the river.

"Time to go, buddy," Chase said as he lifted Hakim to his shoulders.

"So thirsty," Hakim whispered.

"Me too."

One foot in front of the other, desperation driving each step. The terrain became more uneven and treacherous in the dark. *Don't let me fall, Lord.* If he tripped and fell, he might not be able to get up.

"Hakim, have I ever told you my favorite scripture?" Chase asked. "Isaiah. I forget the chapter and verse. But it says 'Those who hope in the Lord will renew their strength. They will soar on wings like eagles; they will run and not grow weary, they will walk and not be faint.' I'm dog tired. We could sure use a pair of wings to fly out of this place."

Chase raised his eyes and there it was, just ahead, the extraction point where he'd been able to rescue Pastor Kwon and his family.

He hastily sat Hakim up against a boulder. The fence looked exactly like he'd left it. It appeared to be intact, but that was an illusion. Chase listened for a hum indicating the wires were hot, but hearing nothing, he disengaged the hooks holding the fence together. A five-foot stretch of fence toppled over, giving him plenty of room to walk through.

"We'll be by the river soon," Chase said, reaching for Hakim. But before he could grab his comrade, floodlights illuminated their position. Chase's arm moved to block the light from his eyes. A North Korean patrol blocked their path.

"Leaving so soon, Mr. Maserati?" a familiar cadence shouted through a megaphone.

Colonel Yong-Sun.

"Stay behind the boulder," Chase ordered as he dove beside Hakim, rifle at the ready.

The patrol began to close in, shouting, demanding their surrender. Chase answered with a shot, taking out one of the lights. Soldiers scattered for cover, returning fire. A bullet pinged off the boulder. Too close for comfort.

"I don't think we're making it out of this one," Chase said.

And the person he thought of was Blade. Words never said, feelings never acted upon. He hadn't learned one damn thing since Cheyenne died.

"You have no choice but to come out!" Colonel Yong-Sun shouted. He emerged from the shadows, flanked by heavily armed soldiers. A triumphant sneer twisted his features.

In his time with the Navy, Chase had seen a lot of bad guys up close, and only a very few took pleasure in torturing people—Yong-Sun was one of those few. He continued to shield Hakim, his mind racing, searching for a way out. But there was nowhere to run, nowhere to hide. They were trapped, at the mercy of a man who knew none.

"Don't come a step further, or you'll be the first one I shoot."

"Ah," the colonel said, "and just when we were starting to understand each other."

The odds were against them. Chase glanced down at Hakim. He could kill Yong-Sun and they would both be shredded by a hail of bullets, or surrender and take his chances. But if he chose the latter, Hakim would be dead within a day.

Chase used the boulder as a shooting rest, aimed at the colonel—

"Love you, my brother." In one last sacrificial act, Hakim heaved himself up, grabbed the rifle out of Chase's hands, and fired.

Chase rolled into a small ball as a barrage of gunfire exploded around them. Bullets peppered Hakim's body, blood and gore spraying outward, the momentum spinning him until he fell face-down into the dirt.

Shaken, Chase tried to crawl to his friend, but a gun barrel to his temple stopped him.

"Tsk, tsk," the colonel said. "You Americans are too hasty, too impatient. And now Hakim is dead."

"You bastard!" Chase screamed.

Colonel Yong-Sun only laughed. "Return him to his cell."

Chase stood, studying the scene. He would never forget his young charge or the suffering he'd endured at the colonel's hand. Even the dirt, greedy for moisture, soaked in his blood.

I swear there will be a reckoning.

TWENTY-SEVEN

April 12 – 5:37 a.m. KST
Camp 14, North Korea

Why do the people I love keep sacrificing themselves for me?

That question plagued him during the ride back to the heart of Camp 14. Diesel fumes burned his nostrils as the transport rocked to a stop. A sharp jab from a rifle butt drove into his ribs, pushing him forward. Chase stumbled out of the truck and nearly ran, almost hoping one of the soldiers would kill him. But that would be taking the deserter's way out. After tonight, he was at war.

Two guards seized Chase by the arms, their grip vise-like as they marched him through the compound for the laborers to witness. Yong-Sun's victory for all to see. But this was a futile gesture. Their empty stares told him these people were long past caring about anyone or anything—except survival. If only he'd been able to save the Kwon family—or even Hakim—his misery would be worth it.

After tiring of their game, the guards made a show of kicking and beating Chase with batons until they reached the cellblock. Aware that the colonel might be watching, they escorted Chase down the dimly lit corridor to the same dank cell he'd occupied earlier.

With a brutal shove, the guards sent Chase sprawling across the cold concrete floor. The impact sent shockwaves of pain through his already battered frame. The door slammed shut with a resounding bang, plunging him into total darkness.

God, I've been here before. Is this how I finish the race you've put before me?

His mind flashed back to a video of his five-year-old niece, Emma, who had started kindergarten at a private school this year. She preened before the camera in her green uniform and recited Joshua 1:9: "Have I not commanded you? Be strong and courageous. Do not be afraid; do not be discouraged, for the Lord your God will be with you wherever you go." He smiled in the dark, remembering Emma flexing her arm muscles before blowing a kiss to her Uncle Chase.

Sometimes, faith was all anyone had in the end.

He slowly pushed himself up, wincing at the pain, sure this last beating had broken a rib or two. Hakim's final image burned behind Chase's eyes—steadfast, determined, and brave. Blood had sprayed in a wide arc as the bullets tore through his body. Then came the thud, awful and final, as Hakim crumpled to the earth, his life snuffed out in a single, merciless heartbeat.

Chase hit the wall with his fist as if pain could drive out the memories.

The countdown to the Day of the Sun hurtled toward him. By now, Commander Kazir would surely be mobilizing the Soldati. Their expertise and resources made the CIA look like amateurs. He must remain vigilant, clinging to the possibility of rescue. But once he was transferred to Pyongyang, any hope of extraction would vanish. Something had to give—soon.

Survivor's guilt would consume him if he allowed himself to wallow in it. Determined to maintain his mental resilience, Chase closed his eyes and pulled up a memory so old it felt like it belonged to someone else. "First thing," his dad had said, wiping grease off his hands with a red shop towel, "you listen. Engines talk, son. You just gotta learn how to hear them." Chase had been twelve, maybe thirteen, crouched beside the rust-bitten '65 Mustang they'd dragged into the garage.

Chase's father, a NASCAR crew chief, lived for fast cars, and hoped he would follow suit. But while Chase inherited his father's love of engines and speed, he also carried a quiet resentment—for all the months racing had kept his father away from home. He'd once sworn to never make the same mistake, never leave his own family behind. Yet when he enlisted, he was gone from Cheyenne for even longer periods. Still, the memories of those long afternoons in the garage, side by side with his dad under the hood of that old Mustang, were priceless.

He visualized the engine block, every bolt, every part—valve covers, pistons, camshaft. He recalled the smell of gasoline and oil, the rhythmic clink of socket wrenches, the way his dad would hum under his breath while working.

Start with disassembly.

Chase could hear his father's patient instructions as he loosened bolts, removed the intake manifold, set each part aside in perfect order. His breathing evened out. The pain diminished. Every time the darkness tried to pull him under, he turned another screw. He rebuilt the engine from memory, part by part, day by imagined day. It gave him rhythm. Purpose. Control.

He repeated the exercise again and again until finally falling into a light sleep. He had no way of knowing how many hours had passed when he heard a rustling outside his cell. He tensed, pushing himself to his feet. The key rattling in the lock seemed unnaturally loud in the silence.

The door swung open, flooding the cramped space in harsh light. Chase winced at the abrupt glare, his vision blurring as he attempted to adapt to the stark change. A figure entered, backlit by the corridor lights.

As his vision cleared, Chase recognized the unmistakable outline of Colonel Yong-Sun. The man's posture was relaxed and casual as he regarded Chase.

"Mr. Maserati," Yong-Sun said, his voice smooth and controlled, "I trust you have had time to reflect on recent events."

Chase remained silent, studying the colonel. Yong-Sun was a puzzle, a man of contradictions. Based on his accent, he had clearly received his schooling in England. How could anyone exposed to the freedoms and values of a Western democracy choose to return and operate a labor camp under one of the most oppressive regimes in the world?

"Not in a talkative mood?" Yong-Sun stepped inside the confined space, his polished boots incongruous against the grimy floor. "That is a shame. I so enjoyed our previous conversations."

"What do you want?"

Yong-Sun's lips curled into a smile. "Want? I merely thought we might discuss the looming Day of the Sun festivities. After all, you are the main event. An entire nation will watch your America crumble."

Chase's jaw tightened, but he forced himself to remain outwardly calm.

"Our people lay flowers at the statues of Kim Il Sung all around our illustrious country. We invite foreign countries to perform for our Supreme Leader. Fireworks explode in the night sky. Of course"—Yong-Sun's tone shifted into quiet menace—"not everyone is there to celebrate. Some have other roles to play."

Chase envisioned strangling Yong-Sun, snuffing out the man's life. But he'd be dead before he took two steps forward. His stint as a SEAL had instilled in him the virtue of patience. The opportunity to strike lay ahead. And the colonel? Justice awaited him—for Hakim.

"Your attempt to leave your accommodations caused quite a stir, *American*." Yong-Sun slapped his thigh with an open hand. "There are those who believe you should face severe consequences."

"Is that why you're here?" Chase asked.

"No, no. I'm simply informing you of the reality of your situation. You've been taught Newton's third law: action—reaction. It's fundamental."

"I was always a dead man walking."

"The choice is yours. I can turn this into something tolerable—or not. My only request? Give me the names of your Christian conspirators. Prolonged defiance, well . . ."

Chase met the Colonel's gaze. "I appreciate the advice. I'll take it under consideration."

Yong-Sun studied him for a long moment. Then, with a slight nod, he turned and exited. The door closed behind him, plunging Chase once more into blackness.

As the colonel's footsteps receded, Chase exhaled slowly. Each inhalation felt like a countdown. His mind drifted to Blade —he'd use his love for her, his desire to see her once more, to fight off the demons that attacked his sanity.

"I'm not done yet," Chase muttered to himself. "Not by a long shot."

CHAPTER
TWENTY-EIGHT

April 12 – 9:08 a.m. KST
Seoul, South Korea

Alec stood motionless in the steam-thick air, water droplets cascading down his lean, muscular frame. As he toweled off, he assessed the damage—bad, but not fatal. It could have been worse —much worse. He cleared a patch on the fogged mirror, revealing a face that looked like a prizefighter's after the match of a lifetime. The sclera of his right eye burned red, giving him the cold, mechanical stare of something inhuman. A harsh reminder of just how careless he'd become.

He had no regrets about killing Camila. Luck and brute strength had allowed him to walk out of that park alive. Alec moved his jaw, the muscles working beneath the stubble of his beard. Gingerly, he touched his split lip. He looked bloody awful.

As he bent to pull on his jeans, his knuckles brushed the denim. He winced at the pain. Camila might have acted independently, but by God, no other soul would dare attempt a coup against him. As the Spaniard, he had to make an example before he lost control of his operations. It was necessary to cull the herd, and this time, only three of his brethren had forfeited their lives. Should history repeat itself, an entire gang would face annihilation. There were plenty of replacements to choose from.

At thirty-seven, Alec felt the weight of his years like never before—each decision a stone in his pocket, dragging him down. Had Martel carried the same burden? Always looking over his shoulder, weighing people's motives, suspicious of everyone and everything?

Stepping onto the balcony, clad in jeans and an olive green polo shirt, Alec inhaled the salty tang of the sea air. Sokcho stretched out before him, a stark contrast to the gritty streets of Liverpool where he'd honed his survival-of-the-fittest mentality. Here, the morning bustle was muted, the crash of waves against the shore a constant, soothing rhythm.

David was already waiting—ever efficient, which Alec found both reassuring and vaguely disquieting. A carafe of dark roast waited on the patio table, its familiar bitterness the only thing that made mornings tolerable.

"Morning, boss," David said.

Alec nodded, pouring himself a cup of the steaming brew. He leaned against the balcony railing, looking toward the lighthouse. "Any updates?"

David cleared his throat. "The assassinations are complete. Each target's successor arranged the hit, as per your instructions."

"Nothing like promoting someone for following orders," he mused. *One less complication to worry about.* "And Mila Krüger?"

In response, David steadied himself on his crutches and produced his tablet. "I picked this up an hour ago," he said, tapping the screen to cue the audio.

A tense, urgent tone filled the air—Alec recognized Mila's voice instantly. "Senator Andrews, the problem is still in the wind. Our sources place her somewhere in Shanghai, but—"

"No excuses, Mila." The man's smooth Southern lilt carried an edge of authority that left no room for argument. "I don't much care for explanations. I expect results. Get it done, or you can forget about your share of René Martel's fortune. That's not a threat—it's a promise."

Alec's interest piqued at the mention of Shanghai and his former mentor's wealth. His mind raced with possibilities. What did he mean by "your share"?

"I cannot function on the pittance you have provided. I need at least fifty thousand more to finalize our arrangement."

The slow, soft Southern drawl hardened. "Remember, I'm funding your legal battle. You owe me!"

As the clip ended, Alec's gaze sharpened. "Why didn't you show me this first?"

"I thought your business interests were more urgent than Mila Krüger."

Alec set his cup down and sat on a cushioned patio chair. He didn't trust David, but he needed the younger man—at the moment. "Senator Andrews. What do we know about him?"

"I've prepared a dossier." David pulled up a file and placed the tablet on the table.

Alec refreshed his coffee and began to read. He scanned each page, absorbing every detail. He drummed his fingers against the table as he tried to connect the dots between Senator Andrews and Blade. What was the endgame here—and whose move had started it?

"Richard Andrews," Alec murmured, scanning the information. "Senior senator from South Carolina. Member of the Committee on Foreign Relations." His eyes narrowed. "What's his interest in Martel's beneficiaries? And why is he after Blade?"

David shifted uncomfortably. "That's unclear. But given his position and connections, he's not someone to be taken lightly."

Alec leaned back. "No, I wouldn't think so." He let the silence stretch before adding, "Pack up. We're going to Shanghai."

"Shanghai?"

"I plan to find out what Blade's up to. And it's bloody well time to settle a few old scores along the way."

As David thudded away, Alec stayed on the balcony, eyes fixed on the endless sweep of the Sea of Japan. Mila and Max Krüger's attempt to seize Martel's fashion empire hadn't bothered him until they set their sights on Blade.

As much as he tried, he couldn't explain—or shake—the possessiveness he felt toward the knife-thrower. Allowing the Krügers—a pair of self-serving tossers—to take her out felt wrong. Ironic, really, given she'd made no secret of wanting him dead.

There were occasions when taking down an enemy required finesse, like an archeologist digging for hidden treasure. He planned to dig until he uncovered the connection between Senator Andrews and Blade. Persistence always yielded something valuable.

Alec prided himself on his adaptability. He'd clawed his way out of the cesspool of Liverpool, recognizing René Martel as a means to prosperity. Martel had given him an education, responsibility, and ultimately the management of the Spaniard's illegal operations. Perhaps there would be something to gain from this American senator.

David plodded forward into the sunshine, gripping his tablet. "We've hit a bit of a snag. Chinese authorities are searching every plane entering or leaving Shanghai. It seems there was some sort of kerfuffle in the city, and an American was killed. Three other people escaped with the help of a Chinese dissident."

"Has the dead American been identified?" Alec asked, afraid of the answer.

"No name yet, but it was a male."

Alec drained the last of his coffee. This must be Blade and the Soldati, he was sure of it. The woman was exasperating.

"Investigate the possibility of flying into Nanjing without undergoing searches. If it's clear, we fly there, then rent a car."

He remembered his first glimpse of Blade on stage in New Orleans. Sexy in her black leather jumpsuit, the light catching her reddish brown hair, the holster she wore on her hip, and the skill she exhibited as she threw knife after knife at her live target. How he desired her then. And if he was honest with himself, he still did.

"I've completed the arrangements," David called from the living area. "We can leave within the hour."

Alec straightened up and rolled his shoulders. "Good. Make sure we're untraceable. We arrive in Shanghai as ghosts."

Alec took a final look at the peaceful Korean seaside. He would be in Shanghai before nightfall. The senator's secret would be his soon, and Blade would be safe. Thank the gods he hadn't taken the kill shot to end her life.

April 12 – 9:31 a.m. CST
Shanghai, China

For the first time since entering this complex as a young girl, butterflies fluttered in Ming's stomach as she entered the rehearsal area, her eyes scanning the expansive space for Qianfan. The familiar scent of chalk and sweat mingled with the faint aroma of jasmine wafting through the open windows. Sunlight streamed in, stretching long shadows across the polished wooden floor.

Memories of the previous night lingered, vivid and electric—Qianfan's tender touch, his whispered words of love, the way their bodies moved in perfect harmony. It had been everything she'd ached for. Yet the sweetness was tainted by the bitter knowledge that it might be the only night they'd ever share.

On the opposite side of the room, Qianfan's lithe form was warming up on an exercise mat, his body a fluid poetry of motion as he executed a series of flips and handstands. Ming's breath caught in her throat as she recalled how those same whipcord muscles had lifted her effortlessly, making her feel as though she were floating on air.

She struggled to contain the rush of emotion, acutely aware of her peers. In the Crimson Silk compound, nothing went unnoticed—walls listened, unseen eyes lingered, and silence carried secrets. One misplaced glance, one telling expression, would undo everything.

"Ming!" Her coach's sharp voice cut through her reverie. "Come here."

She pivoted to find him flanked by a pair of severe-looking men in crisp black uniforms, their shoes gleaming and utility belts equipped with pistols. The presence of the People's Police suggested they were armed with information about Tian. An eerie silence fell over the rehearsal hall as everyone's attention locked onto Ming.

Do not fear. I can do all things through Christ who strengthens me.

"This is Gui Jintao and Kang Yangsheng from the Public Security Bureau," her coach said before retreating, clearly desperate to distance himself from this situation.

Officer Jintao, the taller of the two, fixed Ming with a penetrating gaze. "Ming Zhang, we have a few questions to ask regarding your cousin, Tian Zhang."

Ming's mouth went dry, and her tongue felt like sandpaper. She'd braced for this possibility, but the reality was far more terrifying than she'd imagined. Still, she kept her voice steady. "Tian? Yes, she's my cousin. Is something wrong?"

"You will accompany us to our office for further questioning," Officer Yangsheng said. His eyes appeared bug-like behind thick, wire-rimmed glasses.

She forced herself to look at both men, desperately trying to project an aura of innocence and confusion. "Of course I'll go with you. But I don't understand why you're interested in speaking with me."

Ming's attention darted briefly to Qianfan, who had stopped his routine and was watching the scene unfold with barely concealed concern. She silently begged him to stay put, to not draw attention to himself. If they suspected her, Qianfan must remain above suspicion. The mission—Chase's rescue—depended on it.

Officer Yangsheng's lip curled slightly. "Understanding isn't required. Only compliance."

As they escorted her toward the exit, their footsteps echoed through the hushed rehearsal space. Ming sensed the intense stares of her fellow performers boring into her back, their whispers already beginning to circulate.

Her coach stood frozen, watching as his star performer was led away. The defeated slump of his shoulders told Ming all she needed to know—she was already presumed guilty.

A black sedan waited at the curb. Officer Yangsheng opened the rear door, and Ming slipped in without a word. He followed, the door closing behind him with a solid clunk. Trapped beside her captor, Ming offered up a silent, urgent prayer—for strength, for Qianfan, for Chase, and for everyone depending on her.

"Your cousin has involved herself in a troubling situation," Officer Jintao said from the front seat as the car wove through congested traffic. "We're hoping you can give us insight into her recent activities. You want to help, don't you?"

Ming had skipped breakfast, a decision that seemed wise as waves of nausea surged through her. She reassured herself that these men possessed only one piece of information: Tian's presence at Starbucks yesterday, but how did that implicate her? "I apologize, but I'm unaware of Tian's *activities*. We aren't close."

Yangsheng's laugh was devoid of warmth. "Not close? Your family tells us you are as thick as thieves. You were shopping at the HKRI Taikoo Hui yesterday. It is near the Starbucks Roastery, where your cousin was spotted. A coincidence?"

"I often go there to escape the demands of my profession."

"Is that so?" Officer Jintao's tone made it clear he didn't believe her. "And I suppose you have no idea about her involvement with a group of foreigners? Or about her mother's financial difficulties?"

The pieces clicked into place. Tian's mother had been arrested and now they were casting their net wider, hoping to ensnare Ming as well.

"I am sorry to hear about my aunt's problems." Ming forced her hands together to keep them from trembling. "But I have no time to involve myself in family drama. The Crimson Silk Acrobatic Troupe is my life."

Yangsheng jumped in. "Do you think your cultural performance is what interests the North Koreans? Or could it be something else?"

"I'm not sure what you're suggesting," she said carefully. "I was ordered to perform in North Korea—to share our culture— just like the other performers. We do as we're told."

"I've seen you perform. Impressive. It is an honor to be chosen by our North Korean brothers and sisters."

Did they know about the American and suspect her of treason? "It is a great honor," she managed to say.

The car pulled up to an impressive government building in the heart of the Huangpu District. Ming had walked past this building occasionally, keeping a wide berth on her way to the Bund. Despite her tightly controlled schedule, she would periodically slip away to walk the pedestrian promenade, wishing she were sailing away from her life in China to freedom.

As Officer Jintao stepped out of the car, he allowed Ming a glimpse of the imposing Shanghai State Security Bureau building with its glass high-rise office tower. The glass shimmered in the morning sun, indifferent to those who were imprisoned in the country's fist. Jintao took hold of her elbow and led her up the steps.

All three were silent as the doors closed with an ominous thud, shutting out the vibrant city and plunging Ming into a world of fluorescent lights and sterile corridors. As the two officers marshaled Ming deeper into the bowels of the building, she prayed to be released soon. She could not miss the plane to North Korea—to the grand finale she'd painstakingly planned for months.

Officer Jintao opened the interrogation room door. "After you," he said, giving her a lop-sided grin that reminded her of a bian lian performer she'd once seen in a traditional Chinese opera. The performer changed masks in seconds to convey shifting emotions. The face masks had scared her. It was said in ancient times people wore these masks to frighten off dangerous animals.

She jumped as the door of the interrogation room slammed shut with the finality of a coffin lid.

CHAPTER
THIRTY

What is Finn so excited about?

Blade steered the motorcycle through Shanghai's choked traffic, keeping pace with Finn. Xiu had performed another miracle by securing two bikes in under a few hours. It wasn't her Ducati, but the hum of the engine beneath her, the rhythm of the ride—it felt *normal*. A sensation she hadn't experienced in months.

Jets flew overhead as they neared the Shanghai Hongqiao International Airport. Whatever or whoever awaited them at the private hangar that Thomas had arranged remained a mystery. Finn knew something, but the man could keep a secret.

Finn slowed in front of a nondescript building and parked the bike. Blade did likewise, removing her helmet. The place looked deserted. His steps quickened toward the door. He punched in a code, and the reinforced door slid open with a pneumatic hiss.

"This way," Finn called over his shoulder, as he turned on the lights and strode inside. "Wait till you see what we've got tucked away."

"This had better be good."

"Oh, just a wee surprise that'll make our job in North Korea a bit easier."

At the center of the hangar, a bulky mound lay concealed beneath a tarp. With a flourish worthy of a magician, Finn grabbed a corner and gave it a dramatic tug.

"Holy crap," Blade said.

What emerged looked like a prop out of a sci-fi movie—sleek lines, gleaming metal, and an aerodynamic form that seemed to mock the laws of physics. It reminded Blade of Luke Skywalker's landspeeder, only sharper. Meaner.

"Is that . . . ?"

"May I present Arcturus One, an aerial vehicle built for two. Top of the line, cutting-edge tech." Finn's grin widened, full of mischief and pride. "This beauty will get us in and out of tight spots faster than drinkin' a Guinness on payday."

"Impressive, but is it safe?"

"Its frame is aluminum and carbon fiber, light as a feather and tough as nails. And this feature is fierce—it's controlled by a bleddin' joystick! She has an auto-land function and a ballistic parachute with rapid deployment time."

Blade approached the vehicle cautiously, her fingers tracing its smooth surface. "But how does this fit into our rescue plan?"

Finn's expression sobered, his eyes filling with sadness. "Listen, Blade. This isn't just any old toy. This is our lifeline when shite hits the fan. When things go arseways—and they always do—this is our ticket out."

"There's only space for two people."

Finn nodded. "Field operations are usually banjaxed. No guarantee we'll make it home."

"And you're qualified to fly this thing?"

But before he could answer, Thomas cleared his throat. Blade jumped at the interruption, her reddening face betraying her inexperience.

"It is surprisingly easy to fly. That's why you are both here. To practice." Thomas held up a hand to stall their reactions. "But first, let's talk."

Thomas led the way to an office in the corner. The walls were covered with maps, satellite imagery, blueprints, and handwritten notes, creating a dizzying tapestry of North Korea's geography.

"The Day of the Sun celebration provides our only window," Thomas said, his finger tracing a path across a map of Pyongyang. "According to our sources, the Rungrado 1st of May Stadium is the scheduled venue for the celebration. We have reason to believe Chase will be executed during the grand finale. A public display of American arrogance brought low."

"Bleddin' bastards," Finn muttered.

"Over one hundred fifty thousand are expected to attend. The complex is huge. Once you arrive in North Korea, Ming's network will acquire a detailed map and hopefully the location where they're holding Chase."

A slight ache began at the base of Blade's skull, the enormity of their task penetrating her sound judgement. "And my role?"

"I'll address that shortly. You'll be outfitted with a KPA uniform. Once you arrive in Pyongyang, become one of the throng. Mingle. Be inconspicuous."

"What's our time frame on the day?" Finn asked.

"Once the festivities begin, Finn will locate Chase while you provide communication. That's all you do," Thomas said, looking directly at Blade. "No heroics, and then get the hell out of there."

"How will we communicate?" she said, knowing North Korea had limited internet services.

Thomas fixed her with an intense gaze. "I'll let Xiu explain the details. The devices are primitive by our standards. You'll be able to communicate with each other, but truthfully, you're on your own."

The trio huddled closer as Thomas spread out a detailed schematic of the Taedong River. "You'll escape by boat along this route. Extraction happens here." He pointed to a spot near the stadium. "From there, the captain takes you to the six-person submersible we've used before. "

"And if things go wrong?" Blade asked.

"We improvise and that's where our new toy comes in," Finn said, jerking his thumb toward the Arcturus. "Where're we stashing it, then? Can't exactly park it on the street."

"Still working out the details. Probably west of Pyongyang, nearer to Korea Bay."

"Damn the luck. Luc should be here, figuring out all the details," Finn said. "Once we're inside the Crimson Silk complex, contact will be risky."

Blade's eyes narrowed as she studied the maps and blueprints they would be navigating. "How are we ever going to memorize all this?"

"Step by step—as a team," Finn said.

The distant roar of a jetliner taking off interrupted the meeting, a stark reminder of the ticking clock.

Finn moved back to the Arcturus One, running his hand along its sleek fuselage. "We can do this," he murmured, more to himself than the others. "We have to."

The weight of their mission settled over her like an avalanche of snow burying her in chilly fear. Joe dead. Luc still hospitalized. Father McCann holding vigil. All of it terrible. And what of Chase? She would move heaven and earth to have one hour with him. She had much to say to him—if she was brave enough.

"I'll be back at sixteen hundred hours," Thomas said, packing a few maps into his briefcase. "I expect both of you to know how to operate that vehicle by the time I return."

Finn slapped her on the shoulder and gestured for her to follow.

She didn't argue, didn't protest, just followed his orders. Something was happening, a shift in her psyche. Perhaps this was how Vivienne felt when on a mission. With hands on hips, she looked around and realized she no longer cared about her own safety. Only the team mattered—Finn, Xiu, Thomas, and especially Chase. The soldier and friend who had returned to Geneva to save her life.

So this is what it's like to be part of something bigger than myself.

Blade squared her shoulders and steeled herself for what lay ahead.

THIRTY-ONE

April 12 – 9:23 p.m. CST
Shanghai, China

Alec stepped out of the taxi, his polished oxfords skidding slightly on the rain-slicked pavement. He tilted his head back, marveling at the behemoth of glass and steel spiraling into the night sky. One hundred twenty-eight stories, the tallest building in China, and a symbol of China's ambition to become a global financial powerhouse.

The cool breeze didn't mask the humidity. Alec could feel sweat trickling down his spine. He adjusted his bespoke Savile Row suit and strode toward the entrance—alone. He'd told no one about this visit to Wu Fen. From now on, his whereabouts would be on a need-to-know basis.

Four men materialized from the shadows as Alec entered the lobby, their black suits a stark contrast to the minimalist modern interior. Only a hint of a dragon curled from the starched white collar of each man. Without a word, they descended upon him. Practiced hands raked over his clothing efficiently, searching for weapons, wires, or anything that might threaten their master.

If—*when*—Alec survived this night, he'd assemble a security team just as loyal and competent. These men would die for their Dragon Leader. No doubt of that. Red Pole enforcers were notorious for their allegiance and violence.

"This way," a guard growled, his English clipped and harsh. The group moved as a unit toward a private lift, two guards on each side of Alec. The doors shut with a whisper, and his stomach lurched as the lift rocketed upward at forty-five miles per hour.

Alec had taken a chance on this face-to-face meeting. The Spaniard—a carefully constructed alter ego—was a much more formidable opponent from afar. Now, stripped of that mystique, he hoped this wasn't a trap and that Wu Fen was an honorable man.

A subtle chime announced their arrival to the 120th floor. The doors parted to reveal a foyer bathed in soft amber light; the air held the faint aroma of sandalwood. Alec was escorted through a space that rivaled the British Museum. Ornate gold crown moulding accented the burgundy walls. Display cases with non-reflective glass contained priceless antiquities—swords, delicate porcelain, hand scrolls of silk. One piece in particular caught his eye: an earthenware figure of a woman, just over a foot tall. The brass plaque identified her as *Standing Court Lady*, her full lips and elaborate hairstyle a window into an empire long expired.

Francesca, a woman he'd dated two years earlier, had opened a gateway into the art world. While pursuing her doctorate in Renaissance Studies, she'd led him through Italy's most revered galleries, from Rome to Venice, culminating at the Museo dell'-Opera del Duomo in Florence. It was there he first encountered Donatello's *Penitent Magdalene*—a haunting wooden sculpture that radiated raw anguish and unwavering devotion. The piece struck something deep within him, a resonance he still struggled to put into words. That life seemed eons ago, buried beneath the weight of his current existence.

The final set of doors opened to floor-to-ceiling windows that provided a vertigo-inducing view of Shanghai's skyline, with the Oriental Pearl Tower dominating the vista while the Huangpu River cut a dark ribbon separating the Bund from the new Financial District. Silhouetted against this urban canvas stood the Dragon Leader Wu Fen.

Even from across the room, the man exuded an aura of power and danger that unsettled Alec more than he cared to admit—an intensity that left him feeling exposed and dangerously outmatched. His snow-white hair, contrasted with the neon lights below, created an eerie halo effect that gleamed against the glass. *No angel*, Alec reminded himself. *But then again, neither am I.*

Alec approached, giving a slight bow from his shoulders. *"Ni hao,"* he said, his voice steady despite the adrenaline coursing through his veins. "Thank you for agreeing to meet with me."

"Ah, the Spaniard. I've been looking forward to putting a face to the name."

"Xièxiè," Alec said, thankful he remembered a smattering of Mandarin.

"I hear you've been cleaning house."

News traveled fast in their world. Alec fought to keep his expression neutral. "It's part of the job."

Wu Fen's lips curled into what might have been a smile. "Indeed it is. Tell me, what brings the infamous Spaniard to my doorstep?"

Alec met the Dragon Leader's stare. "Information."

Wu Fen gestured to a pair of leather armchairs. "Please, sit."

As Alec lowered himself, every sound, every shift in the room seemed magnified. Across from him, Wu Fen settled with deliberate calm, his stoicism tempered by a flicker of curiosity.

"I'm trying to locate an American woman," Alec began, shifting uncomfortably in his chair. "She goes by Blade. She's here in Shanghai."

Fen's gaze sharpened. "Blade? An unusual name. And why is this woman of such interest to you?"

Alec crossed one leg over the other. "She may be connected to a recent death. An elderly American man, yesterday. I want her location, the dead man's identity, and her reason for being in Shanghai."

A tense silence fell, broken only by the muted footsteps of a Red Pole approaching with a tray of baijiu and two glasses.

Wu Fen leaned back, steepling his fingers under his chin. "Interesting. And what do you plan to do with this information once you have it?"

"That's my business."

Wu Fen lifted his cup, swirling the clear liquid. "You understand that this comes at a price. If I do this, we're even. No more favors owed."

Alec considered the consequences carefully. Keeping a leader of the Chinese Triad in his corner had provided a certain level of protection when navigating the Asian markets—no small advantage to surrender. But Blade . . . The urgency to find her, to figure out what game she was playing, eclipsed everything else.

"Agreed," Alec said, yet the word felt like a noose tightening around his neck.

Wu Fen nodded, satisfied. "Then let us drink to our arrangement."

The baijiu scorched Alec's throat, igniting a fire down the length of his body. This had to be the most asinine decision he'd ever made.

"I'll have what you desire, day after next, at sunrise. You will be contacted with a meeting place." Wu Fen rose from his chair. "My men will escort you out."

Alec stood, buttoning his jacket. "Cheers then. Much appreciated, sir."

Half-expecting an attack from the guards, Alec followed

cautiously as they wove their way through the opulent rooms and down the dizzying lift. Something irreversible had been set in motion tonight, and Wu Fen was probably laughing at the rookie mistake. The loss of the Dragon Leader's favor would undoubtedly lead to bloodshed down the line.

He walked briskly into the humid Shanghai night, determined to put as much distance as possible between him and Wu Fen's den. Although he thought the older man honorable, he knew from experience that people were unpredictable.

Once he ascertained the location of Blade, what then? Would he confront her? Kill her? Kidnap and subdue her? He removed his suit jacket and began to run. No matter what happened in the coming days, he would never be able to outrun fate.

CHAPTER
THIRTY-TWO

April 13 – 9:58 a.m. CST
Shanghai, China

The morning sun did little to brighten Blade's mood as she trailed behind Xiu and Finn through a maze of narrow alleyways. The Soldati operatives spoke softly, leaving Blade to her own thoughts. Thomas had left the hotel earlier on some secret errand he chose not to disclose.

An old woman eyed them warily as they rounded the corner of a nondescript building, her rheumy gaze following their progress. Xiu rapped softly on a faded red door, glancing furtively over her shoulder. After a moment, the door creaked open, revealing a dimly lit interior that appeared to swallow the daylight.

"Welcome," a lilting voice called from within. "Enter swiftly."

Blade hesitated on the threshold, her instincts screaming caution, like the first time she'd visited a voodoo shop in New Orleans. What she'd found there had mystified and frightened her. There were candles, voodoo dolls, tarot cards, and other items that had confounded her. After being offered a psychic reading, she'd beaten a hasty retreat. But that was not possible today—not with Chase's life hanging in the balance.

The workshop was a cluttered wonderland of theatrical supplies. Racks of costumes lined the walls, a riot of colors and textures. Makeup kits overflowed on every available surface, and the air was thick with the mingled scents of greasepaint and spirit gum.

At the center of the organized chaos stood Madam Bianzhuang. Her delicate features clashed with hair dyed a jarring shade of red, layers of elaborate makeup, and tattoos that snaked across every inch of visible skin. Yet it was the sharp intelligence in her eyes that held Blade in place, making a cool, clinical, and unmistakable assessment.

"These are the ones?" she asked Xiu, skepticism evident in her tone.

Xiu nodded. "The best we have."

Madam Bianzhuang switched on the overhead lighting before circling Blade slowly. "Impossible," she muttered, shaking her head. "To transform this one into a Chinese cleaner? Bah!"

Blade bristled but bit back a retort. This woman was their ticket to infiltrating North Korea undetected. She couldn't afford to antagonize her.

"The man first." Madam Bianzhuang gestured to a weathered barber's chair.

Finn's scowl deepened as he was ushered forward. "I still say this is a waste of time."

"Hush," she chided, "And sit still."

She ran her hands through Finn's black wavy hair, massaging his scalp with strong fingers. Blade stood, fascinated, as Finn closed his eyes and allowed himself to relax into the expert's hands. She'd never seen him so vulnerable. Madam Bianzhuang smiled.

"Beautiful hair. Pity," she said as she reached for the hair clippers.

"Jaysus!" Finn said. "What are you playing at?"

Blade looked over at Xiu and both women started to laugh.

"What's so funny?" Finn asked.

"You sound like a little girl," Blade said, still giggling.

"You aren't Samson, you know," Xiu added.

Blade watched, mesmerized, as Finn's features melted away beneath prosthetics that reshaped the slope of his nose and the line of his jaw. Layers of carefully applied makeup replaced his fair complexion with a warm, golden undertone.

Hours ticked by. Xiu had cleared a table to work on her laptop, fingers lightning fast over the keyboard. Blade, with nothing to do, found herself rummaging through the costume racks, pulling out one dress after another—and wishing Joe were here. His steady presence and quick wit would have lightened the day. He was a master illusionist, and she half-expected him to walk through the door, all smiles and bravado, accepting applause for resurrecting from the dead. But that was impossible.

At last, Madam Bianzhuang stepped aside with a flourish, a satisfied gleam in her eye. "It is done," she announced. "Behold."

Finn turned to the mirror, shock rippling through him. His reflection was utterly foreign—distinctly Asian—every trace of his Irish heritage erased.

"Well, I'll be damned," he muttered.

Xiu's approval was more effusive. "It is perfect! Finn, you're—"

"Unrecognizable," Blade finished softly.

Madam Bianzhuang's scrutiny locked onto Blade. "Now, for my greatest challenge."

Blade settled into the chair, her stomach churning with a mix of anticipation and dread. Cool fingers tilted her chin, examining every angle.

"Contact lenses, of course," Madam Bianzhuang murmured. "A shame to hide such fire, but necessary."

Like Finn, the makeup artist began with her hair. "No wig, too risky."

The woman began to mix different chemicals together.

"Are you going to color my hair?" Blade asked.

"No worry. This is temporary," Madam Bianzhuang said. "But this is not." Taking hold of Blade's hair in one hand, she whipped out shears from her apron and cut off eight inches with the other.

Blade gasped. "What the hell?"

"Who's the little girl now?" Finn said, throwing an arm around Xiu's shoulder.

The makeup artist patted Blade's arm gently. "You will see."

A lump formed in Blade's throat as tears gathered, blurring the world around her. It was only hair, she told herself, but it felt like fragments of her identity had been sheared away and discarded on the floor.

To be trampled upon.

Blade breathed deeply, not trusting herself to speak. Finn and Xiu shifted their attention to a webpage on the laptop, giving her privacy.

As the hours crawled by, Blade heard Xiu and Finn talking, doing something constructive while she endured Madam Bianzhuang's ministrations and further instructions on how to make subtle changes to appear North Korean once they crossed the border. When the process was complete, Blade barely recognized herself. Gone was the knife-thrower from New Orleans. In her place sat a Chinese woman, unremarkable in every way.

Xiu nudged Finn, who had fallen asleep in a lumpy chair. He awoke with a start and jumped to his feet. He scanned the room for any threat, then remembered where he was. His eyes widened as they settled on Blade, a slow smile spreading across his face. He crossed the room in a few strides and leaned close, their faces nearly touching as they studied their shared reflection in the mirror.

"Sure we might just pull this off yet."

Madam Bianzhuang allowed herself a small, satisfied smile before her expression turned grave. "The real transformation begins. I've selected these clothes for you. Put these on and you will rehearse."

Finn and Blade took the proffered clothing and did as they were told.

"Remember," Madam Bianzhuang instructed, her voice low and urgent. "It is not enough to look the part. You must become invisible in your very essence. Focus on the ground, keep your shoulders slumped. You are no one. You wish to be seen by no one. This is the key to your survival."

Blade nodded. But when she caught the worry tightening Xiu's features, a flicker of doubt raised its ugly head. Was she truly ready for this? Could she really infiltrate one of the most oppressive regimes on the planet?

They gathered their supplies—makeup kits for touch-ups and additional prosthetics to use in North Korea.

"We return separately," Xiu instructed. "Blade first. Finn follows in ten. I will be last. Trust your training."

Blade stepped into the late afternoon bustle, a living rehearsal for the performance of her life. With slumped shoulders and bowed head, she perceived each passerby as a potential threat. The disguise held. To the crowd, she was just part of the noise— unseen and unnoticed.

The walk to the hotel seemed endless. When she finally slipped through the lobby unnoticed, Blade felt triumphant. But it was short-lived, tempered by the knowledge that this was only the beginning.

When she stepped into the room, the rush of relief was dizzying.

"Well done," Thomas said, clapping from a darkened corner. "But tomorrow—tomorrow is when the trial begins."

After Finn and Xiu returned, the team reviewed the upcoming timetable. Tomorrow, the Crimson Silk troupe would be on their way to North Korea. They'd be flying in with the performers—blending in behind the makeup and costumes. By then, Chase's exact location should be nailed down.

As Shanghai's neon glow filtered through grimy windows, Blade lay sleepless in her narrow bed. In mere hours, they would masquerade as cleaners, surrounded by people she couldn't communicate with. Ming was their one chance to make it across into North Korea. And somewhere in that hostile land, Chase was waiting—if he was still alive.

CHAPTER
THIRTY-THREE

April 13 – 10:04 a.m. KST
Camp 14, North Korea

The stench of urine and blood and sweat clung to the air as Chase was roughly shoved into the interrogation room by two soldiers he'd never seen before. His stomach churned, memories of Hakim's torture flooding back. The bare concrete walls, the wooden table, the colonel and his knife—it was difficult to believe it was only four days ago.

Colonel Yong-Sun's smug smile did nothing to alleviate Chase's foreboding. One soldier took out a gun and gestured toward the table. Chase considered tackling the man to the ground but thought better of it. He just had to hold on a few more days— long enough for Thomas and the Soldati to pull off a miracle.

Chase winced as he tried to sit on the table, his broken rib making it difficult. Impatient, the second soldier manhandled Chase to a prone position and strapped his wrists and ankles down, just as they'd done to Hakim. Was the colonel going to flay him alive? Or did the sadistic bastard have something even worse in mind?

Every nerve ending pulsed with fire, and he almost wished the colonel would finish him off. He'd seen the result of tortured men and women in the Middle East. Chase flexed against the bonds, testing their give. Tight. These men were professionals. If ever there was a time for prayer, it was now.

"Mr. Maserati," the colonel drawled, his eyes glinting with anticipation, "good news. You are being transferred to Pyongyang in the morning."

"Is that why you have me trussed like a turkey?" Chase said, letting out a laugh at the colonel's apparent confusion. "Never heard that expression? I don't think your Comrade General Secretary will find it amusing if I'm dead on arrival."

Chase was certain the top brass remained oblivious to his escape attempt. Had they known, Yong-Sun would already be en route to the capital, summoned to explain his failure. By Chase's estimation, Yong-Sun had only hours left to gather intel before his reputation crumbled or he suffered a humiliating demotion. The Supreme Leader expected results—not excuses.

The colonel leaned in close, his fetid breath hot on Chase's face. "Before you leave here, I promise you will break by giving me the names of your Christian operatives. Every last one."

Chase had gone through SERE training in a contained environment, where instructors taught about survival, evading the enemy, resisting, and escape. But in the wild, people were unpredictable. Manipulation was his best option. "Go to hell."

The backhand came fast, connecting with a sickening crack that echoed off the walls. Chase's head whipped to the side, his mouth filling with the coppery taste of blood. He turned and spat, crimson blood and saliva landing near the colonel's polished boots.

Wiping his knuckles on his pants, as if making contact with Chase's skin had contaminated him, Yong-Sun stood tall again, towering over him. "There are other ways to extract information, Mr. Maserati."

As if on cue, the rusted hinges of the door creaked open, and a woman in pristine blue scrubs stepped inside. The middle-aged woman looked out of place, as if she'd taken a wrong turn on her way to a hospital. Her meaty hand held a metal tray that gleamed under the harsh light, a hypodermic laid out with clinical precision. The colonel barked rapid-fire instructions in Korean, each syllable heightening Chase's apprehension.

"What is that? What are you giving me?" Chase demanded, his voice hoarse as panic set in. He struggled against the leather bonds as the two soldiers laughed.

The colonel snapped his fingers and the two soldiers rushed forward, their hands pinning his shoulders down.

"No need to fight. You will only hurt herself."

The nurse approached, being careful not to make eye contact, focused only on her task. She brought the needle closer, the tip gleaming inches from his vein.

"Our truth serum is quite effective," Yong-Sun gloated. "Soon, you'll be telling us everything we want to know."

"Wait—" Chase bucked, hoping the broken rib would somehow puncture his lung. If he talked, too many people would die. The Christians in this country would continue to suffer in labor camps or be martyred for their faith.

The needle sank into the crook of his arm. Chase felt the wooden table biting into his shoulder blades. And then his chest burned with pressure—deep, crushing, like a vice clamping down behind his sternum. His breath caught halfway to his lungs. Pain shot down his left arm, hot and electric. The room tilted. His vision blurred. Through the haze of pain, he saw alarm spread across the room as his breathing became labored and erratic. He began to convulse violently, his muscles seizing beyond his control.

Yong-Sun yelled at the woman, his self-assured smile fading into something darker—fear.

Chaos erupted as she ordered the soldiers to cut Chase loose and lay him on the floor. Carefully, the woman turned him on his side, keeping a trembling hand on his shoulder to keep him steady.

Chase heard shouted orders and panic in the room, but he was beyond caring. Dimly aware of the cold concrete against his skin, he saw the outline of a woman bathed in ethereal light above him. Though her features were indistinct, his heart recognized her instantly. Cheyenne. She reached out to him with outstretched arms. He longed to be held, and he was so tired. It would be easy to let go, to slip into that welcoming warmth. To finally rest.

"Stay with us!" the nurse cried out from a great distance away.

"Keep him alive!" Yong-Sun bellowed. "Or I will have your family killed!"

The woman dropped beside Chase, her hands moving over his chest, compressions starting, relentless. She pressed down, again and again, trying to force his heart back into rhythm.

Chase entered the bright light. And then, nothing.

CHAPTER
THIRTY-FOUR

April 14 – 4:42 a.m. CST
Shanghai, China

Restless and out-of-sorts, Alec had abandoned his bed to stroll alongside the Huangpu River, which slithered through Shanghai like a venomous snake, waiting to attack the unsuspecting. He patted the Sig Sauer P320 in his shoulder holster under his puff jacket. There was a certain honor among the Triad, but there were others out to kill him. Being here alone, in the predawn, was foolish. But he had grown tired of hiding and running. Once he found Blade, he'd return home—ready to make his stand.

The Bund unfolded before him, offering a view unlike anything he'd ever known. He settled onto a bench, eyes tracking a Chinese junk as it glided across the inky water. In this sepia light, its massive square sails resembled something ancient and eternal. He drew in a slow breath, the scent of the river stirring memories of nights along the River Mersey—nights pulsing with adrenaline, when survival had been instinct, not strategy. A quiet chuckle escaped him. Strange how that same fire still burned in his chest.

Alec's phone buzzed, snapping him into the present. He pulled it from his pocket, squinting at the screen. The message was brief, cryptic: "Bund Financial Square. Shanghai Bull. Now."

He pocketed the device, removed the gun from its holster, and stuffed it in his pocket. Best to be prepared. The promenade was nearly deserted, save for a few early-morning runners, as he strode toward the statue. At this pace, he'd reach his meeting point in no time.

The bronze bull loomed ahead, its reddish-gold sheen gleaming beneath the streetlight like burnished armor. Alec arrived sooner than planned. He surveyed the plaza, instincts sharp, every shadow a potential threat. The charging bull was meant to symbolize China's strength and economic ascent—but to Alec, it radiated something far more menacing. Not prosperity. Power. And the promise of war.

A figure stepped into view, his movements smooth and deliberate. The same Red Pole from the night before. The dragon tattoo on his neck seemed to writhe in the flickering streetlights. Without preamble, the man extended his hand, a folded slip of paper resting in his palm.

Alec took it and eased back, keeping the young man in his sights for a good thirty feet before he strode away. He had the information he wanted, but at a steep price. Wu Fen allowed him to walk away this time, but Alec would need to strengthen his Asian suppliers or risk a coup.

Sunlight was just breaking over the horizon, its luster shimmering over the river. Shapes came into focus, and people began to filter onto the promenade—early walkers with their pets and tourists catching the sunrise.

Alec opened the paper slowly. It was an address, as expected. He reached for his phone and opened an app to hail a ride. Within the hour, he would be confronting Blade and ending their ridiculous cat-and-mouse game for good. His business was suffering, and by the looks of Blade's life, she wasn't doing that well either. If she didn't see reason . . .

A blue sedan pulled up to the curb and Alec slipped into the back seat. At this hour, traffic was light. After twenty tense minutes, he leaned forward, his voice barely above a whisper: "*Tíng zài zhèlǐ*. Stop here."

The driver, sensing the urgency in Alec's tone, eased the car to a stop, the engine's purr fading to silence. They were a half-mile from the destination—close enough to approach on foot, far enough to avoid detection. Alec pressed a generous tip into the driver's hand, a wordless command to forget this ride. As he emerged from of the car, the cool air felt refreshing. He watched the driver make a three-point turn and head back to Shanghai.

Alec quickly dashed into a copse of trees, moving with practiced stealth. And then he saw it—a *siheyuan*—the traditional Chinese rectangular home with its gently curved roof, nestled in the clearing ahead. From this distance, the place looked abandoned, but appearances could be deceiving.

The early morning was eerily silent, broken only by the occasional snap of a falling branch or the faint cry of a distant bird. He studied the house, searching for any flicker of movement or the faint glint of a hidden camera. Hours crawled by as he held his position, unmoving. His body ached from Camila's vicious attack, and he longed to stretch his limbs.

Finally, a car rolled up and parked in the short driveway. Two figures emerged—a tall Black man wearing jeans and a crisp white shirt with rolled-up sleeves, and a petite Asian woman with choppy black hair that defied gravity.

What the bloody hell are the Soldati doing here?

He waited another excruciating thirty minutes before making his move. With a deep breath, he approached the door and knocked.

The door swung open, revealing a face Alec knew all too

well. Thomas Kazir, commander of the Soldati di Cristo. Recognition flickered in Thomas's eyes.

"Alec," Thomas said, his expression carefully guarded.

"Thomas."

A moment of uneasy silence stretched between them before Thomas wordlessly stepped aside, inviting him in.

As Alec crossed the threshold, a furious stream of Chinese erupted from the adjoining room. The young woman stormed past, shooting him a virulent glare before disappearing down a hallway.

Thomas cleared his throat. "Xiu is a bit preoccupied. Perhaps we should have a private conversation," he suggested, gesturing toward a sitting room. "You and I."

The furnishings were sparse—a few chairs that might have been confiscated from the dump and two rectangular tables covered with papers and laptops.

Barely containing his urgency, Alec sat, his body rigid as he cut straight to the point. "Where's Blade?"

Thomas's expression hardened, the scar along his neck flushing red. "I don't know how you found us—but I can tell you this: Blade wouldn't want you anywhere near her."

Alec changed tact. "Have anything to drink?"

Thomas stood over him with clenched fists. "Were you responsible for Vivienne's death?"

Christians valued truth. Alec decided to test the theory. "Vivienne was collateral damage. My target was Martel. I had no idea Blade would drive to the chalet that night. I could have killed her, but I left her alive."

Best not tell the whole truth about his deal with Vivienne—the trade between her life for Blade's.

Thomas moved to the window, staring into the woods. "Vivienne was a good friend. She did not deserve to die in the freezing cold."

"No, she didn't," Alec agreed. "Blade's been hunting me for the past few months. It's time we both get on with our lives."

Seconds stretched as Thomas deliberated. Alec still had the pistol, but he hoped it wouldn't come to killing either Thomas or the woman.

"Christ says to love our enemies and to forgive those who have sinned against us," Thomas said, turning to face Alec. "I do forgive you, but I cannot help you."

Before Alec could respond, Xiu entered the room. She slammed a laptop down on the table. "You want to help?" she challenged. "Then help us get Chase out of Pyongyang—alive."

What the hell have you gotten yourself into, Blade?

"I'm in," he said simply. "What do you need?"

CHAPTER
THIRTY-FIVE

April 14 – 7:15 a.m. CST
Shanghai, China

Somewhere nearby, a street vendor was flipping jianbing or pan-frying dumplings. The tang of fried dough and scallion permeated the morning air—faint, but enough to turn Blade's stomach. Finn peeked around the corner of the alley, waiting for the cleaning crew to make their way to the Crimson Silk Complex. His watchfulness should've been reassuring, but instead it set her on edge. That she and Finn could successfully impersonate Chinese cleaners still seemed absurd. It felt like a bad joke with deadly stakes.

"You look like hell," Finn whispered.

Blade shot him a withering glare. "Thanks. Didn't sleep much." She touched her face gingerly. "Is the makeup holding up?"

Finn nodded, his expression softening slightly. "Aye, Madam B did a fine job. You appear a right proper Chinese woman, though I'd recognize you anywhere."

Blade smiled, aware her brown contact lens concealed her one distinguishing feature. She smoothed down the simple, dark clothing Madam Bianzhuang had provided. The disguise was flawless. With luck, no one would spare them a second glance.

She stiffened as Finn clamped his hand around her forearm. "Oi," he said, tilting his chin toward a group of people in plain clothes, trudging toward the complex.

"The cleaners?"

"Time to earn our keep." They fell in step behind the group, and although an older couple looked at them quizzically, it wasn't their place to ask questions.

The complex loomed before them, a utilitarian, square brick building that reminded Blade of the FBI Field Office in New Orleans. She'd driven past the building many times as she rode her Ducati on Lakeshore Drive near Lake Pontchartrain. It seemed a lifetime ago as she, too, followed in their wake.

They slipped through the main entrance unchallenged, and for a brief second, relief washed over Blade. But it vanished just as quickly, overtaken by the sharp edge of caution. They weren't out of the woods yet. She forced herself to focus—if things went sideways, Thomas and Xiu were holed up just a half mile away.

The staff, who had entered with as much energy as zombies, were now animated as they rummaged through the central supply closet. They milled about, gathering supplies and chatting in Mandarin. Blade quickly grabbed a floor mop and kept her eyes downcast, shuffling down the corridor. Finn, in turn, reached for a white cloth and a bottle of disinfectant.

He motioned with his head and, thanks to Xiu and the downloaded floor plan, the two set off in the general direction of the main rehearsal area.

Blade moved through the corridor, pushing her mop methodically over the gleaming hardwood floors. Finn moved well ahead of her, maintaining a significant gap between them.

She passed through double doors that led into an area resembling a circus ring with various aerial equipment with its rigging and safety net, tumbling mats, balance beams, and other equipment that she couldn't identify. Finn was already down on all fours, scrubbing a patch on a mat. Another worker stepped in and began to polish the wall mirrors. Blade continued her slow progress across the floor, glancing up occasionally until she spotted a familiar face.

Qianfan.

He wore tight-fitting black shorts and a snug tank top that emphasized a well-muscled body. The video she'd seen of his performance did not do him justice. In the video, Ming was the star, the focal point, and Qianfan was merely an instrument to highlight her. In person, his grace and agility shined through.

Fighting the urge to rush over, Blade maneuvered closer. Qianfan continued his routine of flips and handstands. As she neared, his eyes narrowed, not in suspicion, but in sudden curiosity. He smoothly transitioned into a handstand.

"Ming was taken into custody yesterday," he murmured in perfect English, his words barely audible as he held the inverted position. "She has not returned."

Blade momentarily stopped the rhythmic sweeping motion and stood straight, dumbfounded. "The plan?" she whispered.

"Unchanged," he replied, his voice strained from the exertion. "We leave for North Korea this afternoon. Be ready."

With the room beginning to fill, Blade edged away, cutting a path toward Finn, who was scrubbing down a barre like he'd been doing it for years.

"Ming's in custody," she muttered, bending down to adjust her mop pad. "No word on her whereabouts."

"Listen, this was never about anyone but Chase. There's plenty out there riskin' it all to see us through. We hold steady, yeah? Stay the course."

"What if we can't pull this off?" she hissed.

He stopped polishing the barre and inched away from her, keeping his back to the acrobats as they streamed past. "Then we die trying," he replied grimly.

Blade continued her task until she reached the stairs. Somehow, she'd need to stay hidden until it was ready to board a plane to North Korea.

From an upstairs window, Blade watched Ming return to the complex, her movements heavy with fatigue. Blade exhaled, grabbed her dust mop, and padded downstairs.

The frenetic energy of workers had subsided to a measured trudge as men loaded the last boxes of costumes and equipment into a truck. Qianfan had stationed himself on the first floor in the hope that Ming would return. He lit up as she entered the room. Without hesitation, he ran to envelop her in a close hug. Even from this distance, Blade could sense the attraction between them.

She said something in his ear, then pushed him away gently. Blade observed how the other performers gave Ming a wide berth, as if an invisible force field surrounded her.

"Seems our friend's little chinwag with the police didn't do her any favors," Finn murmured.

When Ming turned, the young performer spotted the pair on the staircase. Blade detected a subtle shift in her demeanor—a slight lift of her chin and shoulders. A gust of wind from a fan caught Ming's waist-length black hair, whipping it across her body. Dressed in a fitted red tank and black leggings, she carried the effortless grace of a runway model rather than an acrobat.

Blade turned to Finn and could see that Ming's beauty had made an impression. "Close your mouth, lover boy," Blade teased, nudging him with her elbow. "You're supposed to be invisible, remember?"

Finn cleared his throat, his cheeks reddening beneath the foundation he wore. "Aye. Let's get back to work."

One of the female coaches clapped loudly, drawing attention from everyone on the first floor. She barked a stream of commands in Mandarin, her sharp tone needing no translation. The entire room erupted into motion—workers grabbing bags, technicians gathering equipment, and performers hurrying to collect their belongings.

Blade and Finn exchanged quick glances, understanding nothing of what was said but recognizing urgency when they saw it. It was time to move out.

As they filed out toward the buses, a stern-faced man wearing a navy blue tracksuit stepped into Blade's path, speaking rapidly and gesturing at a stack of equipment cases nearby.

She froze, heart pounding. Xiu had warned them about this— if addressed directly, make a gesture of acknowledgment and move away without speaking. Blade nodded deferentially and reached for the nearest case, steeling herself against the pain in her wrist as she mimicked what the other workers were doing. The coach's eyes lingered on Blade before he turned away to berate someone else.

Close call.

The bus ride to the airport went smoothly. Once on the tarmac, they helped unload boxes, careful not to draw attention to themselves in the daylight.

As they boarded the plane, Blade spied Ming and Qianfan enjoying an iced beverage in first class while they continued to walk down the aisle to the last row next to the restrooms. As she settled in, Blade wanted nothing more than to curl into a ball and disappear for the rest of the flight. The hair, the makeup, the clothes, the looming trip to North Korea—it was all wrong. If Joe were here, he'd probably tell her to pull up her big girl panties and get on with it.

As the engines roared to life, Finn nudged her and grinned. She'd never noticed his chipped incisor tooth before. Somehow, this small imperfection made him appear less disagreeable, more human. Perhaps this partnership would work just long enough to extract Chase out of Pyongyang.

CHAPTER
THIRTY-SIX

April 14 – 9:16 a.m. KST
Pyongyang, North Korea

His head throbbed, pounding like he'd surfaced too fast from a deep dive. The world swam into focus—stark white walls, the astringent sting of disinfectant, the rhythmic beep of a heart monitor. A hospital, maybe. But the cold bite of metal at his wrists said otherwise.

He tugged at the handcuffs, desperation rising as they refused to give. The restraints clinked against the bed frame, a grim reminder of his powerlessness. Chase studied the room, seeking any clue to his location or a potential means of escape. A dusty window near the ceiling allowed in weak rays of early morning sunlight. He heard the faint sounds of a city stirring to life—a city that must be Pyongyang.

A tinny speaker crackled outside the building, spitting out propaganda in garbled, alien syllables. He couldn't make out the words, but he knew their meaning. The show was about to start. And he was the headliner.

He squeezed his eyes shut, forcing his training to kick in.

Memories surged through him in sharp bursts—a needle, Cheyenne's ghost-white face, the jolt of a military truck over cratered roads. Each bump had ripped through him like shards of glass.

No chance in hell Thomas and the Soldati could extract him from the center of Pyongyang. A miracle wouldn't be enough. Not here. Not now. They'd never find him in a maze of three million people and layers of surveillance. He was on his own.

The creak of a door snapped him back to the present. For a fleeting moment, hope surged as he thought he glimpsed someone familiar. But no—it was her. The nurse from Camp 14.

Chase tried to catch her attention, but she kept moving, intent on taking his vitals. "Where am I?" he croaked.

She ignored him, pulling a blood pressure cuff from a drawer in the bedside table. She made a small clucking sound from her throat—whether that was good or bad, Chase had no idea—and poured water into a plastic cup. She mumbled something in Korean, then produced two pills from her pocket.

"No pills," he rasped, clenching his jaw and turning away.

Strong fingers dug into his chin, wrenching his face toward her. "Swallow," she hissed in broken English. "Or I call guards. They make pain. You want pain?"

Chase glared defiantly. Her hand clamped over his nose, the other forcing the pills past his cracked lips. He attempted to spit them out, but she held his mouth shut, nails digging into his cheeks. Her eyes, cold and clinical, seemed to enjoy this.

"Ah, our guest is awake. Excellent." Colonel Yong-Sun stepped into view, his crisp uniform immaculate.

I can't seem to shake this guy.

Chase tensed. He yanked on the handcuffs, only making them tighter. Blood seeped under the metal.

"Where am I?"

"Pyongyang, of course."

The stench of the colonel's cologne nearly triggered his gag reflex. Chase steadied himself before speaking. "Didn't have anything else better to do than follow me here?"

A scream sliced through the air from somewhere in the building—then abruptly cut off. Chase knew full well the horrors that were unfolding beyond these four walls. He'd seen the colonel's brand of punishment up-close. This was no ordinary hospital. It was a house of horrors.

"The pills will help you rest," Yong-Sun said casually. "We want you healthy for tomorrow's festivities. We cannot have you looking too worse for wear on national television, can we?"

Realization hit him—the broadcast would be a regime spectacle, his execution turned into state propaganda. No wonder Colonel Yong-Sun was here, gloating with that smug grin of his. This was his moment of triumph, a bid for favor with the Supreme Leader.

But Chase wasn't done. "I'm surprised you're still here. I figured after that truth serum debacle, you'd be scrubbing latrines in Pyongyang by now."

Yong-Sun's jaw tightened, the flicker of irritation there for only a heartbeat before he recovered. "The serum worked as I intended," he replied coolly.

The drugs were taking hold despite Chase's desperate fight to stay alert. "You meant to kill me *before* the execution? Keep telling yourself that. Can't get a half-dead American to talk? Doesn't exactly inspire confidence with the top brass."

The colonel leaned in, breath soured by kimchi and rot. Chase fought to keep his focus fixed on the man, committing every detail to memory for the day of reckoning—but the edges of his vision were beginning to blur.

"Your fate is sealed," Yong-Sun whispered. "And with it, the fate of your entire underground network. Did you truly believe you were a match for the might of our glorious nation?"

What did the bastard mean about the entire underground network? Had the Soldati been compromised?

As consciousness slipped away, Chase saw those he loved flicker through his mind like a bittersweet slideshow—his fallen SEAL teammates, young Hakim, and Blade . . . God, Blade. Her smile, warm enough to melt an iceberg, had captured his soul. He wasn't finished—not with her, not with any of it.

In the encroaching darkness of his drug-induced stupor, Chase allowed a fresh mantra to take root. He locked onto the one thing they hadn't taken—his will.

I will not beg.

I will not break.

I will not die here in this godforsaken country.

CHAPTER
THIRTY-SEVEN

April 14 – 3:36 p.m. KST
Pyongyang, North Korea

As the commercial airplane made its approach to the runway, Blade caught her first glimpse of Pyongyang through the oval window. The sprawling cityscape surprised her, a surreal mix of brightly colored buildings and gleaming modern skyscrapers that seemed to defy the country's notorious reputation for poverty and isolation. Towering above it all was a pyramid-shaped building dominating the skyline like a looming sentinel.

"Steady," Finn whispered in her ear. "We're laborers. Nothing more."

Armed soldiers boarded the plane, their faces impassive masks as they walked down the aisle, scrutinizing the passengers. Blade focused on their hands, noting how their fingers hovered near the triggers of their rifles. As they drew closer, she dropped her chin, letting the dark curtain of hair mask her face.

The soldiers passed by them, entering the galley, where they helped themselves to cookies and a soft drink. Blade could hear them gulping down the beverage as they tried to communicate with the attractive flight attendant.

Satisfied with their inspection, the soldiers led the way down the metal stairs. Her throat tightened at the sight before her: a gauntlet of soldiers gripping Type 58 assault rifles, their suspicious eyes scanning the deplaning passengers. A hastily erected security checkpoint sprawled across the tarmac—barriers, scanning equipment, and inspection tables arranged with military precision. The Crimson Silk troupe shuffled forward in a subdued line, each person passing through the metal detector before being patted down by guards. To her right, more soldiers scoured the luggage, their movements mechanical and thorough as they pawed through intimate belongings with cold efficiency.

Blade rubbed her sweat-slick palms against her dark-colored pants. *What if the guards spot the prosthetics?* Finn's athletic build made him an even bigger risk—he stood out among the lean, compact Chinese performers. Thankfully, she'd left her knives in China.

Stay calm. I'm a nobody with nothing to hide.

Blade released a shaky breath, sweeping the crowd until she spotted Ming and Qianfan. Their steady composure anchored her, grounding her in their mission. These two Chinese performers, hiding their Christian faith in a country where belief meant imprisonment or execution, had gambled everything to help them. Their courage, standing against such brutal oppression, humbled her to the core.

Near the airport entrance, an argument drew her attention. The troupe's coach jabbed his finger at an indifferent soldier, his neck and cheeks mottled red with barely contained fury.

"What's happening?" she murmured to Finn.

Before he could answer, shouts erupted nearby. Two guards yanked a worker from the line, his desperate cries dissolving into whimpers as they dragged him away. Blade's stomach twisted into knots.

"This is bad," Finn muttered. "If they start questioning everyone—"

The coach's booming baritone filled the space, barking orders in Chinese, cutting off any further protest. The troupe scrambled into a single formation. Blade's gaze swept the scene, cataloging every detail.

Armed guards began to herd the troupe into groups of ten. Blade fought the impulse to flee, but she reminded herself to remain in character. Workers didn't run, they meekly followed orders. A turquoise bus rolled up, and the performers were quickly ushered aboard.

"There goes our lifeline," Blade said as she saw Ming and Qianfan board the bus.

Sharp gestures and barked commands directed the Chinese workers to haul crates and the apparatus from the plane's cargo hold to a waiting flatbed truck already piled high with equipment.

Finn bent to lift long pieces of aluminum. "Easy does it," Finn murmured as she helped him tie them down. "We're doing our job."

"What could these be for?" she wondered out loud.

Finn gave a curt shake of his head, silently warning her to keep quiet as an armed soldier edged within earshot. He aimed the gun at Blade and pretended to pull the trigger. The other soldiers snickered as she fell to her knees in a posture of submission. The soldier holding the gun advanced, jabbing her shoulder with the muzzle. He laughed. Blade forced herself not to react. If they discovered her nationality, she would certainly be taken into custody or shot. Not to mention what they would do to Finn.

Two more flatbed trucks with side rails rumbled up. The soldier with the gun lost interest as his superior shouted, *"Shàng qù! Shàng qù!"* Workers clambered in with Finn and Blade close behind.

Pyongyang contradicted everything Blade had read about North Korea—there were decent roads and unexpected green spaces. Children dressed in crisp white shirts skipped along the sidewalks, presumably walking home from school. The lack of traffic struck her as unnatural, although there were many cyclists. But beneath this manufactured facade of cleanliness and order lurked something sinister, a darkness she couldn't quite name.

As they drove out of the city into a more rural area, Blade started to see signs of poverty—women washing clothes in a river, ramshackle dwellings with tin roofs, potholed roads. The trucks eventually stopped in the middle of a wheat field, with tents pitched in rows, the fabric billowing slightly in the late afternoon breeze. With no privacy, and not speaking either Chinese or Korean, how would they ever make it out of here without blowing their cover?

The women were separated from the men and assigned tents. Blade accompanied a gaunt elderly woman with a distinct limp into the tent. The woman quickly kneeled on one of the two pallets and lay down, clearly exhausted.

Blade knelt beside her tentmate and tapped two fingers lightly against her own throat, then gave a slow, deliberate shake of the head—silent, intentional. *Let her think I'm mute.* As Chase once advised, get some shut-eye when you have the opportunity. Without hesitation, Blade stretched out on her own pallet and let exhaustion claim her.

It was dark when she was nudged awake by the old woman, who gestured for Blade to follow her. Dinner time. As they approached the chow line, a small voice cut through the din. "Psst!"

Blade looked up to find a young girl, no more than eight,

crouched behind a tent, frantically waving her forward. She scanned the area for Finn, paranoia setting in. Every face was a potential threat.

The old woman squeezed her forearm, encouraging her with an urgent nod. From the corner of her eye, she saw Finn shuffling over, his eyes shifting between the young girl and the old woman.

"Should we?" she whispered to Finn.

"Might be our only chance."

The pair followed the girl to a dilapidated hut on the outskirts of the tent city. Inside, two military uniforms lay neatly folded on a rickety table. A pistol lay on top of one uniform and a knife on the other.

"Our ticket in," Finn said softly.

Relief washed over Blade as she noticed their suitcases in the corner. She turned to thank the girl, but she was gone.

Blade's hands trembled as she changed her appearance to a North Korean soldier. They were two foreign operatives, deep in the heart of the most paranoid regime on Earth, about to attempt a rescue that would be considered suicide by most intelligence agencies.

"We need to go over tomorrow's plan," Finn said as he buttoned his jacket. "We've only the one shot at this. If we miss our window—"

Blade imagined what Chase must be enduring in some North Korean cell. The image steeled her resolve. "We won't fail."

Just as they finished their preparations, the soft crunch of leaves announced someone approaching. Blade and Finn froze, listening. Finn quietly removed the Type 68 pistol from his utility belt. Blade's hand instinctively went to the concealed knife at her hip, a comforting weight against her palm.

Footsteps crunched closer—deliberate and unhurried. Blade pressed her back against the rough wooden wall of the hut. Finn did likewise. The door creaked open, and the harsh beam of a flashlight sliced through the darkness, sweeping across the room. She squinted into the glare, trying to get a better look at the intruder.

"Who the hell are you?"

CHAPTER
THIRTY-EIGHT

April 14 – 4:54 p.m. KST
Pyongyang, North Korea

The armored convoy ground to a halt before the towering Rungrado 1st of May Stadium. Ming counted the soldiers—twenty-four, all armed with rifles, taking positions around their vehicle with practiced precision. Not a greeting—a warning.

"Remember, we represent the People's Republic of China and are honored guests," the director called out in Mandarin. "Tomorrow, an entire nation will be watching you. There is no room for error—not on this stage. Every step you take reflects on our troupe, our country, and our future. Make us proud, our shining stars."

Ming's fingers found the small cross she wore hidden under her leotard, a reminder of why she was really here. As the troupe filed off the bus, she fell into step beside Qianfan, their footsteps in sync with their escort.

"Keep facing forward," Qianfan whispered. "They are studying us."

They had been warned about devices recording their movements. Ming fought the urge to look for the cameras. Instead, she began to count her breathing, trying to slow her racing heart. *Yī, èr, sān, sì.* One, two, three, four. The familiar count before a performance. Except this time, a missed cue could mean imprisonment—or death.

The tunnel opened into the stadium proper. She was no stranger to world theaters, but this was something else entirely. Tier upon tier of seats stretched toward the sky like in an ancient colosseum, the afternoon light painting harsh shadows across empty benches that would soon hold countless spectators.

"Magnificent, is it not?" The government-appointed minder materialized beside them, his hollow smile failing to mask his calculated gaze. "The Supreme Leader will attend tomorrow's festivities." The Crimson Silk Acrobatic Troupe had been assigned many minders for their three-day stay, ostensibly to act as a guide and translator, but in reality they were censors who controlled what was said and seen during their stay.

Ming bowed slightly, careful to maintain the expected expression of humble appreciation. "We are honored," she said in careful Korean, the words tasting like ash in her mouth. She reminded herself that this wasn't just a performance, it was an assignment from God.

This is your plan, Father. Use me well.

A temporary stage loomed in the center of the stadium, its framework hidden behind billowing walls of white silk that rose twenty feet into the air. The silk, stretched taut in some places and left to ripple in others, revealed vague silhouettes of the metal scaffolding beneath.

"There are two hours to rehearse," the director said, clapping for order. "We begin immediately—start to finish."

Performers fanned out across the field, launching into warm-up routines under the watchful eyes of both coaches and soldiers. Ming stretched, her mind a whirlwind of calculations and contingencies. The stadium's design conspired against her—every sound echoed, every movement was visible from multiple angles. She glanced at the apparatus she'd requested. Would it hold up when it mattered most?

Through the controlled chaos of preparation, she spotted Jiahao carrying a box of props. As a stagehand, he was intimately familiar with the maze of apparatuses, ropes, and pulleys. The night Ming had learned about performing in North Korea, she'd had a vivid dream of red silk and an iron cross. She had enlisted the help of her trusted friend and ally to bring that prophetic vision to fruition.

She almost missed his subtle signal—three fingers brushing his chest—their private code.

"I should check the equipment," Ming said as she crossed the field with measured steps, hoping she wouldn't draw suspicion.

"The craftsmanship is impressive," she said in a clear voice as she approached Jiahao. Then, softer, "Were you successful?"

Jiahao tilted his head and stared at her as if she were from another planet. "Obviously. But are you sure about this?"

Ming nodded. "How does this work?"

"Hydraulics. Nothing to worry about," Jiahao said, running a hand through his short hair. "Once you give the signal, I will flip a switch, and the cross will begin to rise. You'll have only seconds to get into position before it continues upward—about thirty feet, well beyond the silk drapes."

"You know the consequence of getting caught?"

Jiahao ignored the question. "If you change your mind, I have installed a safety valve that will reverse the lift."

Her index finger traced the metal, finding the mechanism.

"Ming!" Qianfan's voice cut through the rehearsal area like a whip crack. "We are next!"

Before she could respond, heavy boots pounded on the artificial turf—multiple pairs, approaching fast. A young soldier with dead eyes approached, flanked by two others with fingers draped too casually over their weapons. "What is that?" he snapped, nodding toward the aluminum bars.

Ming's mouth went dry. There was little she could do for her friend as the soldier bent to inspect the bars.

"It . . . it is part of the show. Bars to—"

A sharp cry shattered the tension. Ming spun to see Qianfan sprawled on the stage floor, his face twisted in agony, clutching his ankle. "Something snapped!"

Their coach rushed forward. "Quick, bring the emergency kit!"

Ming gaped in silent amazement as Qianfan commanded the attention of everyone in the stadium, his acting flawless in his apparent suffering. The soldiers hesitated, their conditioning to investigate warring with their fear of allowing injury to one of the Supreme Leader's chosen entertainers.

"His ankle is broken," the director said, clearly flustered.

She ran to his side, aghast that he'd broken his ankle on purpose to draw attention away from Jiahao. How she loved this man who would give so much for their cause. She touched his shoulder as he pounded his fist in pain. An unspoken message passed between them—we face the future together.

"Ming, prepare to perform solo while we assess the program," the director ordered.

"Of course," she said, moving away from Qianfan. Two of the troupe helped him into a waiting golf cart.

Ming took her position and began her warm-up sequence. Above her, the empty stands loomed like silent witnesses. Soon they would be filled with thousands who would see what she had painstakingly coordinated, thousands who needed hope in this dark place.

A soldier's radio crackled with static and harsh Korean words. Ming did not need to understand the language to recognize an order. She focused on her movements, each one chosen for function and beauty, as she silently recited the verse that had led her here: "But the path of the righteous is like the light of dawn, which shines brighter and brighter until full day."

Tomorrow, she would be that light. Even if it cost her everything.

CHAPTER
THIRTY-NINE

April 14 – 6:07 p.m. KST
Pyongyang, North Korea

"I'm John, Pastor Kwon's brother," the man holding the flashlight hissed. "Ming sent me."

Finn kept his pistol trained on the short man as he entered the hut. He was careful to keep his hands in full view.

"This wasn't the bleedin' plan. And what proof have we you're really with Ming?" Finn shot back, brows drawn tight.

"Your contact in the capital has been compromised. If I meant you harm, I would have come with a few more people other than myself," John said.

"Fair enough," Finn said, lowering his weapon. "I'm not one for taking on an operation when it's all gone arseways from the start. We've been flexible—up till now."

Blade felt the same frustration. Coming into North Korea blind was disconcerting. It was like running into a burning building with only a garden hose to put the fire out.

"We must hurry," John said urgently. "You will stay with me

tonight. Tomorrow, fellow believers will help. You may be missed if they do bed checks. Please, follow me."

"Do we trust him?" she asked, studying the desperation etched on John's features.

Finn stared hard at their contact, measuring him. After a beat, he gave a slight nod. "Aye, we do. There's honesty in his face. Besides," he added with grim humor, "we've not many other options, eh?"

The tension in Blade's shoulders eased fractionally, though suspicion kept her on the balls of her feet, ready to strike if necessary. She rushed to the suitcases and removed the kit from Madam Bianzhuang. Finn didn't bother with his. They followed John out into the cool night, Finn's weapon never wavering from the North Korean's back. Overhead, the sky stretched with a canopy of stars so bright they seemed to watch like electronic eyes.

John led them to a cluster of bushes, revealing three bicycles hidden beneath carefully arranged branches. The metal frames were deliberately dulled—no chance of reflection. "Cars would draw attention," he explained, his voice barely audible. "Bikes are ordinary. Just three more shadows in a city full of them. And in Pyongyang, the shadows have teeth."

Blade mounted her bicycle and rode between John and Finn. They pedaled down empty country roads through the endless dark. With no streetlights or warm glow from windows, reality seemed suspended, marked only by the revolution of their wheels against the dirt road. Her muscles, dormant in the past few weeks, protested. Without caffeine or any substantial nourishment, she fought the urge to sleep. Her head jerked awake at regular intervals.

"There she is," Finn said. "Pyongyang."

The capital emerged from the darkness, backlit in the moonlight. Electricity was scarce in North Korea, Blade had read, but the Supreme Leader wasn't going to scrimp on making a good impression on the world.

John's home—really a shack made of scrap wood and corrugated metal—crouched on the city's edge. Although the hour was late, the air still stank of cabbage and coal.

The door opened before they even got off their bicycles. "This is my wife, Nari," John said, beaming at the thin woman.

She greeted them with serene dignity and motioned for them to enter their home. Despite a small fire burning in a coal stove, it was chilly.

"I have tried to seal the gaps, but the cold air always wins," John said with a smile. "Sit, warm yourself."

Blade and Finn sat in the only seats in the two-room shack. Blade followed Nari's movements as she served rice and vegetables in chipped bowls, then poured tea into cups that had known better decades.

After they devoured their meal, they gathered around the stove for warmth. It reminded Blade of sitting with her mother in a ski lodge after a long day on the slopes, the two of them curled up near a roaring fire, cradling mugs of hot cocoa that chased the chill from their bones. She should have cherished those days together, lived more fully rather than fixating on her knife-throwing competitions.

"How did you learn English?" Blade asked softly, wanting to know more about this man who risked not only his own life but his wife's as well.

"From an American missionary. Wonderful man, but he was eventually betrayed. We never heard from him again."

"He just disappeared?"

"Many disappear."

"And how d'you come by the name John, then?" Finn asked.

"I chose the name for John the Baptist at my baptism. I only pray my life will honor him. What he accomplished before his death has not been seen since, except for Christ Jesus himself."

"Aye, and we all know how that ended for John the Baptist," Finn muttered grimly.

The words dropped like bullets in the crammed room.

"In this country, we understand that some things are worth dying for." John spoke softly, each word laden with sorrow and pride. "That truth matters more than survival."

Nari stood and moved about the room, squeezing her husband's shoulder as she passed. Blade caught the glance they shared—brief, but rich with love and quiet sacrifice, a lifeline in a place that gave them nothing but danger. A pang twisted in her chest. Would she ever know love like that? Did Finn wonder the same? Did Chase?

A sharp knock shattered the moment. Everyone froze. Blade's heart leaped into her throat as Finn shifted to stand between the women and the door. John raised a hand for silence, then went to answer.

Their muted conversation was too low to overhear, but when John returned, his expression was bleak. "Chase has been transferred. He's being held in a medical facility within the stadium."

"Why there?" Finn said.

John shrugged. "Rest," he said simply, handing Finn two pallets. "There are matters to settle with our friends. I won't be long."

Finn unrolled the pallets side-by-side near the stove. "We'll need a few hours of sleep," he said, "and we'll not be doing it in the freezing cold." He lay down, patting the pallet next to him.

"I'd rather lay down beside a gator."

"This isn't a proposition. It's common sense, now lay down."

Blade stood over him for a few seconds before succumbing. She hated to admit it, but Finn was right. Their combined body warmth would at least stop her from shivering.

Finn pulled her close. "We'll spring Chase and get the hell out of this godforsaken pit," he vowed. "Every single one of us."

CHAPTER
FORTY

April 15 – 1:47 a.m. CST
Dandong, China

The small dock was silent except for the soft lapping of water against rotting pylons. The crescent moon struggled through a thick curtain of clouds. Only the faintest gleam traced the current of the Yalu River, more suggestion than reflection.

"I can go no further," Thomas said, standing with his hands clasped behind his back as if he had not a care in the world.

Good riddance.

Alec didn't need a damn babysitter, but he had to admit, the Soldati's connections and resources were impressive. Within hours, Thomas had scheduled a private jet from Shanghai to Dandong. And Xiu's abilities went far beyond IT. The young woman had arranged for weapons to be delivered, engaged a smuggler for the boat ride to Nampo, and found a driver to take him to the outskirts of Pyongyang. David could learn a thing or two from her.

"I'll do what I can."

The rigid-hull inflatable boat bobbed gently, a wizened old

man gripping the wheel, his features obscured by a cigarette burning from the corner of his mouth. He flicked the cigarette into the water, where it hissed and disappeared.

The smuggler waved urgently as Alec dropped a waterproof duffel into the boat with a soft thud. Inside were Alec's requested weapons: a Sig Sauer CROSS STX with a high-powered rifle-scope, a Beretta 70 with ten extra magazines, and enough grenades to ensure he'd get out of any situation alive.

A slight smile tugged at his lips. He'd also included Cold Steel Sure Balance throwers. Blade had proven her proficiency with a knife.

The timeline was tight. Three hours on the flight with Thomas, who had simply closed his eyes and slept. Depending on the weather and patrol boats they might encounter, another three to four hours before making Nampo. Two hours to Pyongyang via delivery truck. Just one hour left for getting into the stadium, locating Blade, and helping rescue the bloke. Alec hated tight timelines. It was a recipe for sloppy mistakes.

"You late," the old man said, poking Alec in the chest with a forefinger. "Patrol don't wait for tourists."

"Good thing I'm not a tourist. Let's roll, old man."

Alec donned a wool cap and hunkered down behind the smuggler. The warmth of the jacket and gloves was welcome, a temporary shield against the biting cold. But once they reached land, he'd ditch them both. He needed to move fast, clean, and unencumbered.

Only a white bow wave broke the darkness as the RHIB plowed through the river. "How many runs have you made?"

The smuggler shot him a glare. "You give me money. I get you to Nampo."

"Point taken."

Without warning, the smuggler pushed the throttle forward, and the RHIB took off like a missile. The engine screamed and echoed in the blackness. Cold wind lashed his face, the spray cutting like needles as the boat skimmed across the bay. Clouds obscured the moon as well as Alec's sense of direction.

He lost track of time until the old man suddenly eased off the throttle. The boat's high-pitched whine softened to a whisper. Alec tensed, looking up.

The smuggler's finger pointed dead ahead.

Pale beams cut through the low-lying mist, scanning the gloom in slow, deliberate sweeps. A patrol boat loomed in the distance, a dim shape a kilometer out.

"Cut the engine," Alec ordered, voice low.

"No. We are close. If they spot us, we make a run for it."

The low drone of the boat bled into the night air, its search-light drifting dangerously near. Alec didn't move—just watched, breath held. Far too close now.

The smuggler cursed softly. "If they see—"

The distinctive crack of the boat's 50-caliber machine gun shattered the silence. Tracers lit up the darkness like angry fireflies.

"Bloody hell!"

The smuggler slammed the throttle down, and the RHIB surged forward, a black arrow slicing through dark water. The old man maneuvered the boat in a zigzag pattern, trying to avoid being peppered with bullets.

"Five minutes!" the smuggler yelled.

We won't last that long.

Alec reached for his duffel bag and removed the CROSS STX case. He'd practiced putting the weapon together with his eyes closed—stock locked, bolt slid into receiver, scope snapped into place, and magazine inserted. Same drill. Thirty seconds, rifle up, trigger squeezed, one sharp report, and the searchlight went dark.

Let them try to find us now.

A 5.45mm round hit the boat, splintering the top edge.

Alec put the scope to his eye once again, trying to steady himself against the rocking boat. He pulled the trigger, taking out the soldier firing the 50-caliber gun. Again, he aimed and fired. Another soldier toppled over in the wheelhouse.

"Go!" Alec yelled.

Their boat pulled away as the soldiers' discipline disintegrated into chaos. Alec squinted into the horizon, noticing how it began to darken around the edges. Nampo. There were dozens of ships docked in the port city. The old man continued in his zigzag pattern.

Gunfire cracked through the early morning, but without the searchlight, they were firing blind. Minutes crawled by before the smuggler turned the wheel, angling diagonally toward the shoreline roughly two kilometers out.

"Seodulleo," the smuggler hissed urgently as they neared the shore. Hurry!

Alec instantly grabbed his duffel and launched himself over the side as the smuggler whipped the boat around in a 180-degree arc, never looking back.

The icy water dragged at his legs as he moved quickly to the shore. After ditching his jacket and gloves, he ran up an incline to a dirt road, slipping on the rain-slick ground. Somewhere far off, a dog barked at an approaching vehicle. He glanced at his watch. Still on time.

An ancient olive green truck lumbered down the road in his direction. The driver, a teenager by the looks of him, stopped and gestured for Alec to join him.

The lad didn't speak English, and the truck backfired every few miles. *Crikey, this is a right cock-up.*

He'd missed the sunrise with all the confusion, but now the sun promised a bright new day. Not ideal for an extraction. Damn Blade. After months of psychoanalyzing himself, he still found it impossible to pinpoint the attraction or desire he felt for her.

About twenty kilometers from Pyongyang, the teenager pulled to the side of the road behind an aging delivery truck with a patched canvas cover that stretched over curved ribs supported by a metal frame.

A scarred man, a burn victim judging by the extent of damage, opened the flap. Alec surmised that was the only invitation he was going to get.

What he should do is turn around and forget about Blade and her idiotic attempt to rescue Chase. Could she be in love with him? He was screwed, no matter how he examined this situation. But he hadn't crossed half the world to fail. Whatever it took, he would locate Blade—and maybe, just maybe, earn a measure of redemption in her heart.

"Bollocks," he whispered. "This is going to be a right mess."

CHAPTER
FORTY-ONE

April 15 – 6:21 a.m. KST
Pyongyang, North Korea

Dawn light penetrated the threadbare material that served as curtains. John was already moving about the hut as Blade's eyes fluttered open. It was quiet outside. Finn snored faintly beside her, his normally stern features softened by sleep. Blade stretched slowly, her muscles stiff from the hard floor. She moved his arm away from her waist, thankful he didn't wake. Absently, she traced the tender spot on her ribs where the assassin's blow had struck just days ago.

Blade smelled a mixture of sour cabbage, green tea, and orange blossom—not wholly unpleasant. Strange how the orange blossom reminded her of home. A rooster crowed, and a neighbor screeched at the offending bird.

"Oi, I should have been up hours ago," Finn said, throwing off the flimsy blanket and jumping to his feet. "Why didn't you wake me?"

That's the Finn I know—angry and disagreeable.

"There is time," John said, carrying a tray filled with ceramic cups and a teapot.

Nari appeared silently at her husband's side, bearing bowls of cold rice. Her dark eyes held a depth of compassion that made Blade's throat tighten. They had so little, yet gave freely to strangers without a second thought.

"Eat," Nari urged softly in Korean, the word needing no translation.

As the four ate and drank their tea, John grabbed an old paper bag and pencil to outline the logistics for the day. Sitting cross-legged on the floor, he began to sketch a rudimentary map of the area.

"The stadium," John explained, his English careful and measured, "is on Rungra Island, located in the middle of the Taedong River." John crudely drew an island with two bridges on the north and south sides, connecting it to Pyongyang.

Finn leaned forward, his shoulder brushing Blade's. "How'll we make it there?"

"You'll be taken to the island in a delivery truck. Once there, you will meet one of our friends at Gate 5, precisely at ten o'clock. Look for someone in a white lab coat. The crowd's massive—the stadium holds one hundred and fifty thousand."

Finn gave a low whistle.

A ghost of a smile crossed John's exhausted face. "But this is good. As soldiers, you will hide in plain sight."

"You'll be there?" Blade asked, while studying the crude map. So much could go wrong.

John shook his head. "My work must continue here. Since my brother was killed, our friends rely on Nari and I to lead followers to Christ and then smuggle them into South Korea."

"This contact takes us to Chase?" Finn's question carried an edge of impatience.

Blade placed a hand on his arm, hoping to diffuse his brusqueness.

John's eyes locked onto theirs, hard as granite. "Yes, but be warned—if you are captured, we will kill you or we all die."

The words hung in the air like smoke. Blade felt their weight settle onto her shoulders, another burden to carry. But she understood. One loose thread could unravel everything these people had built.

"And once we've got Chase, this lad gets us to the boat, yeah?" Finn pressed. "He'll take us downriver?"

"Yes. And we have your flying machine hidden if needed."

A whisper of movement caught Blade's attention. Nari pressed something into Blade's palm—a tiny bundle wrapped in faded cloth. "For strength," she whispered, the first English words falling from her lips.

Blade unwrapped the package, revealing a delicate gold cross. Unexpectedly, she blinked back tears at Nari's generosity, even though she wasn't a believer. The emotion surprised her—sentimentality was not high on her threshold list.

"Thank you," Blade managed, her voice rough with emotion. She clasped the necklace around her neck, letting it rest against her skin. Whatever happened today, she would find a way to repay their courage.

Finn checked his revolver with practiced efficiency, the metal catching the weak morning light. "Well then," he said, "let's go get our boy."

April 15 – 9:02 a.m. KST
Pyongyang, North Korea

The stench of fish and melting ice had become almost unbearable after twenty-five minutes crammed in the freezer. Alec's muscles throbbed as he tried to shift without disturbing the layer of carp and mackerel concealing him. The truck hit another pothole, sending icy water seeping through his thermal gear. He forced himself to remain perfectly still, remembering the heart-stopping moment at the last checkpoint when a soldier had lifted the lid and rummaged through the ice. The soldier had helped himself to several fish before slamming the freezer shut, never noticing the man hiding beneath.

Finally, the delivery truck wheezed to a stop. Alec heard muffled voices, then silence. Metal hinges creaked as the driver lifted the freezer cover and began to empty the fish and ice into buckets. Carefully, Alec pushed up on the wooden barrier and uncurled himself from his cramped hiding place.

The scarred man put a finger to his lips, then drew back the canvas flap. His misshapen face creased with concern as he surveyed the loading dock of the stadium.

"Guards," the man whispered in heavily accented English, gesturing for Alec to follow. "Everywhere cameras."

Alec's trained eye swept the service entrance, cataloging every detail. Two soldiers were more interested in the giant monitors than securing the area. Cameras were in plain sight in six-meter intervals across the loading zone. The layout of the stadium seemed straightforward. Finally, a break.

"Medical?" Alec asked as he pantomimed a person giving a shot.

The scarred man pointed down a dimly lit concrete tunnel, then wagged a warning finger in Alec's face. "No, no. You crazy man."

Alec grabbed his duffel bag and placed it in a wooden box, then filled it with ice and fish. The delivery man hefted one to his shoulder. Alec donned the scarred man's jacket and did the same except he walked in the opposite direction and kept to the wall.

Once the tunnel opened onto the concourse, Alec set his box down and melted into the shadows. He noted guard positions, camera angles, and potential escape routes. Spectators poured into the venue for the festival, creating useful chaos. Long queues had already formed at the loos.

A maintenance corridor branched off to his right—possibly useful if things went sideways. After some reconnaissance, he chose a secluded position behind a dumpster, where wooden crates rose ten high. From there, he had a clear view of anyone coming or going from the building where he suspected Chase was being held.

Unsure of the timetable for the ceremony, he removed the Sig Sauer CROSS STX from the duffel bag and started to assemble the scope and suppressor to the rifle. As he unfolded the stock and attached the bipod, Alec heard a scuffing noise. He sat up straighter and listened, his hand shifting to the knife sheath on his belt.

That sound again. Footsteps approached, likely one of the soldiers patrolling the area. Alec gently placed the gun down and unsheathed the knife, ready to spring into action.

Seconds later, a North Korean soldier stepped into view, weapon raised. Alec, with a fraction of a moment to react, grabbed the gun barrel and hoped the soldier didn't pull the trigger. Simultaneously, he plunged the knife blade into his adversary's throat. The soldier gurgled, then fell to his knees.

Not one to take chances, Alec yanked the knife free and plunged it through the man's eye socket and into his brain. His pulse raced, half expecting a contingent of soldiers to surround his hide. The soldier, probably inexperienced, had failed to alert others to his discovery. In dictatorships, people were often rewarded for their deeds rather than their cooperative teamwork.

He shouldn't have bloodied the soldier's uniform. Nothing to do about it now. Alec heaved the soldier over the side of the dumpster and scattered garbage over the body. Someone was bound to notice the missing soldier and come looking. With the Supreme Leader in attendance, would they dare raise the alarm? Alec gambled the North Korean military would not want to be embarrassed.

Bollocks. What more could go wrong?

He would have to find a different hiding spot, but there was no other reasonably secluded area with the sightlines he needed. He'd have to find a spot up above the corridor. Alec remembered a door he thought might be a maintenance room—plain, metal, and tucked just out of sight. The Korean symbols were undecipherable, but his hunch made sense. There had to be a way to a catwalk or platform.

He knocked, not wanting to be surprised by anyone holding a wrench or worse. No answer. The room stood empty for now.

Alec didn't hesitate. A steel ladder led to an access door in the ceiling. Alec climbed fast, hands sure on the rungs, and slipped through the opening.

He lay down on his belly behind a large ventilation vent. Just as he suspected, the stadium had interior catwalks to access the lighting panels and HVAC system. Taking out his rifle, he used the scope to survey the area through a grated walkway. There were two soldiers interspersed along the catwalk, but they were intent on laughing over a cell phone—most likely a video. The spot offered temporary safety, but if he needed to provide cover, he'd become a sitting duck unless he could kill the soldiers around him.

From his current position, he could see both ends of the corridor. The medical facility was on this floor, though he couldn't tell exactly which door led to Chase. He had no doubt Blade was here. Of course she was. The woman didn't recognize the words fail or surrender. He wondered what she'd make of seeing him here, playing on her side for once. Would she be pleased? Or would she simply put a blade in his chest and call it even?

CHAPTER
FORTY-THREE

April 15 – 9:32 a.m. KST
Pyongyang, North Korea

So far, so good.

They slipped through the checkpoints without raising suspicion, soldiers waving them through thanks to the stolen uniforms and Madam B's expertise. But an undercurrent of unease left Blade queasy. Being this deep in enemy territory felt like walking on a tightrope over the Grand Canyon—once committed, there was no turning back.

"Keep your head down," Finn muttered, confidently striding toward Gate 5. "And for the love of all that's holy, try to walk like a soldier."

Blade almost smiled.

As they neared the gate, she noticed the heavy presence of soldiers, who were stationed at regular intervals. A normal precaution for any world leader. They'd been lucky up to this point, riding their bicycles through checkpoints and not being closely examined, but their disguises would not hold up under intense scrutiny.

"Look at them all," Finn said.

Animated columns of people filed into the stadium as if they were attending a circus. Teenagers took selfies, just like they did in America. Yet, they weren't allowed to have unrestricted internet service or freedom of speech or any other right that the Supreme Leader didn't sanction.

"Sweet Jesus," Finn breathed, tilting his chin at a group of soldiers ahead. "They all have rifles." He pivoted sharply and retreated the way they had come.

Blade followed him, her stomach dropping as she scanned the crowd, realizing he was right. Every soldier had a rifle slung over their shoulder or held at crisp attention in front of them. Without that key piece to their uniform, they were instantly marked as outsiders.

"Give me a minute," Finn said, already beginning to veer away from her.

Blade's hand shot out, gripping his arm. "Are you crazy? We can't separate now!"

"Do you want to get us both caught?" he hissed. "Stay here. Back in ten."

Before she could argue, Finn disappeared into the crowd, leaving her alone. Each second stretched as she stood at attention, spine ramrod straight, face impassive. Blade stepped into formation, as if stationed there all along—just another soldier spaced at the proper interval. She imagined roots sprouting from her boots, anchoring her to the earth, keeping her from sprinting after her partner. If Finn didn't return . . . if he was caught . . . if Chase was already dead . . .

A young lieutenant passed by, his dark eyes lingering on her breasts. Blade met his gaze with practiced indifference, years of performing on stage serving her well, even as her heart thundered against her ribs.

The young soldier edged forward, studying every inch of her

with obvious interest. He opened his mouth to say something, but Finn's appearance interrupted him. Her partner now carried two rifles, their metal gleaming dully in the morning sun.

The lieutenant barked out an order she didn't understand but turned on his heel and walked away.

"That was close, yeah?" Finn said as he handed her a weapon.

"Too close," Blade whispered. "Where did you—"

"Best not to ask." His lilting voice was gentle but firm. "Gate 5. Let's move."

They merged into the stream of people entering the stadium. Blade had been to a New Orleans Saints football game two years ago, but the Caesars Superdome was minuscule in comparison to this massive structure, the scale of it almost beyond comprehension. She could see Finn's trained eye noting security cameras, exit signs, and guard positions—mapping possible escape routes if things went south.

She jumped at the sudden blast of the national anthem. Around them, thousands rose in unison—a display of absolute control that made goosebumps race along her arms.

As the anthem played, Blade's thoughts drifted to Chase, her throat tightening. He was somewhere in this complex. Was he still sane after days of torture? Was he still alive?

She cut off that line of thinking before despair could take root. She had to believe he was alive.

Beside her, Finn's trigger finger tapped against the rifle. She guessed he was calculating how much C-4 it would take to bring this whole place down. A demolitions expert in a target-rich environment was like a fox in a henhouse.

John's friend appeared right on schedule, his white doctor's coat out of place. He passed without acknowledgment, but they fell into step behind him, following him out of the stands and into the twisting concrete halls of the stadium.

"Ready then?" Finn asked softly.

Blade nodded, her fingers tightening on the rifle. "I was born ready."

9:45 a.m.

The stadium rose before them like a massive magnolia blossom, its sixteen arched petals reaching toward a steel-gray sky. The frigid air stung Ming's cheeks as she disembarked from the bus. Qianfan moved slowly behind her, adjusting his grip on the crutches as he maneuvered down the steps.

The troupe followed their minders to first-tier seating, which offered a commanding view of the stadium floor below, where the Russian performers were assembling in their vibrant costumes. Every twenty meters, soldiers in crisp olive uniforms watched their progress with cold, calculating eyes. The display of force wasn't surprising—this was the regime's most important celebration, the birthday of their Eternal President.

"Careful," Ming murmured as Qianfan's crutch caught on an uneven step. She steadied him, using the moment to scan the streams of people flowing into the stadium. Somewhere among the masses were the Soldati operatives. She prayed they'd found a way inside undetected.

"I'm fine," Qianfan muttered, though he leaned into her help. He might never perform at this professional level again, and the coaches were furious at his clumsiness. It was a bad omen. But in Ming's mind, it was a gift from God. He would not be on stage with her at the critical moment of her mission.

Ming adjusted her down coat as she sat, fighting a shiver that had nothing to do with the temperature. Already, the stadium thrummed with the energy of people packed shoulder to shoulder —party officials, military officers, and carefully selected citizens, all here to witness the spectacle. And the execution.

"You are too quiet," Qianfan murmured in Mandarin as they settled into their seats. "What aren't you telling me?"

Ming leaned close, pitching her voice low. "My performance is the catalyst for action. My part of the operation is to create a distraction, like you did for Jiahao."

Qianfan's face tightened. "What kind of distraction?"

Before she could respond, North Korea's national anthem erupted from the stadium speakers. The crowd surged to their feet as one. Ming rose mechanically as she viewed the Supreme Leader enter the stadium on the huge Jumbotrons on the east and west ends of the stadium. His white suit contrasted against the entourage of military officials in dress uniform. The world tilted —just slightly—as if her center of gravity had betrayed her.

"Ming—"

One of the minders leaned forward, giving them a warning glare to be respectful. Ming kept her eyes forward until the music stopped. For another five minutes, the Supreme Leader addressed his people, smiling and gesturing as if he were a benevolent leader who loved his subjects. The reality was far different from this carefully orchestrated illusion.

The stadium quieted as the Russian performers bowed and marched into place on stage.

Qianfan wrapped his hand around Ming's forearm and squeezed gently. "Tell me what you are planning."

"The less you know, the safer you will be."

A flash of purple caught Ming's attention. Li, the company's newest member, spoke animatedly with a soldier near the lower steps. Her stomach clenched as Li pulled out her phone, showing the screen to the uniformed man. His eyes narrowed as he spoke into his radio, his gaze sweeping toward their section.

"Something is wrong," Qianfan said.

Ming forced herself to breathe normally as Li pointed in their direction, the soldier nodding with grim satisfaction. The morning performances had begun—a little more than an hour until the rescue operation was set to begin. If they even survived that long.

"Is Li a government informant?" Ming hissed.

Qianfan shrugged. "Whatever happens, it won't alter our plan."

"If I'm taken," Ming whispered, keeping her expression neutral, "you know nothing. You have seen nothing. You suspect nothing. Understand?"

Qianfan only stared at her, his brow furrowed with worry.

Ming's eyes burned as she watched Li and the soldier climb toward them. "Promise me you will protect the others. The underground network needs you."

The soldier was four rows away now, Li trailing behind him like an eager shadow. Three rows. Two. Ming's mind raced, each scenario ending in disaster. But if she could buy the Soldati team enough time, give Chase even the slimmest chance of escape . . .

Over a dozen Russian dancers were spinning and leaping on the stage below, the folk music inviting the spectators to clap in time. Her fellow troupe members beside her, unaware of the soldier or Li, joined in the celebration.

The soldier and Li reached their row. Ming tried to remain relaxed, even though her head pounded from the music.

It was only 10:30.

And everything was already unraveling.

On the final note of the "Kalinka," the soldier took hold of his rifle, gripping it tightly as if prepared for resistance. "Come with me," he ordered.

April 15 – 10:01 a.m. KST
Pyongyang, North Korea

Chase inhaled deeply, the sterile scent of ammonia and disinfectant stinging his nostrils—a grim improvement over the cell in Camp 14. Music seeped through the walls, the muffled brass instruments reminding him of the "Star-Spangled Banner."

Ten days in captivity, according to his internal clock. Every nerve and muscle screamed as he sat handcuffed to a metal chair bolted to the concrete floor. The faces of the dead haunted him in this stark clinical room—Petty Officer First Class Mike Watson, skull exploding from a sniper's bullet in Tel Skuf, Vivienne Martel, killed nearly five months ago near Geneva, and Hakim— he'd never forgive himself. The kid's broken body, bloodied and beaten, because Chase had brought him on this mission. Each failure settled on his shoulders, the yoke too heavy to carry.

Resignation had never tasted so bitter. There was no rescue party coming, no clever escape plan, just the inexorable march toward public execution. No decent burial awaited him. At best, they'd toss him on a garbage heap. *God, please make it quick.*

Now Chase understood Jesus's anguish in the Garden of Gethsemane. Soldiers came to terms with death in their own way, but knowing the hour and method of your execution—that was a special kind of torture.

Once the music finished, the rhythmic chant of *"Manse, manse!"* grew to a deafening roar. *Will this crowd chant when I'm executed? And what of Blade?*

Those fierce amber eyes sliced through his defenses like a laser. He'd tried to deny the attraction, tell himself it was just admiration for her skills, her determination. But when she'd looked at him with that intoxicating blend of challenge and vulnerability, something long dormant fluttered to life in his chest.

The door crashed open and Colonel Yong-Sun strode in with two soldiers following in his wake. He stood over Chase, confident and in command. "Comfortable, Mr. Maserati?"

Chase merely glared, his fingers itching to wrap themselves around the colonel's scrawny neck.

"Shall we get you cleaned up? I believe you soldiers have a crude saying—shit, shower, and shave?" The colonel's boots clicked against concrete as he circled the chair. "But don't mistake this courtesy for opportunity. My most skilled men stand ready."

Yong-Sun nodded at the men. They stepped forward, unfastening the shackles at Chase's wrists and ankles. Blood rushed into his hands, igniting a firestorm of pins and needles. He curled his fingers into a fist. A slim chance to fight back outweighed dying as a spectacle for thousands.

"I am eager to see our Supreme Leader's face when I parade you like a pig led to the loyalty feast."

Chase's head snapped up. "The Supreme Leader?"

"Oh yes." Yong-Sun's grin widened. "He knows nothing of this surprise. Imagine his pleasure when I present him with an

American spy, captured trying to undermine our great nation. My career will ascend to glorious heights."

The burlier guard shoved Chase, and he went down on all fours. His legs cramped from hours of sitting motionless. He rose unsteadily to his feet while mentally cataloging details. *One door, two soldiers, and one colonel with a god complex. Odds are shit, but better than zero.*

Chase steadied himself, placing a hand on each side of the doorframe. *Timing. Precision. No second chances.*

Then he exploded into action.

His elbow slammed into the closest soldier's throat, a brutal, efficient strike. As the man crumpled, and before the second could react, Chase spun, locking him into a chokehold. For one heartbeat, escape seemed possible.

Until white, searing pain punctured his consciousness.

The colonel's knife twisted in his side, driving Chase to his knees as blood bloomed across dingy prison cotton. Red-hot anger surged through him, adrenaline allowing him to lunge at his nemesis before collapsing on the cold floor.

"Admirable," Yong-Sun said, wiping the blade on Chase's tunic. "But I decide when you die, American dog."

The taste of copper flooded his mouth. Through blurred vision, he heard the colonel barking orders in Korean. Soon, medical personnel swarmed around him, their voices harsh and urgent as they worked to stem the bleeding.

After days of torture, surely he'd bleed out soon. Chase felt some vindication at dying before the colonel was rewarded for bringing him to Pyongyang. Yong-Sun would be fortunate to leave the city with his head.

As Chase's world faded to black, his last words to Blade—*join the Soldati family*—sounded lame and cowardly. The regret cut deep.

"I'm sorry," he whispered, though whether apologizing to

Blade or Cheyenne or God, he wasn't sure anymore. Music started once again, something that might have been Russian. Russian in North Korea. He must be hallucinating.

A final prayer rose from deep within—not for rescue or survival, but for forgiveness. For all the lives he couldn't save. For all the love he'd been too afraid to give.

CHAPTER
FORTY-FIVE

April 15 – 10:09 a.m. KST
Pyongyang, North Korea

After passing hundreds of people to reach the medical wing corridor, its emptiness worried Blade more than the soldiers standing guard throughout the stadium or Finn's disposition. No one had given them a second glance, although Blade could feel sweat on her brow. She dared not wipe it away for fear of smearing her makeup.

"This way," Lab Coat said.

Voices bounced off the concrete walls, growing louder. Coming their way.

"Quick!" Their contact yanked open a door. Finn shoved Blade into what appeared to be an examination room, the metal instruments gleaming on a nearby tray. Her heart slammed against her ribs as voices filled the corridor.

Finn edged toward the door, peering through the narrow gap. His body went rigid. "Medical team," he whispered. "They're rushing into a room down the corridor."

Blade shuddered. Every instinct in her body screamed a

warning—the same visceral sense which had saved her from the assassin in New Orleans, the same intuition which had alerted her to René Martel's true nature in Mallorca. She knew with bone-deep certainty Chase lay imprisoned in the room down the hall.

Why would Chase need a medical team?

Images of Chase bleeding and broken just yards away assaulted her. Would they even try to save him? Blade struggled to gain control of her emotions. Of course, they would keep him alive. This was a spectacle—like the *Gladiator* movie—where Maximus stood defiant and proud in the middle of the Colosseum. Tears welled in her eyes as she pictured Chase in this stadium, being executed like an animal.

Not while I'm stilling breathing.

But they were running out of time.

"We need to move," Finn growled as he removed his hat and threw it across the room in frustration. He sidestepped the table, his boots squeaking against the linoleum floor.

Alarmed, Blade took a deep breath to dispel the tears and turned on her partner. "And alert every soldier in the building?" Voice trembling, she said, "We need to be smart about this—rushing in will only get us killed."

"Shhh," Lab Coat said, bringing a finger to his lips. "Keep your voices low. Your English will give us away. And I cannot be taken alive. Understand?"

Finn exhaled loudly and nodded.

"I am Dr. Kim," their contact continued in a whisper. "Ming performs at 11:30. Alone." His hands trembled as he spoke. "Qianfan broke his ankle yesterday, on purpose. Too long a story to tell, but you must act during her performance."

Ten excruciating minutes crawled by. The only sound was the dim, incessant Russian music, punctuated periodically by the crowd's applause. When footsteps approached again, Blade and Finn instinctively moved to flank the door.

Finn quietly opened the door a crack. Through the gap, they could see a uniformed officer stride past, his polished boots gleaming. His fingers drummed an impatient rhythm against his thigh as he walked.

"An officer," Finn whispered.

"Let me investigate," Dr. Kim said, adjusting his coat. "Stay here." His Adam's apple bobbed as he swallowed hard.

As the door clicked shut behind him, Finn turned to Blade. "That corridor's a killing ground—no cover, nowhere to hide."

"There's surveillance cameras everywhere," Blade added. "How will we get Chase out?"

Finn ran a hand through his hair. "The instant we grab him, every guard in this cursed place will know."

"Ya think?"

"If you're so bleddin' intelligent, any suggestions?"

Blade glared, helplessness fraying her nerves. "You're the expert!"

Dr. Kim returned, his face ashen. "American is alive, but he has been stabbed. They are keeping him stable—for the execution."

Blade felt light-headed and grabbed the examination table to stay upright, the cold stainless steel edge biting into her palms. *Chase. Stabbed.*

Finn looked to the ceiling as if he could see straight to the heavens. "How in the hell are we going to get him out of this stadium without killing him? Or us?"

Noises came from the corridor. Blade scrambled to the door and peeked out. "Two unconscious guards being carried away."

"Chase hasn't lost his touch," Finn said wryly.

"There's one guard outside Chase's room, rifle held at the ready."

"Let's crack on," Finn said, bending to pick up his hat. "While there's only one soldier to take out."

"And risk a gunshot to alert the entire complex?" Blade grabbed his arm. "We follow the plan and wait for Ming."

"Every minute we wait is another minute Chase bleeds out!" Finn hissed.

"And if we rush in, we all die!" Blade's voice shook with the effort of restraining herself. The waiting was torture, but rushing in would be suicide.

"Listen to me," Dr. Kim cut in, his quiet authority stopping them both. "Your friend is alive. Ming swore to create such chaos that even the Supreme Leader's guards will be drawn away. We must trust her."

"I'm in command of this mission, and I say leg it," Finn said, poking a finger into Blade's shoulder.

"I will tell the guard outside that two soldiers will come to take Chase when it's time for him to be brought to the ceremony. That should give you the element of surprise you need to over-power him," Dr. Kim said, making an effort to convince Finn. "But then I must go to wait on the boat."

"Finn, listen to him. Please."

He shook his head. "Jaysus, are you thick? That'll never work."

She looked at the clock.

Twenty minutes until Ming's performance.

Before Finn could respond, Dr. Kim produced a crude map, drawn on the back of a sheet of correspondence, from his pocket.

"We are approximately here," Dr. Kim said, pointing to an X on the map. "Gate 10 is here."

Blade traced the escape route with her finger, committing it to memory, then Finn took it and did the same.

"The boat is exactly where I marked. The wheelhouse is painted a bright red. You won't miss it. Once you reach the Taedong River, you will be relatively safe." He hesitated. "There is a backup plan. Your flying machine is hidden on a rusted barge with a blue stripe painted on the side, less than a kilometer downstream. If you cannot reach the boat . . ." He met Finn's eyes. "Get to that barge. But only as a last resort."

"Chase won't make it to the barge if he's wounded." Blade shivered. The portent of a bad omen? A tightness in her chest made her wonder if she was having a heart attack. Finn had been right. She shouldn't be here.

Reading her apprehension, Finn gave her shoulder a squeeze. "*Oi*, you'll do fine."

"It's almost time," Dr. Kim whispered, checking his watch. "May God protect us all."

Blade remembered her mother's words before a knife-throwing competition; when she was jumpy and anxious, her mother would say, "Chin up, aim straight, and try not to stab the judge this time." They'd have a good laugh and the tension would melt away. So many emotions surrounded these few words—Marie's love and belief in her daughter were always spoken at the perfect moment. Blade could hear them now.

She realized with a start she hadn't thought of Alec since joining this mission. Her vendetta against the man responsible for Vivienne's death seemed self-indulgent in comparison to the horror Chase faced. She'd walked away from Chase four months ago, but if he gave her another chance, she'd never leave his side again.

Blade touched the knife strapped to her hip, determination hardening her resolve. She wasn't leaving this hellhole without him. Not this time. Not ever again.

CHAPTER
FORTY-SIX

April 15 – 10:33 a.m. KST
Pyongyang, North Korea

When the armed soldier pointed to Coach Zhou, Ming sat cemented in place, the temporary vertigo making her world spin. He had protested, then tried to retreat in the opposite direction. But there was a second soldier blocking the way. She managed to draw her legs in as the coach scooted past.

Ming forced herself to breathe steadily as she watched the soldier march Coach Zhou down the concrete steps. Her face remained a mask of serenity—a skill honed through hundreds of performances. The soldier kept his rifle trained on the shaking man, a reminder of the constant danger.

Li returned to her seat, leaving Ming perplexed by her smug demeanor. She didn't have the time or energy to wonder what Coach Zhou might have done to deserve Li's wrath. It was just one more example of the treachery entrenched in Chinese society. Ming knew all too well there wasn't much difference between China and North Korea. Both regimes used intimidation, starvation, and torture to maintain control of their populace. She had grown weary of performing, of using her talents to serve as a propaganda piece for a government not worthy of her commitment, patriotism, or talent.

When Director Chen rose and began his descent down the steps, the other performers fell into line without hesitation, their limbs stiff from fear. The sight jogged a memory long buried—back home, years ago, when Ming had trailed behind her grandmother's casket. She must have been five or six, too frightened to get close. Her mother's grip had been unrelenting, dragging her forward step by step. Like her peers, she was expected to obey without question.

In an act of defiance, she remained seated and turned to Qianfan, squeezing his hand with desperate intensity.

"Your hand is freezing," he whispered, his breath warm against her ear. "Are you afraid?"

"No," she lied. "But if something happens—"

"Nothing connects you to the American or the Soldati. Remember what I told you about Peter walking on water? He only began to sink when fear overcame his faith."

Their one night together would need to last for an eternity. This was her burden to carry. Without warning, Ming leaned forward and kissed him, letting her lips linger against his. She memorized everything—the taste of him, the strength in his hands as he cupped her face, the solid warmth of his presence in this cold nation—knowing they might never meet again.

Her gaze swept the filled stadium, landing on the box with the Supreme Leader. This family had usurped God. Most of these people had never heard about Jesus, but after today, she hoped his name would spread throughout the nation.

"Ming," Qianfan said softly, "I love you."

Too choked to speak, she hurried away, afraid she would change her mind.

The salty sting of tears clouded Ming's vision as she searched for Jiahao through the maze of controlled chaos in their staging area. Equipment cases and props created a labyrinth of shadows and light, while costume racks formed corridors of silk and sequins. The bolt of red silk she'd brought leaned against a makeup station.

The harsh fluorescent lights were merciless, exposing dark circles under her eyes from lack of sleep. Ming sat on the small stool, forcing her hands to remain steady as she began her preparation. In the mirror, she could see the Spanish dancers gathered in the wings. The women's black skirts swirled with each movement, ruffles catching the light like the sea sparkling near Pingtan Island. They either held a castanet or fan, and each wore a red flower tucked behind one ear. The men cut imposing figures in their high-waisted trousers and sequined jackets, their wide-brimmed hats tilted forward to add a dramatic flair. They looked happy, an emotion she had only recently experienced—thanks to Qianfan.

The stadium's PA system crackled to life, feedback screeching through the massive arena before settling into a woman's cultured Korean accent. "Please welcome the *Alma del Sur* of Spain as they take center stage to honor our Supreme Leader."

The pit of her stomach twisted, almost doubling her over. The Crimson Silk Acrobatic Troupe would be next. Ming intertwined her fingers to stop their shaking. Silently, she prayed. *Lord, am I mistaken? Am I truly to be a beacon of hope for your people in North Korea?*

The first haunting notes of a flamenco guitar pierced the air. Ming's reflection stared back at her—pale skin, ruby red lips, glittering eyes. A stranger wore her features, a person who dared to challenge the most oppressive regime in the world. Would her parents recognize her if they saw her now? Would they understand why their dutiful daughter had chosen this path?

Her fingers found the zan in her hair, the ornate hairpin her mother had sent to her on her eighteenth birthday. Its weight felt suddenly significant as she slowly pulled it free. Long, ebony strands fell around her like a veil.

Sound took on an otherworldly element as if she were underwater—the strum of guitar strings, flamenco shoes striking the stage, the crowd applauding—all of it creating a surreal symphony.

She could back out—it wasn't too late. But this was the moment she was born for.

11:30 a.m.

The rhythmic pounding of fou drums matched the vibration in Blade's ears. She rolled her shoulders, trying to shake off the tension that had settled there like a lead weight.

Dr. Kim betrayed no emotion as he straightened his white coat. "That is our signal," he said, his accent clipping the words. "The wait is nearly over."

"And if the timing's off?" Blade asked, her grip firm around the rifle.

"Then your friend dies," Dr. Kim said flatly. "And so do you."

"Comforting," Finn muttered from his position by the door, his rifle held close to his chest.

Dr. Kim's hand hesitated on the doorknob. "You will know when to move. The entire nation will know. Trust me."

As the doctor slipped out, Finn immediately threw the lock on the door, as the doctor had instructed.

The soldier shouted and Blade rushed to the door, straining to hear the exchange between the two men. The conversation seemed to stretch forever before footsteps finally echoed down the corridor, coming closer. Was it Dr. Kim, returning to alert them that he'd failed in his first objective? Or was it the guard?

The handle rattled—just a test to make sure the door was locked. Then the footsteps resumed, fading down the corridor. The guard returning to his post. Blade let out a breath.

"How long do we bleddin' wait?" Finn checked his gun for the third time.

"As long as it takes," Blade said, though every nerve in her body screamed for action. She paced the small confines of the examination room, her boots silent on the linoleum floor. Five steps. Turn. Five steps back.

"You're making me head spin," Finn said.

"Would you rather I use the walls for target practice?"

"Keep moving. Just . . . quieter."

Blade drew the concealed knife, finding the tactile coolness comforting. Chase's face flashed in her mind—not as she'd last seen him, strong and vital, but as he might appear after a week in a North Korean labor camp. She pushed the image away. And waited.

CHAPTER
FORTY-SEVEN

April 15 – 11:37 a.m. KST
Pyongyang, North Korea

Ming stood motionless in her ethereal white costume, each crystalline sequin catching the sunshine. The empty space beside her—where Qianfan should have been—left her feeling incomplete, unbalanced. So much time wasted pretending their love for each other didn't exist.

The music opened with a low, ominous rumble of drums, creating a sense of tension and anticipation as five male acrobats took the stage. Their copper-colored costumes, made to resemble dragon scales, shimmered with their movements.

A row of four rings—each smaller than the last—waited onstage. One by one, the acrobats launched themselves through the rings with breathtaking precision: the first somersaulted effortlessly through the largest ring; the second twisted in a corkscrew motion through the next; and the third and fourth flipped simultaneously, their paths crossing in midair like a living work of art. The fifth acrobat executed a triple backflip with a daring half-twist through the smallest ring, landing with feline grace. The quintet continued to dazzle the crowd with a spinning spectacle of agility and strength.

"You do not have to do this," Jiahao murmured, materializing at her side. His youthful features creased with concern. "There are other ways to save our brother."

Ming smiled and touched his flushed cheek. "Bring the red silk, please."

Striding to the makeup station, Jiahao grabbed the bolt of fabric and rushed back. He bowed as he held out the red silk, overcome with emotion.

But before she could accept it, a shadow fell across them. Ming tensed as she recognized Li. She leaned close, her breath warm against Ming's ear as she said, "If God is for us, who can be against us?"

Ming's eyes widened.

Another Christ follower.

A cello's haunting note signaled the beginning of Ming's performance. With no time to process Li's revelation, Ming grasped the delicate material and stepped onto the stage, a fragile nymph with yards of red silk billowing in the breeze, like a sail, sculpting soft, rounded shapes.

Her lithe dance movements were accentuated by her wild, dark hair, which seemed to have its own rhythm. Ming spied Director Chen in the wings, waving his arms, his complexion resembling a ripe watermelon in his anger, but she danced on.

Thirty seconds in, Ming started to wrap herself into the fabric with various twists and turns. Each twist was deliberate and necessary—moves she had rehearsed repeatedly in secret. The hydraulic lift hummed to life behind her as aluminum bars emerged from the back of the stage.

Ming seemed to float to the apparatus and delicately whipped a length of fabric over the vertical beam. Working swiftly, she crafted secure loops and knots that would hold her in place. The crowd quieted, transfixed, as she wrapped the silk around her waist and chest, each turn of the fabric both restraint and safety harness.

As her feet began to hover above the stage, Ming extended her arms outward, grasping the horizontal bar. The hydraulic lift carried her higher, and higher still, until she towered above the stage. Gasps rose from the crowd in a great whoosh as they realized what they were witnessing—a Christ-like figure on a cross.

The wind snapped and twisted the red silk beneath her, a representation of Christ's blood. Ming prayed that her sacrifice would not be in vain—that people throughout the nation would come to *believe*. Her eyes shifted to the Supreme Leader's box. He was gone—the coward. His security detail had probably whisked him away at the first sign of a disturbance.

Her muscles strained from the uncomfortable position, but she held on. The first shouts from the soldiers barely registered as her gaze searched for Qianfan. And there he was, standing among the crowd, his face registering shock and disbelief.

The music stopped in mid-bar.

A shot cracked through the air.

Searing pain bloomed in her shoulder and she lost her grip on the bar. Panicked, she knew death was imminent. And she was afraid. Frantically, she searched the crowd once again to find Qianfan. Her other arm couldn't support her weight and gave way. The cross that had been her anchor now became a prison as she hung in midair, tethered only by the red silk.

She had only seconds. With one final burst of energy, she screamed, "*Geuriseudo Yesu.* Christ Jesus!"

With pinpoint focus, Ming caught glimpses of the crowd— some horrified, others smiling, and Qianfan rushing down the stairs with his crutches.

A man in a military uniform pushed through the crowd, his

body stiff with rage. "Cut her down!" he bellowed. "Cut her down!"

Ming's thoughts turned to the American prisoner and his chance for freedom. To her fellow believers who lived in fear. To the soldiers below, their rifles raised.

"Father, forgive them," she said faintly as the second shot found its mark.

In the stunned silence that followed, broken only by silk fluttering in the wind, Ming's body lay still, but her message—written in both silk and blood—would echo through the hearts of all who witnessed it.

CHAPTER
FORTY-EIGHT

April 15 – 11:46 a.m. KST
Pyongyang, North Korea

A gunshot resounded through the walls.

"That's our signal," Finn said, chambering a round. "Ready?"

Blade nodded, adjusted the hidden knife in her waistband, and picked up her rifle. Time. It was always about timing. Whether throwing knives at a target or planning a rescue, success required perfect execution in a space of mere seconds.

Finn cracked the door open. Still one soldier guarding the door. They moved into the corridor as if they belonged there. The young guard outside Chase's room shifted nervously at his post, his baby face making him look more schoolboy than soldier. Uncertainty flashed across his features before he raised his rifle with inexperienced hands.

Another shot rang out from the stadium floor, the sound muffled by distance but still distinctive. The guard flinched—all the opening Finn needed. He moved like liquid lightning, disarming the young soldier and using his momentum to throw him into the room. The guard's boots squeaked against the floor as he stumbled.

Blade stood rooted in the doorway, unable to take her eyes off the chair, until Chase raised his head. Her heart skipped a beat. "Chase!" She leaped over the two men as they struggled on the floor. "What have they done?"

Finn managed to wrestle the soldier into a chokehold. The young man's eyes bulged as he clawed uselessly at Finn's arm. But Blade barely registered the grappling bodies—it was just noise in the background as she examined Chase.

His face was unrecognizable—every visible inch of skin mottled purple and black where it wasn't split open. His right eye was swollen shut, his left eye, usually so bright with determination, was now bright red and vacant. Dried blood stained a clean, loose-fitting cotton shirt. She gingerly lifted the edge of his shirt to see a bandage over a seeping wound. An IV dripped steadily into his arm—something to relieve the pain, or something to sedate him?

She whirled around at a sound behind her. A nurse in a pristine white uniform threw the door open and ran out, screaming for help. Blade bolted after her, taking hold of her collar and bringing her down. She straddled the nurse, pummeling the woman with unleashed fury, breaking a few teeth and knocking her unconscious, before hauling her back into the room, dropping her before Finn like a trophy.

"Nice work," Finn said.

Blade shook with emotion but took a deep breath before crossing to Chase. She knelt beside him and pressed her lips gently to his battered cheek. His skin burned against her mouth. *Fever*. With steady hands, she cut through his restraints. Even his knuckles were raw and bleeding. Gently, she removed the IV, careful not to cause more pain.

With trembling fingers, Chase brushed her cheek. "Blade? Are you real?" he croaked.

"I'm real." She caught his hand, pressing it more firmly against her. Tears fell freely down her cheeks.

"Steady," Finn said, placing a hand on her shoulder. "You can't help him if you fall apart. We need to move before anyone notices a missing soldier outside."

"What about the nurse?"

"Tied her up next to her friend." He squatted next to Blade, assessing the damage. "Can you walk, mate?"

Chase tried to stand, but he doubled over in agony. A low moan escaped him as he collapsed back into the chair.

Blade met Finn's gaze, understanding passing between them. The mission had just become infinitely more complicated. Their carefully planned escape route required speed and stealth—neither of which seemed possible now.

"Sorry about this," Finn murmured, lifting Chase in a fireman's carry. Blade flinched at Chase's cry of pain. Her fingers curled into fists. She wanted to tear the world apart for letting him suffer like this. His head lolled forward as he lost consciousness, fresh blood seeping through his bandages. *Don't die. Don't you dare die on me.*

"Grab my gun," Finn said.

"Hurry," Blade urged, leading the way to the maintenance corridor. Their footsteps echoed off the concrete walls. A shout in Korean stopped their progress as they reached an intersection with another hallway. A bullet ricocheted off the wall—a warning shot—sending concrete dust flying. More shouts followed.

"Keep going." She dropped into a defensive stance, firing her own warning shot. "I'll hold them here." The words tasted sour in her mouth, but she knew it was their only chance. Finn couldn't fight while carrying Chase.

"Like hell," Finn growled. "I'm not leaving you."

"I can't carry Chase—you can. Get to the boat." She met his eyes, willing him to understand. "Don't wait for me."

In a millisecond, Blade recognized a mirror of her own emotions in Finn's eyes—mistrust, a grudging acceptance, friendship, and regret. The two had come a long way from the disaster in Mallorca, where Shen had died saving her. Perhaps this was a chance to save someone she loved.

Then Finn turned and hurried down the tunnel, Chase's limp form over his shoulders, leaving Blade alone.

The concrete was cold against her shoulder as she steadied herself, listening to the approaching footsteps from the intersecting hallway. After everything—meeting her biological mother only to lose her, hunting Alec Quinn across continents, surviving attempts on her life—it seemed fitting that it might end here, buying time for Chase's escape.

Inhaling sharply, Blade rounded the corner, her weapon raised and ready. But before she could fire, soft pings filled the air. Two soldiers, already dead from gunshot wounds to the head, fell from a catwalk above the corridor, and the rest pointing rifles at her scattered, abandoning all pretense of order. The first to fall was the soldier who had fired the warning shot; his head snapped back, crimson mist dispersing outward as he crumpled to the ground. One by one, they dropped—like ducks in a carnival game—precision shots felling them with chilling efficiency until there were none left alive.

Blade stared up at the catwalk where the shots must have come from. Nothing stirred. The corridor remained silent—for now. But reinforcements were surely on the way. Who could have helped her? Friend or foe? Whoever had intervened seemed content to remain hidden.

Blade didn't waste time questioning her luck. She turned to run, hoping to catch up to Finn and Chase before someone else did.

Until she heard a bullet whiz by her ear and an order, in English. "Stop, or the next one will be through your head."

"Bloody hell, what are you playing at?" Alec muttered, tracking Blade through his scope. She was surrounded, North Korean soldiers forming a tightening noose around her.

She pivoted in a measured circle, shoulders squared, clearly weighing her options.

"Don't be daft," he whispered, though he knew better. Since Switzerland, since Vivienne's death, he'd studied her every move. She was a force of nature—beautiful, intelligent, relentless, and utterly unpredictable.

But instead of surrendering, her hand darted to her waistband.

He watched in disbelief as a knife spun through the air, end over end, before it found its mark—straight into the commanding officer's shoulder. He wondered if that was the target she was aiming for, or a near miss. Either way, it was a fine throw.

The wounded soldier barked orders through clenched teeth. His men closed in with mechanical efficiency, weapons drawn. Not to execute her, but to take her alive. One of the minions roughly threw her to the ground and searched her, seizing both rifles she carried.

Below, the thunderous crack of a battering ram echoed through the corridor. The maintenance door splintered inward and boots pounded up the metal ladder he'd used earlier. Alec took aim and fired at the first soldier who breached the opening. The access door closed with a bang as the dead soldier tumbled down. *The next tosser will think twice about coming through.*

Alec collapsed his rifle with practiced ease, mind racing through scenarios, each one worse than the last. Extracting her now bordered on impossible. The building would be crawling with soldiers, all of them on high alert after that knife throw. And Blade . . . well, she'd never make it easy on anyone, least of all herself.

He vaulted across the catwalk, rolling over steel support beams until he was well away from the firestorm. *What a cock-up!* He slammed his palm against the roof's edge. From this vantage point, Alec spotted soldiers taking up positions at both ends of the corridor. Standard protocol—control the choke points, limit movement.

A ventilation shaft caught his eye. Not perfect, but a way to get out before they sealed off the perimeter. If he didn't reach the outside of the stadium, he'd be in the same predicament as Blade. They would relocate her soon, try to break her for information, and then kill her. His duffel bag pressed against his leg, heavy with enough firepower to maybe, just maybe—

"Right then," he said, securing the bag against his body. "Time to improvise."

CHAPTER
FORTY-NINE

April 15 – 12:01 p.m. KST
Pyongyang, North Korea

A female soldier shoved Blade into a metal chair—the same one Chase had occupied—with so much power, she almost tipped backward. A half dozen soldiers crammed inside the small room, and Blade found it almost comical to see the soldiers jockeying for position to be near the one she'd wounded. He was definitely the one in charge.

A gunshot cracked from above. "Please let whoever helped me get away," Blade thought, forcing her expression to stay blank as rough hands seized her and cinched zip ties around her wrists.

"I cannot have you throwing any more knives, can I?" the North Korean soldier said in perfect English, gesturing to the blade still protruding from his shoulder. Blood had soaked his uniform jacket, the stain reminding her of a Rorschach test, but he seemed completely unfazed.

Blade glared at the nurse standing just behind the soldier in charge. Blood from the nurse's broken teeth painted her chin crimson as she lunged forward, scalpel raised high.

"Meomchwo!" The officer's order split the air like a thunderclap.

The nurse froze mid-stride, her rage instantly dissolving into naked fear. Without a word, she backed toward the door and vanished, her footsteps clapping down the concrete hallway.

He released a breath. "I am Colonel Pak Yong-Sun," he said, circling her chair. "Your friend and I spent many hours together. Though he proved to be remarkably stubborn."

The colonel's hand struck Blade with devastating force, snapping her head to the side. The metallic taste of blood flooded her mouth as her vision blurred.

That was only the beginning.

"Camp 14 is a place for unwanted guests like you. Being a woman won't earn you special treatment or fairness there. I promise, within minutes of your arrival, you will tell me everything I need to know. I was too soft with your friend—that mistake ends with you."

"Sadist," Blade said, meeting his gaze, defiant despite the blood trickling from her nose. She didn't bother to wipe it away. What was the point? She would shed more blood before this was over.

He leaned in close. "I look forward to breaking your spirit."

But here, in this hell with its blood-stained floor, she found herself yearning for a miracle—hoping Chase had made it to the boat, to freedom.

His index finger brushed her cheek. Acting on pure instinct, Blade snapped at it with her teeth, nearly catching flesh. "Untie me and I'll help get that knife out of your shoulder."

He grinned before turning to one of his minions. "Call a doctor while I make arrangements to take this woman to Camp 14."

"But, sir," a young soldier interrupted, "won't the Supreme

Leader want to question the woman himself? Or his security staff?"

The temperature in the room seemed to drop by ten degrees. The colonel's face went terrifyingly blank, like a mask sliding into place. Without warning, he yanked the knife from his own shoulder and, in one fluid motion, buried it in the soldier's throat.

Blade watched in horror as the soldier's eyes opened wide with shock. He clutched at his throat, blood spurting between his fingers before he collapsed.

The colonel, still expressionless, turned back to Blade as if killing another human was an everyday occurrence. "You will give me answers," he snarled, flecks of spittle flying from his lips, "or you will learn the true meaning of regret."

Blade stared at the growing crimson stain on the concrete floor, the casual brutality of the murder turning her blood to ice. This wasn't just another interrogator. This was a monster, completely unhinged, who would deliver on every threat he made.

And she was completely at his mercy.

12:33 p.m.

Fog distorted Chase's reality. His CPO had warned of experiencing hallucinations after being drugged, and Chase believed he was having one helluva drug-induced hallucination. One where Blade had found him, where he could still feel her lips on his skin.

He kept his eyes closed for another minute, immersing himself in the experience. Was he on a boat? Yes, definitely a boat, traveling with the current. Through the haze, Finn's brogue filtered through, low and urgent. "Critical condition . . . needs immediate surgery . . . losing too much blood."

Chase blinked. Soft light filled the cabin through water-stained windows. An IV line snaked from his arm, clear fluid dripping steadily from the bag above. Strange, he was unrestrained. White-hot, searing pain shot through his side as he tried to sit up. Stabbed. Then he remembered—he'd been stabbed by Yong-Sun—the bastard.

His training kicked in automatically: control the breathing, compartmentalize the pain, assess the situation. Chase concentrated on his surroundings. An Asian man came into view, his forehead creased with concern.

The doctor's eyes suddenly widened as he noticed Chase was conscious. He reached out, tapping Finn's shoulder sharply. "He's awake."

Finn spun around, satellite phone pressed to his ear, his face haggard and splattered with what looked suspiciously like blood. "The Arcturus One is her lifeline. You weren't there—you didn't see what those bastards are capable of!"

Chase's heart slammed against his ribs. "Blade?" The word came out as a hoarse whisper. He struggled to rise, but the doctor's firm hands pressed him back.

"Aye. We'll meet you at the rendezvous point," Finn snapped into the phone, ending the call.

"Finn?" Chase asked, unsure if he was seeing an apparition or his best friend.

"Oi, the sleepin' beauty awakens. Just as we're ready to bolt from this godforsaken place." He gestured to the man in the white coat. "This is Dr. Kim—he's the one who led us to you in the stadium."

Dr. Kim grabbed Finn by the elbow and pulled him a few feet from Chase. "Your friend will die before you make it to South Korea," he hissed. "I know a place, a clinic, thirty minutes from here. Underground. Christians."

"I've been ordered to fly Chase out of here. I reckon we're about two hours from South Korea."

"He isn't stable and shows a steady decline."

"Where is she?" Chase demanded, struggling to sit up. Fresh agony ripped through him, but he didn't care. "What happened to Blade?"

Finn practically shoved the doctor out of the way before sitting on the bed. "Listen, mate, Blade created a diversion so we could get away. Stayed behind to buy us time."

"You left her?"

"I had no choice. It was leave with you or we'd all become prisoners. Once we reach South Korea, I'll slip back into Pyongyang and track her down."

The pilot cut the engine. They had arrived at the barge.

The moment of decision.

Doubt crept into Finn's expression as he weighed his orders against Chase's condition. The rhythmic slap of waves against the hull filled the silence. Time was running out—for all of them.

"Sometimes," Dr. Kim said softly, his voice carrying the weight of experience, "one must not follow orders, but follow one's heart."

Chase recognized the war raging within Finn—duty versus conscience. The right choice versus orders. Using what little strength remained, Chase seized Finn's wrist. "Won't make it," he ground out. "Promise . . . promise me you'll find her."

Finn gripped Chase's hand, clammy and hot. "You have my word, brother. I'll bring her home."

Relief flooded through Chase as his eyelids grew heavy. A resurgence to live coursed through him. He loved Blade, and if given the chance, would never let her go. *Lord, keep her safe.*

"Doctor"—Finn's words seemed to come from the bottom of a deep well—"tell the captain to change course. We're heading for your clinic."

CHAPTER
FIFTY

April 15 – 1:43 p.m. KST
Pyongyang, North Korea

The crowd's bloodthirsty roar was deafening as Blade shuffled through a maintenance corridor, but it was growing fainter—like her chances of escape.

Ming. What had she done to garner the attention of the soldiers and the wrath of those in attendance? The two shots she heard must have struck the beautiful, graceful woman who had risked everything to save Chase. At least he had made it out of the stadium—of that, she was sure. Otherwise, the colonel would be crowing about his victory over the West.

The shackles clamped on her wrists and ankles bit deeper with every awkward movement, the metal already rubbing her skin raw. Colonel Yong-Sun's phalanx of guards pressed in close, their boots striking the concrete in perfect unison.

A bitter wind cut through her sweat-soaked blouse as they emerged into the gray afternoon. Her muscles burned as they approached an ancient bus, its rusted frame a relic of the Cold

War era. If this bus represented Yong-Sun's current status, then he was in deep shit.

"Keep moving, American bitch!" Yong-Sun's pistol jabbed between her shoulder blades, hard enough to bruise.

The chains reduced her to a shuffle-hop as she approached the steps. A meaty hand seized her arm, hauling her up and throwing her onto a cracked vinyl seat. A sharp tang of body odor and diesel fuel filled the stale air around her. Despite the chill, she was thankful for the open windows.

She tracked Yong-Sun pacing beside the bus, his wild gestures punctuating shouted orders in Korean. The colonel reeked of desperation. His career—and possibly his life—hung by a thread. The Supreme Leader wouldn't take kindly to having his precious Day of the Sun celebration disrupted. Heads would roll—Yong-Sun would be fortunate to see another sunrise.

The colonel dropped into the seat across from her, face mottled with rage. "My career," he snarled, spittle flying, "is finished. And you—you and your Christian dogs will suffer for it."

The engine coughed to life, belching black smoke as it lurched away from the stadium. Soldiers took positions through-out, weapons at the ready. As they crossed the bridge into Pyongyang proper, Blade saw dozens of commemorative wreaths and floral baskets placed around statues of Kim Il Sung.

The cityscape gradually gave way to empty fields. Few cars or trucks were on the road. This was the one day where people were given ample food to eat. Blade imagined families celebrating their good fortune. She wondered how an entire population could be brainwashed into accepting such an oppressive government. The grim reality: history kept repeating itself.

Her pulse spiked when she spotted the truck. It sat askew across the narrow road ahead, its hood propped open. Too soon for the Soldati—they'd need time to mount a rescue. But maybe . . .

Yong-Sun bellowed an order in Korean, causing the driver to jump, and gestured for him to go around the truck.

The soldiers tensed, each one taking a position at an open window, rifles raised as the vehicle slowed to a crawl toward the shoulder of the road. The engine whined in protest, gears grinding as they edged past the abandoned vehicle. Blade searched for any sign of movement.

A deafening explosion lifted the front of the bus. Dust and metal shards flew in all directions.

Blade's forehead slammed into the metal seat frame as the world tilted sideways. Her ears rang as instinct screamed at her to get down, but chains yanked her upright. Yong-Sun clenched a handful of her hair as he dragged her to the rear, using her as a shield. His breath came in panicked gasps against her ear.

"You planned this," he hissed. "You and your American friends."

Before Blade could respond, the air erupted with the distinctive chatter of automatic weapons fire coming from the front of the bus. She watched in horror as the soldiers jerked and fell, their bodies shredded by the merciless spray of bullets.

Through the chaos stepped a man dressed in black tactical gear, his face hidden under a balaclava, moving with fluid precision through the carnage. The masked intruder advanced steadily up the aisle, weapon trained ahead with lethal intent.

Yong-Sun pressed his pistol against her temple. His body trembled against hers. "Back!" he shrieked, his voice cracking. "Or I kill her!"

The black-clad figure did not hesitate as he fired a single shot.

Something warm and wet sprayed across Blade's face and neck. She'd smelled death before, but that didn't stop the bile that threatened to spill from her open mouth. Yong-Sun's body bounced against the emergency door, then crumpled in a heap, but Blade didn't turn to look. She remained frozen in her chains, barely breathing as she stared at her mysterious savior.

With deliberate slowness, the stranger reached up and pulled off the balaclava, revealing a man she'd hunted for months.

"Cheers, Blade," Alec said softly, his green eyes glittering in the dim light. "Fancy meeting you here."

The dead silence that followed was broken only by the *tick-tick-tick* of the bus's cooling engine, counting down the seconds until her world would change once again.

CHAPTER
FIFTY-ONE

April 15 – 2:51 p.m. KST
Outside of Pyongyang, North Korea

Blade's nemesis, the elusive prey she'd hunted for months, stood only five feet away—and she couldn't move. Smoke filled the small confines of the bus and stung her eyes. She could see his lips moving, but she couldn't hear anything except the beating of her heart.

She stood, stupefied, as Alec shoved past her and dropped beside Yong-Sun's body. The dead man's eyes stared empty and void, a look of macabre surprise on his face. It was difficult to believe this diminished human being had inflicted so much pain upon Chase.

Alec searched the colonel's body, until relief crossed his face. He held up a key.

Green eyes bored into hers, holding her hostage. "We have to get out of here," Alec said as he unlocked the shackles.

Her wrists burned where the metal had cut into flesh. Rage, terror, and revenge exploded within her. Screaming, she whirled and kicked the dead body over and over, until she felt arms around her, pulling her away. Metal glinted under the seat, and Blade dove for a discarded rifle. She brought it up and aimed it at Alec.

"Stay where you are," Blade warned. She moved her index finger into the trigger guard.

Alec stood straight. "Get on with it if you're going to kill me. Otherwise, we need to get the hell out of here."

"Vivienne's last words were your name. Before I kill you, I need to know why."

"We don't have time for this."

"*You* don't have time."

Alec sat on one of the bus seats, letting out a breath. "Vivienne tracked *me* down. She wanted Martel. I agreed to give her intel about certain operations, but I wasn't going to forfeit my life for her vendetta. How do you think Vivienne found out about Martel's plan for you?"

"You lured me to Mallorca, knowing Martel planned to kill me."

"Vivienne planned to get you out well before anything happened to you—and kill Martel in the process."

"It was you at Gstaad, wasn't it? You were the one in the snowsuit."

"I had every reason to end you right then . . . but the thought of a world without you stopped me cold."

"You expect me to believe that?" She'd been foolish to trust Alec when she first met him, swept up with his good looks and a lucrative job offer that almost got her killed. She wouldn't make the same mistake twice.

"Believe what you will. But you're here, breathing and alive."

Movement caught Blade's attention through the narrow window—a snowshoe hare darting across the open field, its white coat sharp against the muddy earth. The sight triggered Joe's words: "Forgiveness isn't about them, kiddo. It's about freeing yourself from the weight you carry. Some burdens aren't meant to be held forever."

Blade lowered the rifle, but a slight shift from Alec spooked her. In an instant, she brought the rifle up and fired.

The shot missed Alec by an inch as he lunged for her. She stumbled back and tripped over Yong-Sun's body. But she managed to stay on her two feet. Alec, on the other hand, had miscalculated and struggled to find his footing.

The tight space worked against her, but Blade pivoted and snapped a *chassé frontal* kick into his chest, sending him sprawling backward.

"I don't want to hurt you," Alec said, using a seat as a barrier between them.

"Too late."

She leapt onto a seat and then, fueled by a rage that gave her almost supernatural power and balance, made another leap to the top of the backrest frame, delivering a *fouetté* whip kick to his temple. He staggered but didn't fall, rage igniting in his eyes as he reached for her.

Pivoting, Blade feinted a panicked shuffle backward, baiting him to step closer. The moment his weight shifted, she struck. Her right leg lashed out in a powerful *chassé bas,* her heel slamming into his ribs. The impact forced him to stumble forward, snarling in pain.

"Stay down," she warned, her voice steady, but he wasn't listening. Alec lunged.

But this time, he caught her around the ankles. She fell hard. Blade tried to roll, using her elbows for momentum, but his weight and tactical advantage left her staring into his eyes.

Alec straddled her, holding her arms above her head. "Bloody hell, Blade. I came to North Korea to save you. Don't you get it?"

"If that's true, then why try to run me over in New Orleans?" she spat, tasting blood. The memory of the black SUV forcing her

Ducati off the road burned fresh in her mind. "Was that hit meant to finish what you started or to send me a message?"

"That wasn't me."

"Then who was it?"

"I'll tell you everything I know—but first, get in the truck. Someone's bound to come this way."

Blade's laugh held no humor. "And I'm supposed to trust you? After everything?"

"You don't have to trust me," Alec countered, frustration bleeding through his controlled exterior. "But you need me. You're good—damn good—but you can't fight your way through an army of North Korean soldiers alone."

Blade considered. "There are two checkpoints between here and Pyongyang if we use the same roads. But if we can find a way around, I've got a ride out of the capital that will blow you away." She picked up discarded rifles as she made for the bus door. "Coming?"

3:27 p.m.

The smell of manure and damp earth permeated the small village. A few small huts and a barn dotted acres of cultivated land ready for planting. Seeing no farm machinery around, Finn assumed the work was done the old-fashioned way—by using oxen and plow. A hard life for hard people.

A woman had met Dr. Kim at the riverbank, her face anxious as she spied his charges. Finn guessed what Dr. Kim had relayed. Bad news traveled fast. "She is afraid. A search is already underway for an American man and woman. Anyone harboring the couple will be executed immediately and their families sent to labor camps."

Inside the tiny clinic, Finn paced the worn wooden floor,

gripped by memories of standing vigil at the hospital when his sister was injured by a bomb. He prayed Chase would live to fight another day. His sister hadn't been so fortunate.

Every few seconds, his gaze darted to the closed door where Dr. Kim and the woman operated on Chase. Through the thin walls, Finn could hear the murmur of voices speaking rapid Korean and the metallic clink of surgical instruments. The place looked unsanitary as hell, but Dr. Kim had kept him alive—so far.

Don't you dare die on me, you stubborn bastard.

Outside, a dog barked in the distance. Finn froze, his hand instinctively reaching for his weapon. But it was just one more sound in this godforsaken land. With the people starving, the mutt was lucky to not be on a skewer.

The empty minutes gnawed at him. He'd never left anyone behind—ever. Christ, how he'd hated Blade at first. Too bloody impulsive, no discipline, never followed a single order without argument. He'd been dead wrong about her, though. The lass had more grit than any soldier he'd served with. Her sacrifice had allowed them to escape. And by all that was holy, he'd honor his promise to Chase.

After a couple of hours, the door creaked open. Dr. Kim emerged, his surgical mask hanging around his neck, dark circles under his eyes. Finn's heart hammered against his ribs as he studied the older man's face.

"Your friend is stable," Dr. Kim said. "There was some damage to the kidney, but I managed to stop the bleeding."

Finn released a breath, relief spreading throughout his body. The doctor continued to look grim. "What aren't you telling me?"

"The beatings were extensive. Three broken ribs, possibly more bruised. He is severely dehydrated. He needs at least a few days to recuperate and IV fluids."

"Jaysus," Finn said. "How long can you keep us hidden?"

"Not long. Someone will talk. They always do." Dr. Kim

strode to the window and peered out. Dusk cast a gray hue over the countryside, adding to the sense of desolation. "But I may have an answer. Your friend will need to play dead."

"Play dead?"

"We have done it before—smuggled Christians out in coffins. The border guards are less likely to search a coffin, especially with the proper paperwork. Death certificate, transport documents." Dr. Kim's expression grew distant, and Finn wondered how many lives this quiet man had saved. "We move them into China, where other believers retrieve the coffins and take people to safe houses."

"Is it possible, in his condition?"

"I would administer a strong sedative. It's risky, but the best solution under these circumstances. However, we must move quickly. The truck leaves in two days. If we miss it . . ."

"What about me? I'm not letting Chase out of my sight. Not until he's safely with my people."

Dr. Kim gave Finn a withering stare. "Two dead people from this settlement would be suspicious."

Finn shrugged. "Then I'll figure out another way, but I'm going."

"I am too tired to argue," Dr. Kim donned his mask once again. "Let us talk in the morning. Now, let me check on your friend before I get some sleep. The next forty-eight hours are critical."

Finn felt guilty, pressuring the doctor. But damn it, Chase couldn't defend himself. Thomas would be waiting for an update, but there was time for that. Right now, he needed rest.

Somewhere out there, Blade was either fighting for her life or dead. And here he stood, unable to help her, preparing to hide his comrade in a coffin in a desperate gamble for their lives.

CHAPTER
FIFTY-TWO

April 15 – 3:33 p.m. KST
Outside of Pyongyang, North Korea

The truck's suspension groaned as Alec wrenched the wheel hard left. They skidded off the highway onto a dirt road barely wide enough for the vehicle. A plume of tawny dust erupted behind them, leaving a trail anyone could follow.

Blade's ribs screamed in protest as they bounced over deep ruts carved by decades of oxen-pulled wagons and mechanized farm equipment. Vast acres of plowed land, flooded to prepare the soil for rice planting, stretched to the horizon.

She gripped the dashboard, stealing glances at Alec as he compulsively checked the rearview mirror.

"I know who tried to kill you in New Orleans," he said finally.

The memory of trying to outrace the black SUV, taking the turn too fast, her Ducati spinning out of control, then waking in a hospital room, came flooding back once more. "Tell me."

"Mila Krüger and her son—René Martel's illegitimate heir. But here's the kicker: Richard Andrews, senior senator from South Carolina, is bankrolling the whole operation."

"Andrews?" Blade straightened her spine, frozen, remembering the last time she'd heard that name.

"Member of the Committee on Foreign Relations. Ring any bells?"

She thought of her last conversation with Vivienne—how she'd gone on the attack and said things she couldn't take back. A lump formed in her throat, making it impossible to speak for a few seconds. When she finally replied, her voice sounded husky to her own ears. "Vivienne told me my biological father's name was John Andrews. His father was an ambassador for the United States. But that's all I know. Do you think Richard could be related? And if he is—why would he want me dead?"

"Never underestimate the thirst for money and power. Mila and Max are money-grubbing wankers. But why is a senator interested? This makes no sense."

"The Krügers' lawyer has hounded me for months, pressuring me to sign away any claim to Martel's fortune—as if I'd touch a single euro of that scumbag's money."

Alec kept his expression still, concentrating on the road. "Then why not sign?"

Blade shrugged. "Not sure. It's hard to explain. Finding you became my only priority. I couldn't care less about Martel's fortune. Let his empire rot—it deserves to crumble after all the lives he destroyed."

There was a beat too long before Alec answered. "I have my man digging into Richard Andrews, Mila, and her runt, Max. I say we turn the tables on them and do a bit of hunting ourselves. After we get out of this scrape, of course."

Through skeletal trees, the Taedong River appeared, a serpentine ribbon of muddy water flowing toward Pyongyang.

Alec drove the truck into a thicket of trees and killed the engine. "We'll get out here and walk the river until we find a boat. Quicker and less likely to be seen."

Blade spotted a clothesline at a nearby farmhouse, simple work clothes blowing in the breeze. "We need a better disguise to blend in," she said, gesturing to his tactical gear and her torn and bloodied North Korean Army uniform.

Moving through shadows, they grabbed what they needed and changed quickly. Blade couldn't stop thinking about the implications of Alec's revelation. Was it possible that the Andrews family —her family—had essentially paid to have her killed? How had they discovered her relationship to them? And why was she a threat? Blade rubbed her temples, hoping to alleviate the pressure in her head.

After ditching the truck, they walked along the shoreline. A small fishing boat tied to a weathered dock came into view. While Blade kept watch, nerves crackling, Alec worked to hot-wire it. Her gaze traveled to his forearm, where his tattoo of a black rose rippled in the sunlight. It had been four months since he'd left a black rose on her bed, daring her to find him. And here they were, stealing a boat in hostile territory. The motor sputtered to life, and they slipped into the current.

Nearing the capital, Blade could see a patchwork of pastel-colored buildings of pinks, blues, greens, and yellows. The cheerful facade of the city did not fool the world. The regime was ruthless and oppressive. Every time she closed her eyes, an image of Chase, beaten and bleeding, would take center stage. She wondered if she'd ever sleep again,

The river grew busier as they passed the stadium. Alec hunched lower, donning a straw hat left in the boat. He guided them near the shore, eyes scanning for the barge.

"There," Blade pointed to a line of barges. "Blue stripe— that's exactly how Dr. Kim described it."

Her heart rate quickened as they navigated through the increasingly crowded waterway. Dozens of boats now dotted the channel, but she kept her head lowered, mindful of maintaining her cover. Not that she needed to worry—the North Koreans were only too happy to mind their own business.

Alec secured the fishing boat to the barge and both leapt onto the deck. Under tarps, they found the aerial vehicle—sleek, built for stealth, with room for two. She exhaled, releasing the bottled-up emotion she'd held at bay.

"Keep it covered until nightfall," Alec instructed.

Blade turned toward the sun lowering in the sky. "Do you think we'll be able to fly in the dark?"

"I'm not coming with you. Thomas promised not to divulge my whereabouts, but I like to stay one step ahead. Besides," he said, lifting the duffel, "the least I can do is create a little havoc. A payback of sorts."

"From the moment you locked me in that room on Mallorca, I've hated you. And now you do something decent. I-I don't know how to feel about you."

"I brought something for you." He reached into the bag, pulled out the Sure Balance throwers, and handed them to her, his calloused fingers lingering against hers.

Surprised, Blade tossed one of the knives from one hand to the other. "It's heavier than my usual throwers, but it will work."

Alec's eyes glinted in the last afternoon sun. "We have a common enemy. If we make it out alive, I propose we meet in one month. Noon. Strawberry Fields. Come alone."

Blade took a few moments to think. "Agreed. It's been a while since I've visited Central Park."

"Sokcho's almost three hours southeast," Alec said, pointing in the direction. "You'll see the Taebaek mountain range before the coastline. Land somewhere near the lighthouse. Someone from the Soldati should be there."

"When shall I leave?"

Alec smiled. "You won't miss my calling card."

April 15 – 8:06 p.m. KST
Pyongyang, North Korea

Blade stood at the edge of the barge, scanning the city, her fingers drumming against the metal railing as fireworks splattered across the night sky. The kaleidoscope of color cast an eerie glow on the water, but this wasn't the distraction Alec had promised. Not yet.

She'd escaped Yong-Sun, but her proximity to Pyongyang made her edgy. She paced the length of the deck, trying to calm herself by tossing a knife from one hand to the other. Patience had never been her virtue. The Arcturus One waited in the shadows behind her, low and silent, its matte surface blending into the industrial dark. The experimental aircraft was her ticket out of this hellhole—if she managed to pilot the damn thing.

Another flare of color painted the sky. Alone and exposed to unseen danger, she felt like a scared young girl, unsure of herself and afraid of being captured. Of never telling Chase how much he meant to her. *I could use Vivienne's strength right about now.* Blade had barely brushed the surface when it came to Vivienne, but her friends had spoken of a brave, courageous, determined, and competent soldier who knew no fear.

The past week had been a blur of preparation and subterfuge, leaving little time to process her tangled emotions. But in quiet moments such as this, they crashed against her in waves. She loved Chase—that much was clear. His character, his unwavering faith, the way his gaze made her feel precious and wild all at once.

Then there was Alec.

Blade ran a hand through her hair, frustrated by the complexity of it all. She'd hunted him for months, driven by rage and grief over Vivienne's death. Yet here he was, risking his life to save her. The memory of those green eyes and the gentle brush of his fingers against hers as he'd handed over the throwing knives confused her even more.

"What game are you playing?" she whispered into the wind.

A distant boom drew her attention to the horizon. This explosion was different—deeper, more dangerous. A column of fire shot skyward, painting the clouds in shades of orange and red. Two more explosions followed in quick succession.

The signal.

Blade yanked the heavy tarps off the Arcturus One. The sleek aircraft gleamed dully in the moonlight, its unconventional design both beautiful and terrifying. Four hours of rushed training with Finn hardly qualified her to fly this beast, but she had no choice.

She climbed into the cockpit, her hands trembling slightly as they moved over the controls. The preflight sequence Finn had drilled into her head played on repeat. Master switch. Ignition.

The engine hummed, a deep vibration that traveled up through her bones. Blade gripped the flight stick, forcing herself to breathe. She couldn't afford to second-guess herself.

"Trust your instincts," she muttered, echoing Joe's advice over the years.

As if in response, the Arcturus One lifted smoothly from the deck, hovering for a moment before Blade angled it east toward Sokcho. Toward Chase. Pyongyang fell away beneath her, a maze of darkness punctuated by bursts of light and flame.

She didn't look back. Dared not. Whatever complications lay ahead, they would have to wait.

All that mattered was reaching Sokcho before dawn.

8:18 p.m.

The Arcturus One sliced through the night above Pyongyang, its experimental frame reminding Blade there was room for two. Even with the protective carbon fiber safety cell, cold air seeped into every gap in her thermal gear.

Another explosion bloomed behind her. Blade risked a glance back as searchlights stabbed through the black smoke. Alec had promised a distraction, and he'd delivered. The thought of him down there, facing off against North Korea's elite forces, sent an unexpected pang through her chest. After everything he'd done, all the betrayals, why did she care whether he lived or died?

Focus.

Blade kept the vehicle low, nearly grazing the tops of concrete buildings. Each near miss sent a jolt of adrenaline through her system. The Arcturus responded to the slightest touch, more like an extension of her body than a vehicle.

Beyond the city limits, darkness swallowed everything. The wan moonlight barely penetrated the gloom, offering little guidance as she pushed the strange craft forward. She'd been airborne for over an hour; her shoulders burned with tension. The Arcturus One was faster than her beloved Ducati, but at least motorcycles stayed firmly on the road where they belonged.

Thomas's words echoed in her mind: "The modified battery

will get you to South Korea. Three hours, max." She checked the power readout—still good—but the margin for error was razor-thin.

Blade forced herself to stay at treetop level, though every instinct screamed at her to gain altitude. Flying higher would provide safety, give her room to maneuver if something went wrong. But greater heights would also mean radar detection, and she had no illusions about her chances against North Korean air defenses. The Arcturus might be cutting-edge tech, but it was designed for stealth, not combat.

The vaguest shape of the Taebaek Mountains loomed ahead, the massive peaks stretching over five thousand feet into the clouds. This was the only viable route across the DMZ. But as the seconds ticked by, the mountain range grew closer. Blade tried to swallow, but her throat was bone dry. Flying above the mountains wasn't an option—the maximum height the Arcturus could reach was fifteen hundred feet. The valleys remained her sole option, an obstacle course of tight corridors of stone—where one miscalculation would prove fatal.

A sound cut through the Arcturus's quiet hum—the distinctive whine of jet engines. Blade's heart slammed against her ribs as she jerked her head left, then right. Nothing but darkness. Then a flash of metal caught the moonlight. With trembling fingers, she activated the jammer. If that was a North Korean interceptor, the electronic countermeasures were her only defense.

The missile's launch lit up the night. Blade banked hard toward a narrow gorge. The missile detonated against the mountainside, the shock wave buffeting the Arcturus like a leaf in a hurricane. But the gorge proved too small for the larger jet to follow, and Blade pressed her advantage, weaving through the rocky terrain with desperate precision.

Time no longer mattered. Only survival.

She finally saw a faint beam of light—the lighthouse. South

Korea. Freedom. The mountains fell away to reveal the coastline, and Blade scanned the area below, searching for a safe place to land. She was almost certainly in South Korean territory now, but she wouldn't be truly safe until she was standing on solid ground.

Somewhere down there, Thomas's people would be waiting. All she had to do was make it the last few miles without dying.

CHAPTER
FIFTY-FOUR

April 15 – 11:08 p.m. KST
Sokcho, South Korea

The Arcturus One rattled violently as Blade fought the controls; wind sheer slammed into the hull like a battering ram. She could just make out the lighthouse beacon. She tried to steer toward the light, but the wind kept throwing her off course.

"Come on, girl," she muttered. "We've flown too far to crash."

Below, the Sea of Japan churned black and deadly, white-capped waves crashing against jagged rocks. Sokcho's lights glimmered tantalizingly close, but landing there meant questions that Blade was unprepared to answer. Her arms trembled with fatigue, the strain of the past twenty-four hours catching up with her.

She gritted her teeth, fingers clenching around the flight stick. The parachute had to deploy now, or she'd be nothing but a smear against the rocks or thrown into the sea.

With a sharp yank, she pulled the lever.

For a moment, nothing.

The parachute exploded open with a thunderous crack, jerking the craft backward so violently her neck snapped hard against the headrest.

"Too fast," she whispered, adjusting the vehicle's angle of descent. "Too damn fast."

The beach rushed up to meet her, a pale strip of moon-washed sand between black water and darker shadows. Blade tried to keep the Arcturus One steady, but exhaustion had stolen her strength. The aerial vehicle hit the ground with bone-jarring force, cartwheeling once, twice, before shuddering to a stop mere yards from the surging tide.

Blade could only sit there, hand still locked on the flight stick, heart hammering against her ribs. Alive. She was alive.

A figure materialized from the darkness, running toward her on the wet sand. Even through the ringing in her ears, she recognized the voice calling her name.

Xiu.

Blade fumbled with the safety cell's release, her fingers clumsy on the mechanism. By the time she crawled from the wreckage, Xiu had already gathered the billowing parachute and used a broken propeller to hold it down.

"You made it," Xiu said, her face a mask of professional detachment. "Any injuries?"

Blade forced herself to stand, fighting a wave of vertigo. "Chase. Where is he?"

Something flickered across Xiu's features—pain, perhaps, or fear. "He's critical but stable."

Blade shook her head and took a step forward, ignoring how the beach seemed to tilt beneath her feet. "I asked where?"

Xiu's dark eyes burned like glowing coals. "Let's go before the police show up. Unless you think you can explain this mess."

"We're not going anywhere until you answer my question."

"Chase and Finn are still in North Korea. His injury required surgery."

"In North Korea?" Blade repeated, finding it hard to believe.

Xiu crossed her arms over her chest. "He is being smuggled out the day after tomorrow—in a coffin. The network has a route into China, but it is risky as hell."

"A coffin?" The fog inside Blade's head was slowly lifting.

"Only way to get him across the border without raising suspicion. I plan to be there when he arrives."

Blade looked up sharply. "I'm going with you."

Xiu's expression hardened. "No, you are not."

"That's not your call to make."

Xiu stepped so close, Blade could feel the woman's wrath emanating from her body. "Is it not? *You* are not one of us, Blade. You never will be. Chase needs a woman who understands his calling, his commitment. Not someone who abandons everything to pursue personal vendettas."

The accusation stung, but Blade held her ground. "You don't get to decide what Chase wants or needs."

The wind whipped between them, carrying stinging particles of sand, but neither woman moved. Blade studied Xiu's face in the harsh moonlight, seeing something akin to hatred.

"Do him a kindness," Xiu spat. "Go home. Let him heal in peace. Some of us actually deserve to be there when he wakes up."

Blade watched Xiu stalk off, her mission complete. The younger woman's words echoed in her mind, weaving through memories of Chase's quiet smile, his steady faith, and the fierce loyalty he'd shown when he came for her at the hospital in Geneva.

As Joe often said before a show, "In for a penny, in for a

pound." She'd never walked away from a fight, and she didn't intend to start. Whatever Xiu thought, whatever anyone thought, Blade knew one truth with absolute certainty: she would be there when Chase woke.

I dare anyone to try and stop me.

April 16 – 7:52 a.m. CST
Dandong, China

Horizontal rain pelted the windshield as Blade and Xiu approached Dandong. After more than forty-eight hours of blinding fear, it was difficult to keep her eyes open. The steady rhythm of the windshield wipers lulled her into a trance, but somehow she forced herself to remain awake.

The flight from Yangyang to Shenyang, then the drive to this border city seemed endless without a break. Her muscles ached from the grueling journey, and the silence between them had stretched like a rubber band ready to snap.

As Xiu parked the black sedan, Blade studied the woman's profile. Blade had known Xiu was in love with Chase since arriving at the safe house in Rome four months ago. Even then, Blade sensed the woman's animosity toward her. Not only did Xiu feel threatened, but she also blamed Blade for her brother's death. There was an invisible wall between them, as impenetrable as the DMZ itself.

Thomas greeted them on the street, his broad shoulders tense under his crisp, now soaked, white shirt. His face brightened with relief. "Thank God you both made it." He embraced each woman in turn. When he stepped back, his expression hardened with urgency. "The network just confirmed movement. Finn and Chase will depart at 0700 hours tomorrow."

"How is he?" Blade asked, her throat tight.

"Let's go inside, where it's dry."

A girl brought them each a towel, which they put to use immediately. Blade felt a sense of dread as she waited for Thomas. She braced herself for bad news.

"Chase is stable, but in bad shape. If all goes according to plan, Chase and Finn should be in Dandong by noon tomorrow."

"Do we take him to a hospital here?" Blade asked.

"I'll have a medical team standing by in Shenyang with a plane fueled for Rome," Thomas said, taking a seat on a wooden chair, "assuming Chase is strong enough for the flight."

"And if he is not?" Xiu snapped, her usual composure cracking.

"What we always do—adapt." Thomas's tone left no room for argument. "Rooms have been prepared for you. Rest. We have a long day ahead."

Blade started to protest, but fatigue consumed her, making each step an effort. A staff member led her down a dim hallway to her room, where peeling wallpaper and the musty scent of neglect told their own story. From the bedroom window, she could see the Yalu River and a clear view of North Korea. The countryside appeared like any other, but the evil she'd witnessed would forever shape her view of the world.

Even after a hot shower, sleep proved elusive. Her mind raced between the Andrews' involvement in her attempted murder and thoughts of Chase. The two twisted together in her dreams whenever she dozed off—Chase bleeding out while faceless killers emerged from the shadows, Alec Quinn's mocking laughter echoing in the distance.

Xiu's earlier words lingered. "Have you not caused enough damage? Let him heal in peace."

Maybe Xiu was right. Maybe the kindest thing would be to help with the rescue and then disappear again. Chase deserved to find happiness with someone undamaged, someone who wasn't haunted by ghosts and hunted by assassins.

Rolling onto her side, Blade knew she'd never be at peace until she faced her feelings for Chase and discovered the truth about who wanted her dead.

She wasn't sure which outcome terrified her more.

CHAPTER
FIFTY-SIX

April 17 – 7:05 a.m. KST
Outside of Pyongyang, North Korea

The morning air bit with unexpected ferocity, but Finn barely noticed the cold. His attention remained fixed on Chase's breathing, each rise and fall of his friend's chest a reminder of how precarious their situation had become.

Dr. Kim moved to the window, watching as the last villagers disappeared down the rutted road, clutching bags of rice and medicine he'd distributed to ensure their absence.

"The village is clear," Dr. Kim announced. "We must move. Please, follow me."

Finn had no choice but to follow the doctor to the idling delivery truck. He'd wanted nothing more than to leave this damn country, but he never figured he'd be leaving in a box.

"Expect four hours on the back roads to reach Sinuiju," Dr. Kim said. "After one final checkpoint, you cross into Dandong. Our network in China manages everything beyond that point."

"Give it to me straight, doc. Does me mate have a chance to make it there alive?"

"His vitals are strong and he no longer has a fever. I will give him a sedative, which should allow him to sleep through the trip."

"And what if somethin' goes wrong? What if he—"

"Then it is as God wills it."

The words ignited Finn's long-contained rage. He seized the doctor's coat in both hands. "God's will?" he snarled. "Was it God's will, then, that left him swingin' in chains? That broke his ribs and—"

"Finn," Chase rasped.

Both men turned. Chase stood a few feet away, holding his side. "Release him," he managed. "Not his fault."

Finn released his grip on the doctor and strode to his comrade, putting an arm around his waist and leading him to the truck fender. "What the hell are ya doin' outta of bed, are ya mad?"

Chase sat, leaning over to catch his breath. Sweat trickled down his face, and his hands shook from the exertion. "We're wasting daylight."

The doctor shouted for the driver, who came running. After giving orders in Korean, the driver unloaded one of the coffins using a wooden ramp.

"You want me to get in that?" Chase asked.

"We've been in worse shite. Remember the bleedin' sewage tunnel?"

"I think I prefer sewage."

Finn grinned. His buddy still had a sense of humor. "Ready?"

Chase managed a ghost of his old smile. "The sooner we get to safety, the sooner you can find Blade, you Irish bastard."

Finn huffed out a breath that wasn't quite a laugh. "Aye, and don't think I won't drag her back by the scruff if I have to."

If only he'd been able to keep the sat phone. But he'd handed it off to the network—they needed it to coordinate with contacts on the Chinese side. That left him relying on strangers, with no way to reach Thomas, no way to know if Blade had made it to the

Arcturus One. He prayed she'd somehow made it out safely, but with all the gunfire he'd heard . . .

Finn looked down at Chase, saw the steel in his friend despite the agony that clouded them. His mate was hangin' on by one hope: that Blade was still alive.

Finn squeezed his shoulder, careful to avoid the worst of the injuries. "I never break a promise, mate. I'll bring your girl back."

They were out of options. Now it was just a matter of faith—not in God, but in each other. And in the mad hope that it'd be enough to see them through the next few hours.

⸻

1:03 p.m.

"They should be here already," Blade muttered, pressing her forehead against the cool glass, scanning the empty street.

"Patience," Thomas said from behind her, his calm voice a stark contrast to the tension in the room. "Our network knows what they're doing."

The waiting was excruciating. Every minute that ticked by felt like another nail in Chase's coffin—a thought that made her stomach lurch.

"Anything?" Thomas asked.

Xiu's fingers flew across three laptops, monitoring radio frequencies and satellite feeds. "No reports of arrests or . . ." She swallowed hard, dark circles under her eyes betraying her exhaustion. "No reports of bodies being recovered, either."

At the window, Thomas's powerful frame was coiled tight with tension. His hand unconsciously traced the scar on his neck. "Doctor Chen!" he bellowed down the hall. "They're here!"

Blade froze mid-stride, her heart hammering against her ribs. They were late—too late?

All four burst through the back door into the afternoon heat. Blade's legs nearly gave out when she saw Finn's expression as he threw open the truck doors. The coffin lid lay discarded on the floor.

"Need a doctor!" Finn shouted.

Blade surged forward, but Thomas's iron grip caught her arm. "Stay put while the doctor works."

Finn caught her eye—she could read his mix of relief that she'd made it out, overlayed with his continued panic for Chase.

Dr. Chen vaulted into the truck with surprising agility for his age. His movements were precise as he checked Chase's vital signs. Blade's vision tunneled, the edges going dark as she waited for the verdict.

Finally, the doctor looked up, his weather-lined face beaming. "You can transport him to Rome, but we need to move quickly."

"Let go," Blade said, jerking her arm from Thomas's grasp.

She kneeled beside the coffin, believing she was peering down at a dead man. Chase lay motionless, his skin a waxy pallor. His chest rose and fell—he was alive—but her traitorous eyes told her otherwise. She reached in to touch his cheek and almost recoiled when his eyes fluttered open.

"Blade?" he whispered.

The word drew everyone's attention back to Chase. Tears blurred her vision, but she didn't care. His hand groped for hers.

"I thought . . ." She couldn't finish, her throat too tight.

"Not getting rid of me that easily." His cracked lips attempted a smile. "I made a promise to myself in that hellhole. To tell you . . . I love you."

Behind them, Xiu breathed a small, pained sound before turning away. But Blade barely registered it; her world narrowed to Chase's face, his touch, the miracle of his survival.

Thomas barked orders about transport and medical care, his

voice fading to background noise as Chase's fingers tightened around hers.

"No more wasted time," he murmured.

Blade leaned close. "No more wasted time."

CHAPTER
FIFTY-SEVEN

May 5 – 11:03 a.m. CEST
Siena, Italy

Joe's urn rested in dappled shadows cast by a solitary olive tree, its ancient branches swaying gently in the morning breeze. Blade stood motionless, inhaling the fragrance of the white lilies and red roses adorning the heavy wooden table. The symbolism of that lone tree in the castle courtyard struck her anew—like Christ standing alone, a singular beacon of hope and sacrifice.

She was alive.

Perhaps there is a God in this universe, one who watches over and waits for his children. The thought gave her comfort as her hand found the gold cross Nari had given her, now resting against her heart.

With reluctant fingers, she touched the cool metal of the urn. Joe's final moments in Shanghai played through her mind—his last embrace, his knowing smile before she abandoned him. She swallowed hard against the lump in her throat. She'd never told him what he meant to her, never thanked him for being the father figure she'd desperately needed. At least she had his magic diary

—his final gift to her. The leather-bound book, heavy with his secrets, lay on her dresser. She'd open it soon, but not just yet.

Joe would have appreciated this simple celebration of life with only his newfound friends present: Thomas, Xiu, Chase, and Finn, whom he'd bonded with in only a few short days. The grizzled old magician had jumped at another chance at adventure. Blade truly hoped there was a heaven, where Joe could once again perform the art of illusion.

Thomas's rich Nigerian accent carried across the courtyard, his prayer rising to meet the cloudless Tuscan sky. "As we remember our comrades Joe Mancini and Ming Zhang, you promised us a reward in heaven. In John chapter fourteen, verses two and three, Jesus says,

'My Father's house has many rooms; if that were not so, would I have told you that I am going there to prepare a place for you? And if I go and prepare a place for you, I will come back and take you to be with me that you also may be where I am.'"

The words of the scripture blurred as memories of Vivienne's ceremony, mere months ago, crashed over her. Two losses, two permanent hollows carved into her heart.

A warm hand found hers, calloused fingers interlacing with her own. Chase. He stood beside her, still moving stiffly, his bruises fading from violent purple to sickly yellow. But he was alive. The simple act of standing shoulder to shoulder anchored her to the present moment, keeping her from drowning in the undertow of grief.

"Ming Zhang," Thomas continued, his voice thick with emotion, "your sacrifice has ignited a revival in the darkest of places. After what we've all been through, our motto, *Lux en Tenebris Lucet*, has never been more critical in this fallen world. *We* are the light in the darkness. As Ephesians instructs, we must put on the whole armor of God, that we may be able to withstand in the evil day, and having done all, to stand firm. Make no mistake, we battle every day for our brethren and we must not grow weary.

His words triggered a cascade of flashbacks: the chaos of their escape, the deafening gunfire, Ming's final performance that had given them their window of opportunity. The Chinese acrobat's death, broadcast on North Korea's state television, was still sending shockwaves through the oppressive regime.

Blade stepped forward, her voice steadier than she felt. "I've decided to inter Joe's ashes at my new home in Bolgheri—at the winery Vivienne left me." She could picture Joe there, sitting on the terrace of the rustic stone farmhouse, watching the sunset paint the vineyard in gold. "He would have loved it there."

As Thomas concluded, the weight of unworthiness threatened to crush her. Why had she survived when others hadn't? What cosmic lottery had she won to deserve Chase's allegiance, Joe's ultimate sacrifice, or Vivienne's unselfish love?

Chase squeezed her hand gently, as if sensing her thoughts. She allowed herself the luxury of leaning into his strength, grateful for this moment of peace before the impending storm.

Later, in the castle's garden, Blade sought refuge on a stone bench, allowing the afternoon sun to warm her. White wisteria and jasmine cascaded over the arbor walkway, their scent mingling to produce an intoxicating aroma. Bees hummed lazily between blossoms, indifferent to her turbulent thoughts.

How could she tell Chase the truth—that she wasn't ready for a commitment? And after what he'd endured, neither was he. She loved Chase, but was it enough? The Soldati di Cristo and those who labored under Thomas's leadership were called by faith and hope. Even after all she'd been through, she was still unsure of her own spiritual beliefs. Was there a God orchestrating divine appointments? Manipulating events for his divine plan?

Then there was still the meeting with Alec in New York next week, which she'd deliberately hidden from everyone. Another secret. Another betrayal. Blade twisted Marie's wedding ring around her finger, her conflicting emotions warring with each other.

She heard Chase's measured footsteps before she saw him—slower, more deliberate than before his captivity.

He lowered himself carefully onto the bench. "Thought I'd find you here."

The tenderness in his voice nearly broke her resolve. Blade drew a steadying breath. "I've been thinking of flying back to Florida, to see my father." The lie tasted bitter on her tongue.

Chase turned to face her, his expression neutral but his eyes sharp and alert. "I'm well enough to travel. Would you like some company?"

She looked down at her hands, unable to maintain eye contact. "I think we should put some distance between us." Words tumbled out before she could soften their edges. "We've both survived traumas, and I won't pretend to be someone I'm not."

A muscle ticked in Chase's jaw. "Meaning what, exactly?"

"You're a soldier who believes in God. I'm an entertainer who's still trying to believe in herself." She took hold of his hand. "I can't join your fight—not yet. And I won't ask you to abandon what gives your life meaning."

Chase shifted, his movements still stiff from surgery. "So you're running. Again."

"I'm not running." She met his gaze. "I'm giving us time to figure out our true feelings. I love you, but I need to know it's *real*."

There was a long moment of silence as Chase contemplated what she'd told him. A hawk screeched above them, its wings extended to soar on a thermal updraft. Blade envied the bird its freedom, and she longed for the day when she could move forward with her life without doubts and misgivings.

Chase's next words surprised her. "If you need time, take it." He spoke softly, but with the conviction of someone who had walked through hell and emerged changed. "But hear me clearly. I'm in love with you. No doubts. No reservation. Your beliefs, your past—none of it matters. I want to build a future together. With you."

Church bells tolled across the valley, sending shivers down Blade's spine. His thumb moved in gentle circles over the back of her hand, a quiet language that needed no translation.

"Chase—"

"I lost my wife because I was an arrogant man who thought he knew what was best for both of us," he said, each syllable heavy with buried grief. "I won't make that mistake again."

The sun began its descent behind the castle walls, painting the garden in shades of amber and gold. They sat wrapped in comfortable silence, both aware their time of healing was coming to an end.

A storm was gathering on another continent—one that would either answer all her questions or destroy everything she held dear.

And the Andrews family—her family—might hold the key.

God help them.

They had no idea what was coming for them.

THE END

AUTHOR'S NOTE

I hope you enjoyed the book as much as I loved writing it.

If you have a moment to spare, I would appreciate a short review on the retailer's website where you bought the book. Your feedback not only helps me grow as an author, but it also helps other readers discover the story.

Thank you!

ACKNOWLEDGMENTS

First and foremost, thank you, dear reader. My greatest hope as a writer is that something in these pages resonated with you—a passage that sparked laughter, stirred emotion, or offered a glimpse of yourself within its pages. I'm deeply grateful you chose to spend your precious time in Blade's world.

Family is a theme I return to again and again in my writing, and I'm incredibly lucky to have mine at the center of my life. To Mark, my husband and best friend—thank you for standing by me through every high and low. I truly can't imagine this journey without you.

A huge thank you to my daughter Monica—my confidante and partner in crime. You're the one I trust with my words first, and I treasure your wisdom and insight more than I can say. To the rest of my wonderful family—Phillip, Jeff, Alex, Kaylee, Ayden, Noah, and Devyn—you enrich my life every single day.

And to my editor, Kristen Tate at The Blue Garret, thank you for making my story stronger. Your sharp eye and thoughtful feedback helped me grow professionally. I'm already looking forward to collaborating with you on Book Three!

Now, I must begin to write Blade's next adventure . . .

ABOUT THE AUTHOR

Nannette Potter is the award-winning author of the Blade Broussard international thriller series. An adventuress at heart, she lives vicariously through her fearless and impetuous characters who balance their lives on a knife's edge. When not writing, Nannette treasures time with family and travels the globe, where she dreams up future high-stakes conspiracies. She lives with her soulmate and husband Mark in California's Central Valley, where she's an active member of Sisters in Crime and Central Valley Fiction Writers.

www.nannettepotter.com

www.ingramcontent.com/pod-product-compliance
Lightning Source LLC
Chambersburg PA
CBHW032358310726
48973CB00007B/2064